CHOICES

Praise for *Choices*

"John House's compelling and suspenseful hostage drama, *Choices*, will keep you turning pages long after you should have been tending to other business. Get ready for a dramatic journey that will sweep you from coastal Georgia into the dark reaches of the Okefenokee Swamp."

--H. W. "Buzz" Bernard, author of *Eyewall* and *Plague*.

"Edward Majorski, MD, is good at handling emergencies, but things are dramatically more frightening when the emergency involves the doctor himself, trapped in a convenience store stickup gone horribly wrong. Scary story, hard to put down."

-- Louis N. Gruber, author of *Jay* and one of Amazon.com's top reviewers

CHOICES

By John House

ThomasMax

Your Publisher
For The 21st Century

ISBN-13: 978-0-9859255-1-2
ISBN-10: 0-9859255-1-5

Cover design by ThomasMax.

First printing: December, 2012

Published by:

ThomasMax Publishing
P.O. Box 250054
Atlanta, GA 30325
www.thomasmax.com

To all members
of law enforcement for their
splendid work at a difficult job

ACKNOWLEDGMENTS

In the process of getting a novel written, there is no substitute for long hours alone at the word processor. Doubt creeps in during revision regarding point of view, grammar, and style.

I am thankful for Emily Carmain of Noteworthy Editing for her invaluable editing and comments. She takes on the difficult task of correcting my errors and allows me the freedom of creativity.

Thanks to Lee Clevenger of ThomasMax Publishing who taught me how to get my work to my readers.

No writer works in a vacuum. My sincere thanks to authors; Cheryl Norman, Harold "Buzz" Bernard and Louis Gruber for their help and comments.

A special thanks to David L.Robbins, author of *The Devil's Waters*, *War of the Rats*, *Broken Jewel* and other thrilling novels. David is not only a successful author but also a much sought after teacher of writing. He is the founder of the James River Writers and a co-founder of the Podium Foundation which encourages artistic expression.

And finally huge thanks to my readers for your wonderful response and comments on Facebook. I write for you.

CHAPTER ONE

On a Christmas Eve, Jayco Dubois, standing at the rear bumper of a Jeep Cherokee, threw his cigarette butt into the growing pile at his feet. It was his last one.

He was not happy waiting at the corner of Newcastle and Gloucester at seven p.m. on a day too hot for the season. He was not happy in Brunswick on the southeastern coast of Georgia. He was not happy with the salty smell of the marshes that reminded him of his troubled childhood.

But *he was happy* he was no longer in prison and vowed he would never go back.

Stepping away from the Jeep, he walked across a sidewalk of inlaid bricks, which according to the nearby historical marker were brought to the new world centuries ago by those seeking freedom from debtor's prison. From his standpoint, things were no different. Life still consisted of the "haves" and the "have-nots." He was of the latter. Tomorrow would change everything. He had a plan to improve his life. And damn the consequences.

He approached the passenger side of the car, reached in and cupped his hand over the nose and mouth of Charlie Williams. Jayco let go a belly laugh when the stocky man inside the car erupted with a fit of coughing. "Wake up, Charlie. Don't look like Tupac is coming."

His friend, Tupac Garcia, of half-black and half-Spanish descent, was an hour late for their scheduled meeting. Jayco and Charlie had driven all night to reach Brunswick to meet him. Jayco wasn't privy to the reason Tupac chose the city as his new beginning when he was released from prison several months ago.

He leaned against the car, crossing his arms across his chest. "I don't like this city. Just like the place in hell where I grew up. Too damn hot for Christmas. Bet Tupac changed his mind. Can't say I blame him," Jayco said. "You remember—his letters say he's got a good job and plans of staying straight. That's not for us, is it, Charlie? We've got the chance of a lifetime. We score big and head for the good life in Mexico." He glanced back at Charlie, saw his friend nod his head in agreement, just before his chin dropped to this chest again. Jayco shook his head in disgust.

Released from prison within days of each other, Jayco and Charlie had hung around the area until Jayco located a buddy on the outside that owed him—owed him big-time. The man came through with a shotgun and two 9mm automatics.

In prison, they had hatched a plan to knock off a convenience store on Christmas morning. Not just any convenience store. This one, Jayco learned from a fellow inmate was special. Plenty of cash in the register from Christmas Eve sales. Then the bonanzas in the safe under the checkout counter. A mother lode. A one-in-a-million heist he had dreamed about all his life. Pull off this job and retire for life. A hit and run job, steal another car and be on their way to Mexico in a flash. He could manage it with just Charlie, but it would go smoother with Tupac along. Charlie wasn't the brightest star in the sky though he did supply a lot of muscle.

Jayco reached into his shirt pocket, and then slammed his hand against the side of the car, remembering he'd smoked the last of his cigarettes. "Damn, why don't Tupac come on?" In spite of his earlier remarks about understanding Tupac's absence, he seethed with anger. Prison mates don't let each other down. He would respond if Tupac needed him. Tupac owed him the same allegiance.

He ran off another stream of profanity when the passenger door suddenly opened, smacking him on the knee cap. He grabbed his knee, rubbing it vigorously while hopping about on the sidewalk. "Damn you, Charlie. Are you blind, and stupid? Can't you see me standing here?"

His anger quickly dissipated. He ran his hand over the stubble on his partner's head. "Didn't mean it, Charlie?" Jayco was prone to violence and wouldn't hesitate to kill someone over a lesser offense. He had a soft spot in his heart for Charlie. He understood Charlie's pain over name-calling. Didn't make it less truthful, but being called "stupid" hurt him.

"It's okay," Charlie said. "We gonna keep waiting for Tupac? I'm getting nervous. We stay parked on this empty street much longer and the cops might decide to check us out. Won't take them long to identify this Jeep as stolen."

"I know—I know. Ten more minutes and we'll leave. Sure would like to—" He paused when across Newcastle Street a figure emerged from between two buildings. Jayco watched the tall man walk toward their location. It was definitely Tupac; the gait was the tip-off. God knows he had witnessed that walk enough times in the prison's exercise yard. He waited until Tupac reached them before he spoke. "How long you been over there watching us?"

"About thirty minutes. Long enough to see no one else was interested in you. And I saw Charlie whack you on the knee with the door." Tupac laughed, and then wrapped his long, muscular arms around Jayco and Charlie in a bear hug. "Great seeing you guys on the outside."

"Same here," Jayco said. "Let's find a Denny's. I'll bring you up to speed on what me and Charlie got planned. We want you with us. Up to you, though."

It took less than fifteen minutes for the three men to locate the popular chain restaurant. They sat in a corner booth, sipping coffee while they awaited their orders.

Jayco placed his cup on the table. "Ready to hear it?"

Tupac nodded.

Jayco spoke without interruption for the next several minutes. Though no customers were seated near their booth, he leaned close to his friends, concerned his exuberance would make his voice too loud. He studied Tupac's face, trying to determine his interest. Finishing his summation, he raised his hands, palms up.

The response was silence.

Not a patient man, ten seconds was more than Jayco could take. "Well, what do you think?"

Tupac placed his hands flat on the table top. Maybe an unintentional gesture, but it riled Jayco.

"What—you surrendering already? We ain't done nothing yet."

Tupac raised his eyes to Jayco and Charlie. "You know I won't leave you hanging. But—and this is big—have you thought hard about what you are about to do? You get caught in armed robbery—it makes you a three-time loser. They'll put you away for the rest of your natural life; even more, if they can find a way to do it."

Jayco started to speak, pausing when the waitress appeared with their order. He kept his eyes down as the food was placed on the table. When the waitress left, he answered. "Yeah, I've thought about it. I don't plan on getting caught."

Tupac applied a liberal amount of black pepper and hot sauce to the eggs and grits on his plate. Old habits die hard as most prison inmates attest. He spoke through tight lips. "How reliable is the information? You know inmates tell whoppers, anything to build up their reputations."

"The details were specific. The guy's been there. He's seen the money and watched the exchanges. At least a hundred grand at each swap and usually a few packages of 'Meth' and 'crack' left over, for a bonus."

"What's in it for the guy who gave you the information?"

"He's in for ninety-nine years plus life. Ain't ever going to get out. He told me everything in exchange for my word I would take twenty thousand in cash to his mother. Made me swear on a blood oath."
Jayco watched as his friend struggled with the decision.

Tupac cleared his throat, his voice subdued. "Promise me there'll be no shooting. We get in and get out, like you said."
"That's what I said, ain't it? The guns will show the guy behind the counter we mean business. We'll clean out the safe and be out of there in five minutes."

Jayco saw his friend nod his head. He first looked at Charlie and then back at Tupac. A big grin spread across his face. "Okay if we flop at your place tonight?"

CHAPTER TWO
Christmas Day
7:00 a.m.

Doctor Edward Majorski entered an alcove off the nursing station at the Southeastern Health System ER. He dropped his weary body on the edge of the cot used for the on-duty physician. Stretching his six-foot, two-hundred-pound frame over the thin mattress brought a smile of relief to his face. Another twelve hour shift completed—his second in the past thirty-six hours.

Single, and with no family in the immediate area, he always volunteered to take the Christmas Eve shift so the married ER docs could be home with their families. Working two shifts so close together had put him on edge. Thinking back on the day, he regretted the times he had barked at the nurses for minor incidents—something totally out of character for him.

He ran his fingers through his dark, tangled hair in an attempt to appear presentable to the next patient. His appearance became less important when he saw Paul Swartz, another bachelor ER physician, enter the room. Paul was his relief and would cover the ER until he returned at 7:30 Christmas night.

"Glad you came early, Paul. I'm whipped."

"Figured you might be. How do you plan to spend your free twelve hours of Christmas Day?"

Majorski swung his legs off the cot, got to his feet and rolled his neck around on his shoulders to ease the tense muscles. "Believe it or not, I plan to stop at any store I can find open, get a carton of milk, a box of Corn Pops and after eating my fill, sleep until time to come back tonight. If I'm not here by seven, better have the desk clerk call and wake me up."

"If only I was older and sensible like you," chided Swartz. "I spent Christmas Eve eyeballing the chicks at different parties until about two hours ago. I'm whipped and my day is just starting. But don't you worry about me. You eat your Corn Pops and have pleasant dreams."

Majorski grabbed his overnight bag, gave a mock salute and started for the door. He gave Swartz a parting shot. "I'm not worrying about anybody today except Majorski."

CHAPTER THREE

Christmas Day

7:30 a.m.

Angry shouts erupted from the doorway. Heavy boots struck the tiled floor like rifle fire, echoing through the convenience store. The few customers fled in panic, knocking over display racks of Diet Coke and Pringles.

Doctor Majorski dropped face down in front of one of the large coolers at the rear of the building. Where could they go? Three armed men blocked the only visible exit, all equipped with enough firepower to face a small army.

Majorski hugged the floor, ignoring the sticky residue. His heart pounded against his sternum. Dizzy from hyperventilating, he slowed his breathing, inhaling through his nose and exhaling through pursed lips. The carton of milk he'd just removed from the cooler remained clutched in his right hand. Fighting the onset of panic, he recalled another time when the overflow of adrenalin figuratively drove him to his knees. He strained to hear what the men said to the store clerk; his attempt futile against the wailing of an infant in the arms of his frantic mother. The baby was the only voice of protest. The other customers cowered in terrified silence.

Majorski steeled his nerves against panic and crawled forward for a better look. A large black man blocked the front entrance. The shotgun cradled across his chest made him appear a giant. Even without the gun, Majorski didn't want to tangle with him.

He froze in position when the two other men, waving AK-47 rifles and sporting 9mm automatic pistols in their belts, powered their way to vantage points at the rear of the store. Majorski recognized the weapons from his addiction to war and crime movies and knew the guns were capable of killing everyone in the store in a matter of seconds.

Aggravated voices from the front of the store diverted his attention away from the two men in the rear. He turned his head in time to see a boy with stringy, blond hair reveal his youthful indiscretion by arguing with the black man. Majorski grimaced at the sound made by the shotgun barrel against the side of the boy's head. The protest ended when the boy went down like a pole-axed bull.

Amidst the chaos, WYNR, Channel 102.5 FM played on in the background. Kenny Rogers sang about peace on earth and goodwill to men.

Majorski risked raising his head to assess the situation. He took stock of the other people caught up in the madness. At the end of an adjacent counter, a woman in a business pants suit, her hair pulled back in a tight bun, had her arms around a teenage girl. The girl, obviously terrified, buried her face against the woman's shoulder in an attempt to stifle her weeping.

The fact it was Christmas Day didn't seem to matter to the acne-scarred man standing guard near the checkout counter. A twitching finger moved in and out of the trigger guard of his automatic weapon. Majorski thought the man anxious for someone to piss him off. In the present situation, it wouldn't take much.

"Get over here and lie down," acne-face ordered the patrons in the store. "You," he motioned to the man behind the counter, "move away from the cash drawer and get on your knees facing the wall."

Majorski kept his eyes on the balding rotund man behind the counter who glared at acne-face and stood his ground. Apparently this wasn't his first robbery.

Shifting his gaze toward the back of the store, Majorski noticed a door. But where did it lead? Storage room; maybe a restroom. It didn't appear sturdy enough to be an exit. No one guarded the door so maybe it was only a storage room. Even as he calculated his odds of making it to the door, he knew he wouldn't leave the others. I'm not a hero, he thought, but maybe I can do something to help. He rested his head on the floor.

The tension mounted in the room. Majorski could feel it—could taste it. He watched the black man point the shotgun at the owner. "Are you deaf, old man, or just stupid? The 'man' said get on the floor."

Reacting to the shout, Majorski turned his attention back to the men nearest him. Acne-face was almost running in place, constantly shifting from one leg to the other. He appeared to study the patrons on the floor and then shouted to the black man guarding the front, "Tupac, check everyone for cell phones."

Tupac held the shotgun in his left hand. He started the search, beginning with the women. "Dump your pocketbooks on the floor."

The women complied. The older woman trembled so hard she dropped her purse twice before she was able to empty the contents. She wrapped her arms around her daughter, pulling her closer when they were subjected to a pat-down. The girl cried out in terror and her mother defiantly pushed Tupac away.

Tupac moved efficiently through the store, collecting cell phones. No one refused. "Got 'em all."

"Check the kid," Jayco said. "He's moving again."

Tupac rolled the teen onto his back, searched the pockets of his jeans and extracted several items. "Got fake ID cards along with about twenty dollars in cash." He kicked the kid in the butt to get his attention. "Get over against that stock shelf. Stay there like a good boy and you won't get yo' head slapped again."

The frightened boy slid along the floor, collapsing against a rack of beans and corn. A trickle of blood ran down the side of his face, dripping like a faucet, one drop at a time, onto his shirt.

Majorski took in the scene, watching the old man behind the counter stand and wave his arms as he shouted at the robbers. "You damn punks take what you want and get the hell out of my store. Don't hurt any more of these fine people. They haven't bothered you."

"Oh God!" whispered Majorski. He sensed things were about to go down the crapper. Before he could react, he saw acne-face swing the rifle toward the owner.

"Shut up, you old bastard. I'll tell you what to do. Open the cash drawer and that safe under the counter."

"I'm getting tired of this crap," yelled the old man, opening the register. He jerked all the bills from the drawer to toss them on the counter top. He leaned toward the safe, reached beyond it and stood with a handgun extended toward the black man.

Majorski leapt to his feet, waving his arms as he screamed at the man behind the counter. "Don't." His actions were too late.

The old man fired a single shot.

The bullet struck Tupac high in the right chest, knocking him from his feet.

Majorski changed his direction toward the closest man with the rifle. Out of the corner of his eye he saw the storeowner swing the gun toward Jayco. Majorski realized he was too late when the automatic rifle barked three times.

The old man clutched his chest, his heavyset body slamming against the cigarette rack before slumping to the floor.

A high-pitched scream followed and the blond teenage girl jerked away from her mother's arms and ran toward the front door.

Majorski continued his charge, terrified of the rapidly deteriorating situation. He launched his body just as Jayco swung the rifle and fired, striking the older woman in the back as she attempted to restrain her daughter. The force of the bullet pushed the woman forward, slamming both her and her daughter to the floor.

Majorski's momentum carried him into Jayco sending them both sprawling across the floor. The two men grappled for control of the rifle. The struggle was brought to a quick halt when Majorski felt another rifle barrel jammed into his back. He spun toward his assailant, staring into the blank eyes of the stocky man who had entered the store with the other two men. Majorski released his hold on Jayco's rifle and crawled away from him. Within seconds he was staring into the muzzles of two rifles.

The man called Jayco was frantic and Majorski saw the man's finger tighten on the trigger.

"Let it go, Jayco. We got to check on Tupac." The stocky man put his hand on the rifle in Jayco's hand and pushed it away from Majorski.

Jayco pulled at the rifle, struggling to free it. During the entire time his maniacal eyes never left Majorski's face. Finally realizing he couldn't overcome his friend's strength, he relented. "Okay, Charlie. I'll let this bastard live for now. But before we leave, I'm gonna waste him."

Charlie remained in position over Majorski until Jayco had moved away to check on the other member of the threesome.

Majorski and the man called Charlie watched as Jayco knelt beside the wounded man, avoiding the pool of blood beneath Tupac that flowed across the floor, mingling with the lifeblood pumping steadily from the entrance wound to the woman's back.

Jayco spun toward Charlie. "Check out the back room. Make sure the door is locked and block it with some boxes; then get back in here. Tupac is down, he's hurt bad."

As soon as Charlie left the room, Jayco jumped over the counter, his arms shaking in fury.

He jammed the barrel of the AK-47 against the skull of the storeowner and fired three rapid rounds, splattering blood and brains across the lower counters and floor. "You crazy bastard," he screamed at the dead man. "Why didn't you do what you were told? Look what you've caused."

Then, within seconds, Jayco's demeanor changed. His voice sounded surreally calm. "I fixed him for you, Tupac. He won't hurt you again."

The injured man had pulled himself to a sitting position against a stacked display of engine coolant. "Let's get out of here. I can't catch my breath. I won't be any more help to you."

Jayco swept the rifle from side to side around the store, his trigger finger flexing repeatedly outside the trigger guard. "Anyone else want to be a hero?" He ducked behind the front counter, emerging with a large ring of keys. He motioned to the lanky kid nursing the large welt on his head. "Take these keys and find the one that fits the front door. Lock it." He pitched the keys to the boy, who in spite of his nervousness made a one-handed catch.

"Tupac, keep your shotgun trained on the front door. If anybody in this room approaches the door, blow them away. I'm opening the safe, one way or another." He saw Tupac nod. The barrel of the shotgun rested on the floor. Jayco doubted his friend could lift it if required.

The kid, his hands trembling, attempted several times to insert the correct key. After each failed effort, he squeezed his eyes shut in anticipation of a bullet striking his back. On the fourth try he was successful and spun the bolt into place.

Jayco motioned for the keys. "Reverse the sign on the front door. We are closed for business as of right now."

The boy lifted the string holding the sign on the door. His hands were still trembling and he dropped the plastic sign before securing it in place. While backing away from the door, he noticed a truck pull up to the fuel pumps. He realized the pumps were on. Without saying a word, he returned to his place on the floor.

* * *

Outside, a 2005 maroon Toyota Tundra truck stopped at the row of pumps closest to the street. A man with salt-and-pepper hair, dressed in slacks and a golf shirt, stepped down from the king cab, inserted his credit card, removed the nozzle and began pumping gas. He replaced the handle, closed the gas cap, retrieved his receipt and climbed back into his truck. He drove off without a single glance in the direction of the store.

Charlie glanced out the window and saw the truck drive away, but before he could relay the news to Jayco, another car had pulled up to the pumps. He scurried closer to the front window, focusing on an elderly driver who positioned his vehicle on the store-side refueling island. He watched the man finished refueling, and then turn toward the store.

Charlie yelled. "Everyone get down and stay still." Removing the 9mm automatic from his belt, he watched the old man peer at the "closed" sign, ignore it and pull on the door handle. He repeated the action several times before he backed off.

Charlie heaved a sigh of relief when the man ambled toward his car. The relief was short-lived. The man returned to the store and tried the door again, banging hard with his fist against the glass. His face twisted in a frown when he got no response. He peered through the small openings between advertising posters on the door.

Charlie positioned the muzzle of the automatic about two inches from the glass. Though he was at a bad angle to the old man, he was prepared to fire if necessary. His finger tightened on the trigger. He heard the roar of his pulse in his ears. He held his breath, and then sighed in relief when the man turned and walked away.

He remained in position until certain the car was gone and then scrambled back to the checkout counter, pulling Jayco away from the unopened safe. "Jayco. The gas pumps are on. Cars are stopping for gas. An old fart just came up to the door and tried to get in. He pushed his face against the glass and looked around."

"Crap. Did he see anybody?"

"I don't think so. He didn't hurry away, but he was old. Maybe he was going as fast as he could."

Jayco jerked the Atlanta Braves baseball cap from his head and hurled it across the room. "Find the switch to turn off the pumps and the outside lights."

Ignoring the command, Charlie stumbled forward, his chest heaving. He jerked Jayco's arm, spinning him around to face him. His words tumbled out of his mouth. "We need to get out of here."

"I know, Charlie. Calm down. Just do what I told you. I'll shoot the lock off the safe and then we'll get Tupac up and leave through the back door."

"Can I take some chips and crackers?" Charlie asked.

Jayco stared at his simple-minded friend. "Sure, Charlie. Take as much as you want. Make sure you get the money off the counter. Not much there, it'll have to do."

Jayco fired repeatedly at the combination lock on the safe, ignoring the ricochets of bullets and metal. The safe, though badly damaged, remained closed. He lowered his head in defeat, cursed his rotten luck and went to his wounded friend. His concern intensified when he saw the mask of pain on Tupac's face and the amount of blood saturating the torn sweatshirt.

"Think you can get up if I help?"

"Don't know. Can't get my breath. Let me wrap my arm around your neck and we'll try it."

Jayco placed the rifle on the floor within easy reach and squatted beside Tupac. He draped his friend's arm around his own neck, securing a tight grip on the wrist. "Ready?"

"Not really. No choice though. We've got to get out of here." Tupac put pressure on Jayco's neck at the same time he pushed up with his legs. He managed to get a foot off the floor before he collapsed hard, screaming in pain.

"I'm sorry. I can't do it. Get Charlie and y'all drag me to the car. Don't stop even if I beg you. We stay here—we end up in prison again."

Jayco gently removed Tupac's arm from around his neck and straightened up. "No way I go back to prison. I'll take 'suicide by cop' first."

CHAPTER FOUR

8:30 a.m.

Majorski lay immobile on the floor by the coolers. All around him was clutter. Stacked cans and boxes near the entrance and at the end of each aisle barely left enough space for a single customer to pass. Large sections of paint peeled from the concrete walls. Ceiling tile stained with watermarks around the vents and streaks of rust on the covers of the fluorescent lights added to the total picture of disrepair. The tile covering the cement floor was worn through, especially in front of the checkout counter. Months of dried-on pollen and dirt mixed with oil vapor created a distorted view of the scene outside the building. Advertising placards obscured most of the inside of the windows; the uncovered spaces exposing the worst of the filth. Not a picture of a thriving business. Why would these men select this store to rob?

He faced a difficult choice. Exhausted from his just completed twelve-hour shift in the emergency room, he could easily remain at his spot on the floor and not get involved any further. He'd made his heroic gesture. It didn't accomplish anything except nearly costing him his life. *I'm no Rambo*, he thought. Not a single person in the store knew him. Finally, his compassion and sense of duty overcame his fatigue and he rose to a kneeling position.

He directed his words to the man who had fired the rifle and had threatened him. Jayco—that was the name the stocky fellow used when he broke up their brief scuffle. "Mr. Jayco, I'm a doctor." He spoke in a reserved tone. "Please let me do what I can for the wounded."

Jayco snarled, "What kind of doctor?"

Majorski accepted the reply as an opening and cautiously stood up, his eyes focused on the rifle in the man's hands. "I'm an emergency room physician at Southeast Georgia Health System Hospital. Please allow me to examine the injured."

A harsh laugh escaped from Jayco as he glanced at the body of the storeowner. "Don't waste your time behind the counter. That sucker is long gone." He turned his gaze toward the blond teenager, who was sprawled across her mother, her shoulders shaking from deep sobs.

He nodded to Majorski. "Check my buddy. Fix him up first. Then you can check on the woman. Don't try to be a hero again or I'll put a bullet in you."

Being a hero was the last thing Majorski wanted to do. He moved in the direction of Tupac, halting abruptly when he heard Jayco scream at him.

"Stop! Go around the back of the counters and keep low. Another car has pulled up to the pumps outside. Charlie, help him move Tupac and the woman behind all the displays where they can't be seen."

Majorski did as instructed. The injured man, known as Tupac, grunted in pain when Majorski placed his hands under the man's arms to move him. Once he positioned Tupac behind the counters facing the large coolers, he returned for the woman. It was apparent she was slipping in and out of consciousness and opened her eyes when Majorski tried to change her position. She didn't complain. With help from the daughter and Charlie, they moved her to a space a few feet from Tupac.

Returning to the front of the store, Majorski grabbed a box of Pampers he had seen when he picked up the woman. He hurried back and knelt at her side. He pulled her blouse out of her pants and tore it from the bottom to the neck line. He packed several of the absorbent pads against the entrance wound. With a gentle touch, learned from dealing with injured people, he rolled the woman onto her back. He placed his fingers along the side of her neck, noting a rapid and barely palpable carotid pulse.

He shook the young girl's shoulder to get her attention. "Your mom is going into shock. Find something to elevate her legs and anything to cover her to preserve her body heat."

"Thank you," the girl said shakily. "Her name is Lucille Dixon. Mine is Samantha. I'm her daughter."

Lucille Dixon stirred briefly at her daughter's voice. She attempted to open her eyes, her lids fluttering a few times before she mercifully slipped back into unconsciousness.

"Leave her. Check on my partner like I told you."

The harsh voice was enough for Majorski to know who issued the demand. He clenched his teeth, swallowed his anger and slid along the floor to the black man. The man's medical condition had deteriorated; he struggled with each breath. Removing a pen knife from his pocket,

Majorski split the man's Jacksonville Jaguars jersey at the sleeve, and then tore it completely up to the reinforced neck line, which he cut through with the knife. With his patient's help, he slipped the jersey off and tossed it aside.

The smooth entrance wound an inch below the right clavicle was obvious. Majorski shifted Tupac's position, exploring for the exit wound. He lifted the man's right arm, discovering as expected, a mass of shredded muscle and skin; still bleeding profusely. The bullet apparently passed through the upper lobe of the right lung causing it to collapse. The missile's trajectory continued, striking the scapula, altering the course of the bullet before it exited in the right axilla. Large chunks of tissue had been blown away and a mixture of air and blood bubbled from the space, increasing each time the man gasped.

Majorski felt the cold metal of a rifle barrel press against his neck.

"Move over against the wall," Jayco ordered.

Majorski complied.

Jayco kneeled at his friend's side, affectionately rubbing Tupac's short, kinky hair. "You hanging in there?"

"I'm good. Not breathing so hot though."

"Don't worry. Me and Charlie will get you out of here."

Jayco jabbed Majorski with the barrel of the rifle. "Get something to patch up his chest. We're getting the hell out of here before the cops arrive."

Unnoticed, the white teenage boy had slipped up to the front of the store, watching the pumps for another customer. He called out, "Too late. I see flashing blue lights turning the corner."

"Fuck," Jayco bellowed. "Everybody stay where you are. Charlie, help me pick up Tupac. We'll get out the back.

Majorski palpated the side of Tupac's neck, noting the rapid, weak pulsation. "He can't go with you. He'll be dead in an hour if a chest tube isn't inserted."

Tupac raised himself on his arms, his face contorted in pain. "Don't leave me. I can make it with you. Let's get out of here."

The room seemed to spin around Jayco. How did everything get so fucked up? An early morning hit, not many customers and a safe full of drug money. *For God's sake, it's Christmas morning. What are all these people doing here?* "Charlie. Check out back. If it's clear, we'll grab Tupac and take off. We can't use our car; check the old man's pockets for his car keys."

Less than a minute later, Charlie returned. "No good. Cop cars are already in the back lot. Two cops are outside their car with weapons drawn. They know something is going down."

Jayco ran his hand across his sweaty brow while assessing the deteriorating situation. "Find all the posters and paper you can—get the girl and the kid to help you. Cover all the glass up front. Hurry before the cops can look in and get a count."

Jayco paused. "Wait. What do we have in back?"

Having anticipated the question, Charlie was ready with the information. "There's a restroom without a window, and a storage room with an exit to the back parking lot. The back door is steel and has a heavy bolt in addition to a lock in the handle. It's heavy. It'll take a lot to break it down."

Majorski ignored the chatter of the two men. He checked Lucille's pulse again, closed his eyes and after a moment of silent prayer, stood and faced Jayco. "You are going to lose your friend and Mrs. Dixon as well, if you don't come to some decision soon. You have all the cell phones. Use one of them to call 911 for an ambulance. You still have the rest of us for hostages."

Jayco spun away, walked a few steps and stopped. He wrapped his arm around his head as if in pain and continued his silent vigil. Several seconds passed before he spoke. "No. Nobody leaves. If they die, they die."

Tupac didn't flinch from the words, accepting his fate. He screamed in pain when Samantha collided with him in her mad charge toward Jayco.

"You cold-hearted bastard." She slammed her fists into his face. "You can't just let my mother die. Do something."

Jayco bristled in anger. "You crazy bitch, I'll show you what I can do." He drew back the rifle to smash into her skull, halting when an amplified voice boomed from outside the store.

"This is the Glynn County Sheriff's Department. We know you have hostages. The store is completely surrounded. There's no possibility of escape."

No one inside the store moved or spoke.

The voice from outside continued. "A negotiator is on the way. Stay calm. Don't do anything foolish. When the negotiator gets here, he'll listen to you. We can work this out before somebody gets hurt."

"Little late for that, asshole," Jayco murmured.

Majorski recognized a potential opportunity. "Here's your chance. Let the EMTs take your partner and Mrs. Dixon so they can get the help they need to survive. You can negotiate your release using the rest of us. The police will honor your goodwill gesture."

Jayco spat. "Sure. Like a 'goodwill' bullet through my fucking head."

"Man, it's over," Majorski pleaded. "You won't leave here alive except by surrendering. Don't let your friend die for nothing."

Jayco swallowed hard, glanced several times toward the flashing blue lights penetrating the paper over the front windows before answering. "You said you're a doctor. Fix my friend. We'll take the girl as a hostage. They will let us leave."

Majorski shook his head and sat on the floor. "I won't do it. The cops will never let you leave here with hostages, and you know it."

"Do what I say or I will shoot her now!" Jayco jammed the gun under Samantha's chin. "I mean it. This is a SIG SAUER 9mm loaded with hollow points. I pull this trigger and her entire head disappears."

Majorski was trapped. He had to do something to calm the maniac. "I don't have what I need to fix him. We need an ambulance to take him to the hospital."

"Are you fucking deaf? I told you—" Jayco's voice stopped when the lights went out, the refrigerator motors died and the warm air from the vents above him stopped flowing.

"Bastards." He hunkered down behind a wooden counter for protection from imagined snipers with night vision goggles. His nostrils flared as he directed his venom toward Majorski. "Call those cops. Tell them to turn the power back on or I'm wasting a lot of people—starting with you."

Majorski took the phone from Jayco's hand. His fingers trembled when he dialed 911. The familiar ring occurred only twice before a feminine voice responded.

"911 Emergency Center."

Majorski swallowed hard, pausing to carefully choose his words. He recalled too many stories of 911 operators ignoring what they considered to be prank calls. "Hello. I'm Doctor Edward Majorski. I'm an emergency room physician at Southeast Georgia Hospital. At this moment, I'm involved in a hostage situation in a convenience store."

"Yes, sir. We were briefed on the situation. How can I help you?"

Majorski breathed a sigh of relief. "Thank you God," he

murmured. This lady seemed on top of her job. "The police have turned off the power to the building. The three men with guns demand the power be turned back on or they will start killing people."

He allowed himself a brief smile on his subtle ability to notify the operator of the number of bad guys. His bravado was short-lived. He recoiled from a blow to the side of his head from the stock of Jayco's rifle. Showers of multicolored lights filled his vision, followed by a stark blackness. He fell to his knees, high-pitched ringing in his ears. Roughly jerked back to his feet, he nearly fell again but the barrel of the AK-47 shoved against his ribs kept him upright. He felt Jayco's hot breath on his ear, the voice distant.

"Stop being a smart ass. Just tell them what I tell you and nothing more. If I didn't need you to fix Tupac, you wouldn't be hearing this warning. You'd be dead."

Majorski became aware of a warm sensation on the side of his head, a sure sign his scalp was split. He removed his handkerchief and applied pressure to control the bleeding. He fought against the nausea and the pain, desperate to stay focused for the benefit of the others.

The fluorescent lights flickered for a moment before filling the room with a bright glow. At the same time the motors of the refrigerator units kicked on, followed by the usual steady hum.

Jayco smiled, nodding his approval to Majorski. "All right. Now tell the operator to put you in touch with whoever got the lights back on. Tell them what you need to fix Tupac."

Majorski picked up the cell phone from the floor where he dropped it when struck. He was not surprised to discover the operator still on the line. "This is Dr. Majorski again. I need to talk to the person in charge at the scene."

The woman knew her stuff, quickly responding. "I can't patch you through to them directly, but I got a read on your cell number. I'll relay the information."

"Thank you," answered Majorski, fighting against another wave of nausea and dizziness. He closed the cell phone and slumped to the floor.

CHAPTER FIVE
9 a.m.

Lieutenant Buddy Spalding stood alongside a Buick LeSabre, a classic and his personal car. His uniform was wrinkled, a certain sign of his hasty departure from his home. A robbery and hostage situation was not his favorite way to start Christmas morning. He pulled himself up to his full six feet and hastily tucked his shirt tail into his pants.

His large frame carried his two hundred forty pounds easily. "Stout, not fat," he reminded his friends. His assessment of the crime scene included a five-minute session with the alert citizen who notified the authorities of seeing blood on the floor of the locked convenience store. Unfortunately, the man didn't see anyone inside the store and couldn't give any additional information.

"Okay, people. You know the drill. Get the barricades up and get all these people behind them—especially members of the media. Those vultures will be here soon. Let them know if I catch any of them beyond the barricade, they'll get a quick trip downtown."

"You're looking at a First Amendment problem if you totally exclude the media," someone volunteered.

"To hell with the First Amendment! I'm trying to keep this thing contained."

He spun in a tight circle searching for Trooper Hank Ginn, his assistant. "Hank. I want sharpshooters in two locations facing the front and another two covering the rear. Get someone with a radio in the apartment building across the street. Instruct them to watch for anyone trying to escape through the roof. Tell the shooters to lock and load— safeties on. Get me three men with twelve-gauge shotguns loaded with double-0 buckshot behind the patrol cars. No firing from anyone without a direct order from me."

Ginn rapidly relayed orders to a corporal beside him; at the same time he had another officer on his cell phone. Within minutes the barricades and men were in place. "Orders completed, Lieutenant. I also have men taking down tag numbers to send to the Department of

Motor Vehicles to get names of the people inside. We'll get prints from the doors and steering wheels in hopes of getting a match."

"Good work. Get some wreckers in here and haul away the vehicles in front of the store after the CSI guys finish with them. Now what am I forgetting? And where the hell is Lieutenant Watkins?"

Ginn shrugged his shoulders. He wasn't privy to the whereabouts of Grant Watkins, the department's negotiator. "Sorry, sir; I don't know. I need an order to clear a spot behind the barricades for the Crime Bus."

"You got it. Make arrangements for portable floodlights in case this situation goes into the night." *God, I pray it doesn't.*

* * *

Majorski leaned against the cold, thick glass of the refrigerated cooler. The condensation accumulated on the lower part of the unit provided temporary relief to his pounding headache. With his head lowered and the injured side against the glass, he faced away from the others in the store. The forced separation from the injured was tearing him up inside. But without the proper equipment he could do little for them even if that asshole Jayco allowed him near them. He remembered once before his involvement in a life or death situation had made him feel impotent, and he had sworn never to put himself in that position again; but here he was. "Why me, God?" he spoke out loud, not realizing he had done so.

A soft angelic voice responded from much closer than heaven. "I would say because He knows you can handle it."

Majorski turned toward the young woman with the baby and was shocked that the baby was no longer crying; instead, it was sleeping soundly. "How in the world did you get the baby to sleep with all this commotion?"

She patted the front of her sweater, smiling as she answered. "Oh, it wasn't too difficult although I was surprised he would nurse during all the yelling and screaming. I guess he was too hungry to care about anything else. I'm Tracy Adams and this is my son, Luke."

Majorski stared at the woman's exposed swollen breast, realized what he was doing and jerked his eyes away, his face turning a shade of pink. "I'm Edward Majorski. Sorry we meet under these circumstances. I imagine your husband is frantic if he's waiting on you to return from a quick trip to the store."

Tracy smiled, her eyes locked on the handsome man who appeared in his mid-thirties, yet dressed like a preppie; a white shirt with buttoned down collars, snug fitting jeans and black loafers without socks. "Think about what you said. If a husband was at home, do you think I would be in this store on Christmas morning with a baby?"

"Sorry," Majorski replied. A sheepish grin spread across his face. For a reason he couldn't understand, the news pleased him.

"No need to be sorry. There are a lot of single moms these days. Guys don't always accept responsibility for the results of a brief fling and not all women are willing to rush off for a convenient abortion. I won't lie. Though it makes my life more difficult –Luke's worth it." She looked down at the baby, pulling the blanket closer to his chin.

Tracy eased her breast from the infant's mouth, repaired herself and, clutching Luke in a tight embrace, she scooted across the floor, sliding on her backside. "Let me take a look at your head."

She handed the sleeping baby to Majorski and helped him position his arms to support Luke's head properly. With her hands free, she gently pressed her fingers on the lump, avoiding the open wound in the center. She noticed Majorski wince, in spite of his obvious attempt to appear macho.

"The laceration isn't bleeding anymore. It's about two inches long and superficial. No artery involved."

Good news; however, the laceration was the least of his worries. At the moment the worsening headache and the dizziness caused him more concern. As long as he kept his head down, the dizziness didn't seem so bad. When he raised his head, it triggered brief episodes of vertigo. In spite of his problems he became curious about Tracy's apparent knowledge of lacerations. "Do you have medical training?"

"I am ... was a medical assistant in a family practice clinic. I quit after Luke's birth."

"I can't imagine what it must be like," Majorski said. "I don't have enough time in my life for a pet rock, much less a baby."

Tracy beamed. "God provides for us, especially when things are challenging. Maybe He put you in this situation for a reason. We aren't supposed to understand why things happen to us. He has a purpose for everything and everybody." She paused as though deciding whether to go on.

"I guess you've had plenty of challenges," Majorski said.

"I was devastated when I discovered I was pregnant," she replied.

"Working long hours had drained me so I went for a long weekend on St. Simons Island with my girl friend; her parents own a condo on the beach."

"Lucky you. St. Simons is a fantastic place. Sorry, I interrupted you."

Tracy smiled. "Yeah, watch that—I'm coming to the good part. We went out one night; I met a cute guy at Brogan's bar and grill. After a few drinks we went for a ride in his BMW convertible, and we parked near the beach under a full moon. Too many nights alone, too much alcohol and a romantic setting led to Luke's conception."

Majorski gazed at her with interest, picturing the beautiful woman with such long legs having a sexual encounter in the small BMW. He carefully avoided any appearance of being judgmental. "Did you tell the father?"

"No. My friend did. She located him later through an acquaintance. Long story short, he wasn't interested in talking to me. I didn't push it. My parents live in Atlanta and are staunch Southern Baptist. They weren't happy from the beginning about me moving to Brunswick. So, when I ended up pregnant and unmarried, I was on my own."

Majorski felt another wave of nausea pass over him. He carefully handed Luke back to Tracy, taking care to support the baby's head. He remembered the importance of the support from his medical school rotation in obstetrics.

He lowered his head and the nausea passed. He continued the conversation to take his mind off his discomfort. "Luke's a beautiful baby. Have your parents seen him?"

"No ... not in person. I sent them pictures. I think Mom will eventually come around. I'm not so sure about my dad; he's pretty stubborn."

"Like most fathers," he replied. "I wouldn't worry too much. Once he holds Luke in his arms, his stubbornness will disappear like ocean fog in the morning."

"I hope so," Tracy said. "I want Luke to know at least one set of his grandparents."

"Well, it'll happen, or it won't. Either way, Luke seems to be in good hands."

Tracy laughed out loud at the pun, immediately stifled it and peered toward the front of the store, afraid she had drawn unwanted attention to herself.

Majorski touched her arm to reassure her. "How are you getting by—I mean—-since you aren't working?"

Tracy shifted Luke to her opposite arm. "My boss is a great guy. He made sure my insurance stayed current and he gave me a severance payment that should pay the rent and food until I can return to work. And no, I'm not sleeping with him."

Majorski held up his hands, palms out in mock defense. "Hey, I had no such thoughts. I promise."

Tracy raised her eyebrows and then smiled. "Would you mind holding—"

Samantha Dixon crashed headlong at their feet, cutting off Tracy's words. "Please do something for my mother. Her skin is cold. Please make them get help for her."

Majorski made his way to Lucille, touching her arms and legs. Her extremities were cool to the touch, a sure sign her body was shunting blood away from non-vital organs in an attempt to keep the heart and brain functioning. He rose to his feet, staggered momentarily and weaved his way through the boxes to where Jayco was sitting. It took considerable effort to avoid a rancorous attitude.

"If you won't let the injured go to the hospital, at least let me ask the authorities for medical and surgical supplies. I know I can save your friend. It might be too late for Mrs. Dixon. Still, I'd like to make an attempt to save both of them."

Jayco looked at him suspiciously. "I thought you said you were an ER doc."

"I am. Most ER docs can do what Tupac needs. I also had four years of general surgery training and an additional two years of thoracic surgery—chest surgery—before I started working in the emergency room. That training will be of some benefit to Mrs. Dixon. Maybe I can slow down the bleeding to give her a better chance of survival."

Jayco dug the cell phone from his pocket, passing it to Majorski. "Call 911 again. Have them put you through to the honchos in charge. Tell them what you have in mind and what you need. Give the phone to me before you hang up. Ain't nothing happening unless me, Charlie and Tupac get something out of it."

Majorski took the phone, noticing his sweaty palms. *I'm getting myself in deeper,* he thought.

Several minutes after Majorski talked to the 911 operator, the cell phone rang. He clicked it on, answering as he did when in the on-call room at the ER. "Doctor Majorski."

There was silence for several seconds before a gruff voice spoke. "How do I know that? You could be one of the hostage-takers."

Majorski thought about the situation before he answered. "I am Edward Majorski. I'm on the emergency room staff at Southeast Georgia Hospital; Gary Colberg is the CEO of the hospital. Call him. He'll verify it. Now, who are you?"

There was another pause, a few seconds—seemingly like minutes. "Lieutenant Buddy Spalding. I'm the officer in charge at the moment. A negotiator is in transit to this location since hostages are involved. How many people are in there? I understand there are three perps with guns. Anybody hurt?"

"Officer Spalding. There's a gun to my head so I can't answer the questions you've asked." He was certain the officer picked up on the tension in his voice. "Instead, let me tell you what I need. Two individuals are seriously injured. One other per—" he felt the muzzle of the gun press harder against his scalp "—son, uh, doesn't need treatment."

"What are you asking?"

"The persons in charge in the store refuse to allow the wounded to be released to an ambulance. I pleaded with them and they have agreed to let me do what I can here in the store. I need to talk to a physician or an EMT to arrange for medical and surgical supplies; that is, if you agree."

The prolonged silence worried him. Did the person on the other end of the line really care what happened to the wounded or was he more interested in getting the situation over with so he could go back to enjoying his Christmas day?

"Okay. I'll agree to you talking to an EMT here. Understand, we're not actually giving you anything until the negotiator arrives. Concessions must be made before we turn over the supplies."

Majorski peered up at Jayco, who scowled at him. "I've got good hearing, Doc. I heard the last remark. Tell the bastard, I'm the one in charge and I'll determine if any concessions are made, unless he wants a blood bath."

Spalding interrupted before Majorski could relay the information. "I heard. Just stay calm. I'm going to put an EMT on the line. Tell him what you need and we'll go from there."

CHAPTER SIX

9:30 a.m.

Jimmy Harris, the teenage boy knocked out earlier by Tupac's angry blow with the shotgun, watched his assailant's head sag lower onto his chest. "Man, you're bleeding to death. Tell your friend to let the EMTs come get you. They don't know you are one of the robbers. Even if they find out, you'll be alive."

Tupac tried to focus on the kid's words but his mind drifted, preoccupied with the effort to breathe. "Nice of you to care, especially after I smacked you. I ain't leaving Jayco. Not your problem anyway. Just sit there and don't cause any trouble."

Jayco's voice boomed across the store. "He giving you a hard time, partner?"

"No. I'm still with you. The pain ain't so bad now. Damn hard to breathe though."

"Hang in there," Jayco said. "The doc will help you when the supplies get here."

A high-pitched squeal came from the area near Tupac, directed toward Jayco. A belligerent Samantha Dixon screamed at Jayco. "Why don't you let them take my mother? She can't do anything to hurt you. She will die if she doesn't get help soon."

Jayco snarled, "Shut the hell up, you little bitch. If you hadn't run for the door, she wouldn't be hurt. So sit there and shut up. Don't bother me again or I'll put a bullet in you, too."

Samantha wrapped her arms around Lucille, whispering words of love for her.

* * *

10 a.m.

Jimmy Harris visually surveyed the store. Assured all three gunmen were distracted, he crawled across the floor on all fours and propped against the counter next to Samantha. Flexing his knees, he tucked his heels up against his butt, wrapping his arms around his long legs. He was uneasy about striking up a conversation with such a beautiful girl. Nevertheless, he sensed she was devastated by Jayco's verbal barrage and needed someone to console her.

"I'm sorry about your mom. It's obvious you love her a lot. I can tell by the way you worry about her and the way you challenged that asshole. I wish I had your courage."

Samantha stared at him, her eyes filling with tears. She looked away, wiping the moisture away with the sleeve of her blouse. "I do love her; unfortunately, I haven't always shown it to her. As a matter of fact, I've been a total bitch, especially this morning. I pitched a fit because she didn't have the mix to make me pancakes on Christmas morning like my father always did. She didn't get upset. She got dressed and came here. At the last minute, I felt guilty and decided to come with her. Now if she dies, I will never forgive myself. I've made the past year a living hell for her."

Jimmy hesitated, not wanting to pry but Samantha appeared eager to talk. "What happened to her?"

"Well, for a long time I blamed her for my parents' divorce, and for ruining our lives. But the fact is, my dad left her for a younger woman. Mom never saw it coming. Dad worked out of town a lot, so she never suspected anything, right up to the day he told her he was leaving her. She was so stunned; she didn't fight it and didn't ask for alimony. The court ordered my dad to pay child support and he did for a few months."

Looking down at her mother's unconscious face, she took a deep breath before going on. "When he stopped, Mom was too proud to beg him and she would never report him to the courts. I pray to God I'm half as decent as she is when I grow up." Her voice shook. "And that is definitely the key phrase—when I grow up. So far, I haven't shown much evidence of doing so."

"Don't be so hard on yourself. How old are you?"

"I'm seventeen. I'm not driving yet because Mom can't afford the added insurance. Between her and my friends I don't have any problem getting where I want to go."

"I'd be glad to drive you around, if you ever need me."

Samantha's eyes brightened and the corners of her mouth turned up. "Who are you? Are you one of those mysterious angels like we see on television? The people who show up in people's lives and make everything better. My God, I haven't talked this much about my personal life even to my best friends."

He reached out, taking her hands in a soft grasp. "Believe me, I'm no angel. The name's Jimmy Harris. I'm only mysterious to my parents who wonder how they could have possibly conceived someone as stupid as me. My story is a lot like yours, except worse. I dropped out of high school my senior year. I was on the honors program, and had multiple offers for college scholarships. I just got bored. I hang out with friends and go home when I'm totally broke and hungry.

"My parents hope I'll go back to school," he said. "They've never rejected me, and when I show up at home, they take me in like things are normal. No demands, no ultimatums. I guess they figure I'll grow up someday, too."

Samantha squeezed his hands. "Glad to meet you, Jimmy Harris. I'm Samantha Dixon. You and I make quite a pair."

She leaned back against the counter, her head resting on a stack of packaged egg noodles. When she turned her head toward Jimmy, the bags made a funny crunching sound. They both grinned.

"So, what do you do now?" Samantha asked.

"Just about anything I want to, unless it costs money." Jimmy laughed at his own lame joke. "I bum around, do odd jobs, just enough to make spending money for cigarettes and beer. I never work more than a couple of days on the same job. Gets too boring. Computers excite me; not much anything else. I would love to be a programmer but the honchos in charge insist I go to school first."

Samantha sighed. "I know how you feel. School is a drag sometimes. My mom is always on me about my grades. I don't have any brothers or sisters to compare with or it would be worse. She's tough; even more since she and Dad divorced."

Jimmy stretched his legs straight out, rubbing his thighs as he did so. "Do you miss your dad?"

"Oh God, yes! He was so cool and took up for me. I guess I take after him because he's such a free spirit. Too much so for my mom's taste. She liked that in him when they were younger. She grew up and Dad never did. His trips out of town got more frequent and eventually he found someone who didn't mind his craziness. I've never met her, though. Dad never brings her with him when he visits, which is rare."

She suddenly burst into tears. "I've put Mom through hell and now she might die before I can make it up to her."

"Don't say that. She'll be fine. The doc looks like he knows what he's doing. He doesn't take much crap off that scumbag called Jayco. This mess will be over soon and they'll get her to a hospital."

CHAPTER SEVEN

Leaning against the hood of a patrol car, Spalding surveyed the crowd gathered so early on Christmas morning. Why did the misfortune of others draw onlookers like flies to honey? This aspect of his job he disliked. That, and the damn media, he thought when he saw Kathleen Quick approach him, her ever-present cameraman in tow. The tall, curvaceous redhead was an investigative reporter for a television station out of Savannah yet she lived in Darien on the Altamaha River. Her following was so great the station made sure a helicopter was always available for her. *She's got spies everywhere*, he mused. How else could she always be the first media person at any crime scene? Well, at least, the first with a camera.

Spalding flagged down a trooper and gave him instructions for clearing some of the accumulated vehicles behind the barricades. He needed more space. His attempt at looking busy did little to forestall Quick as she barreled in, her microphone soon in his face.

"Lieutenant Spalding. A few words for our viewers, please. What exactly is taking place at this location?"

Spalding knew better than to ignore her. Doing so only made her more determined and lessened the chance for her cooperation later. "There's not much we can tell you at the moment. An attempted robbery, obviously botched, resulting in a hostage situation."

Unsatisfied with the bland statement, Quick lowered the mike, used hand signals to reposition the cameraman, and plastered a grim look on her face before she continued. "We've heard reports of gunshots and injured victims. Were any of your men or any of the perpetrators injured as a result of a shootout?"

Here we go, Spalding thought. The bitch already placed him on the defensive. The goddamn media loved to beat up on the cops. It made their ratings soar. Goddamn media and goddamn liberals, they deserved each other.

"No shootout took place. I can categorically state shots were not fired by the police. As for injuries, I can't comment since we do not have access to the interior of the store at this time."

Quick withdrew the microphone for a moment, speaking directly to Spalding. "I've interviewed a witness who states he saw blood on the floor in front of the checkout counter."

"That's strictly unconfirmed supposition." He motioned for her to raise her microphone again. "We respectfully request that our citizens stay away from the scene. It makes our job more difficult and we certainly don't want innocent bystanders to be hurt. If the viewers will stay tuned to your station, we'll relay up-to-date information through your reports." *Maybe that will satisfy the shark.*

Apparently it did. Quick turned to the camera and gave a final report with the promise to be back on the air with any further news breaks. When she finished, she slashed her fingers across her neck to signal the cameraman to kill the feed. She spun around to face Spalding. "Oh, Buddy, what a piece of work you are. You knew I couldn't push you after such a great plug."

"I was hoping," Spalding replied.

"I guess our dinner date with Grant is off for tonight?"

"Certainly looks like it. The bad guys could suddenly have an attack of conscience and decide to give up, but I wouldn't count on it. The longer this thing drags on the more we'll need Grant's skill in negotiation."

"Okay, the two of you are off the hook for dinner tonight. Don't think you are rid of me. I'll be hanging around at least until prime time coverage is over."

Spalding forced a smile. "Why in hell does Grant Watkins stay married to you?"

"For the oldest reason in the world; I'm great in bed." Quick laughed as she walked away. The cameraman followed her like a well-trained dog.

CHAPTER EIGHT

10:15 a.m.

Majorski stood at the front entrance peeking through a six-inch square of glass not covered with newspaper and poster board. Dark, low hanging clouds drifted in from the southwest, bringing a steady drizzle, adding to the misery of the morning. A kaleidoscope of colors reflected off the wet pavement from the flashing red and blue lights of police vehicles, first responders and fire trucks. He thought of times in the past when he had witnessed similar scenes and had spent no more than a few seconds pondering what had occurred; he'd hardly given a thought for those undergoing possible life-changing moments.

Only a couple of hours had passed since this nightmare began and already it seemed like forever. If it felt that way to him, how must it feel to the wounded? He wasn't as concerned about the chest wound as he made the perps believe. His attempt to panic them into giving up had failed. The injured woman was a different matter. Every minute brought her closer to bleeding out.

The flashing lights played off the white walls of the store, adding further misery to a bad situation. He made a mental note to tell the negotiator to have them turned off. The mere presence of so many official vehicles in front of the convenience store should be clue enough to Joe Citizen that their tax dollars were hard at work and not venture too close. Not that it would stop those neurotic people who fed off the gore and the misery of others.

Majorski placed both arms around the top of his head in an attempt to relieve the constant pounding. The pain increased his tension; the agonizing wait for the surgical equipment and the senseless debate between the negotiator and the politicians didn't help. It was more convenient to place the blame on others rather than accept his anxiety over the impending surgery. Why me?

He looked at his trembling hands and sweaty palms. Even thinking of his past failures depressed him so much he couldn't function. He had tried to put it behind him. He worked hard in the ER, hoping to accumulate enough money to enjoy life. All those years in training, scraping by, sacrificing his youth, while his friends who didn't go into medicine were driving new cars, going on trips and raising families. Fate owed him more. He wanted to enjoy ski trips to Colorado, hiking parts of the Appalachian Trail, scuba diving, and all the other things young men did before marriage and children. Delayed gratification, and now he might never enjoy any rewards. Why had God put him in this situation?

Time wasn't available to formally present his question to God. Majorski saw someone approaching the store.

"I need the keys," he called out to Jayco. "I think our supplies are here."

Jayco held up the circular steel ring that held numerous keys. "No funny stuff, Doc. If you run or someone crashes through the door, I'm taking out the girl and her mother."

"I offered to help," Majorski answered. "I can't do that by running away." He caught the keys thrown his way, inserted the proper key after three tries, slid back the bolt and eased through the partially opened door.

The man outside waited until they were face to face before he spoke. "I'm Sergeant Walker, assistant to Grant Watkins, the chief negotiator."

"Well, Sergeant Walker, I'm Doctor Edward Majorski. You obviously know who I am and why I'm waiting outside this store at this moment. So where are the supplies? A lady is dying inside the store and you assholes are playing political games."

"Don't kill the messenger, Doctor Majorski. Lieutenant Spalding needs more information before he can release the supplies."

Majorski's face turned beet red, his neck veins engorged as thick as ropes. "You tell the son of a bitch if Mrs. Dixon dies because of his incompetence, I'll make sure the media knows all about it, plus her family, and then he, along with the county, will be in civil court for the next ten years."

Walker staggered back from the emotional outburst, his mouth gaping open. He tried to speak, changed his mind, did an about-face and quickly retreated behind the barricades.

* * *

The recessed lighting in the spacious office accented the fine furnishings, wall coverings and plush carpet. The desk across from Spalding was of highly polished cherry wood and he presently sat on a leather couch where he had been deposited by the secretary of Victor Lynch, the mayor's personal assistant. Spalding rubbed the smooth grain of the leather, deciding it was genuine, and no fancy counterfeit. The cost of the couch alone would pay for new desks and chairs for at least four of his detectives. He couldn't imagine the cost of the cherry desk. It resembled one he had seen in a furniture store and advertised as made in one of the first class manufacturers in North Carolina. He suspected the money used to pay for it was diverted from the county budget. The funds spent would have provided cubicles for all his personnel.

He wasn't in the office to discuss furnishings or budgetary concerns. He was there to get his ass reamed out by the flunky, who had the mayor's ear, for allowing the hostage crisis to continue to this point. The mayor didn't like adverse publicity and anything other than a swift conclusion to the matter would be unsatisfactory.

Moments like these were always challenging to Spalding. He was a straightforward, action type and lacked the ability to schmooze the politicians who constantly needed their egos stroked. It was a major accomplishment to get through each encounter without bashing in the face of some pompous asshole.

The door to the inner office swung open and Victor Lynch entered like POTUS into the Oval Office. "Spalding, I'm glad you were able to get here so quickly. Sorry to keep you waiting."

Spalding clenched his jaws, swallowing the response he so badly wanted to give. "What do you want, Lynch? I need to be at the scene. Why didn't you come to me if you wanted an update?"

Lynch maintained his pseudo smile, a trait mastered by all politicians who used it to mask their true feelings. "Actually, the update will be given by me. I've just come from a session with the mayor and the rest of our advisory team. You should be grateful that we're willing to interrupt Christmas with our families to help out in this situation. The mayor initially was adamant about leaving this problem in the hands of the law enforcement. Then the information reached us about the demand for medical supplies, so we put our heads together and developed a solution to your problem."

Spalding stared at the little man in disbelief. "I am the officer in charge. I am open to suggestions, but no one develops procedure except me. I'm not going along with anything that endangers the lives of the hostages. I'm sure Grant Watkins will agree with me. The perps are demonstrating willingness to negotiate by requesting the medical supplies for the injured. It is imperative that we base any further plans on the premise they will be willing to negotiate surrender. The approach taken is my call and mine alone. Do you understand?"

Lynch stood behind the safety of his desk; the smile erased from his face. "The mayor told me I would have problems with you, so read my lips. You'll follow the 'suggestions' of the mayor to the letter. If you don't, you will be replaced. Your next assignment will be riding on a three-wheeled scooter, issuing parking citations along Newcastle Street."

Spalding's shoulders slumped in resignation. He despised the little bastard perched behind the desk. At the moment he would like nothing better than to jerk the asshole from behind the desk and beat him unconscious. Risking his pension in a pissing contest wasn't acceptable. "Exactly what are the mayor's suggestions?"

Lynch sat down and settled back in his high-back chair, a smug look plastered across his face. "Actually the plan is my design; however, let me point out it has the mayor's total approval."

Spalding wanted to puke—either from what he heard or from his feelings of total impotence.

* * *

A shrill sound from inside the store startled Majorski and he pulled open the door.

Jayco motioned for him to re-enter the store. "Answer the damn thing."

Majorski walked to the counter to pick up the receiver of the land line. The phone rang several more times before he reached it. "Doctor Majorski."

Spalding hesitated, gathering himself before he spoke. "I'm still working on the supplies you requested. I can't make the decision without consulting with my superiors."

Majorski turned his back to Jayco and spoke as quietly as possible. "What the hell have you been doing? The situation is under control for the time being. Everyone is calm. The injured aren't interested in your politics. Please don't screw things up by attempting any drastic measures. Just give me the supplies before someone dies."

Spalding concentrated on the first part of the conversation. "I hear what you are saying. No SWAT teams breaching the store."

"You got it! Get me those supplies, now."

"What's taking so long?" Jayco screamed from his perch.

Majorski replaced the receiver. "No problem. I made sure they had a complete list of the items I need."

Majorski paced in front of the store, unaware his image was on every television screen in the Brunswick area. He stopped and swung his leg at a newspaper box outside the front door of the store. The metallic and plastic contraption crashed against the building before tipping on its side. He heard Jayco screaming obscenities inside the store and felt certain the verbal garbage was directed at him. The constant harangue with Jayco was taking its toll. . He was ready to snap. For thirty minutes they had argued about whether or not he would go outside unaccompanied to await the supplies. Had Tupac not coughed up blood, scaring Jayco out of his wits, Majorski was sure he would still be inside.

Choosing to ignore the screams of the psycho, Majorski continued his back and forth movements, periodically staring at the people crowded behind the barriers. A knot grew larger in his stomach, not from fear of Jayco or the men who surrounded the store, but from fear of—in his mind—killing another patient. His fingers trembled at the thought of putting another victim under the knife. He thought such an event was behind him forever.

He sat down with his back against the concrete wall below the front windows. The tension in his neck was unrelenting and he closed his eyes searching for relief. Instead, he relived the worst moment of his life as it flashed in his mind again.

Surgical suite three became deadly silent, disturbed only by the rhythmic clicks of a mechanical ventilator. The customary banter and off-color jokes ceased as the tension mounted in the room. Doctor Majorski placed his surgical instrument against the tumor in the patient's left lung, noting the lateral motion from the pulsation of the aorta. He looked up into the eyes of Doctor Elder, his preceptor and mentor, searching for assurance he was making the proper moves. He tilted his head forward, bringing the bright light of his surgical head lamp directly into the wound, highlighting the exposed tumor. Moisture trickled down his back, across his tight buttocks and through the coarse hair of his legs, seeking the path of least resistance.

The intensity of the moment created exhilaration and anxiety. This was his case, his patient and his opportunity to impress Elder; a chance to demonstrate his skills and knowledge; and possibly, "seal the deal" to be chief resident of the thoracic service at the medical college for the upcoming year.

Retracting the lung with his left hand, he worked his fingers deep into the fissure between the tumor and the aorta. The fragile tissues parted with ease and with renewed confidence he worked his fingers deeper. Once the tumor was separated from the largest blood vessel in the human body, the removal of the malignancy would proceed much easier.

His fingers met resistance; he spoke without looking up. "More counter-traction, please."

The maneuver helped, allowing him to increase the pressure against the tumor with his fingers. There was no give. He moved his fingers superiorly along the edge of the lung and increased the pressure. It worked. The fibers separated and he took a deep breath of relief. His elation was short-lived as a geyser of blood shot out of the operative site, splattering the goggles and masks of both surgeons. The operative field disappeared in a lake of blood.

Majorski quickly grabbed a vascular clamp, slipped it into the bloody field, probing blindly against the surge of blood in an attempt to locate the tear in the aorta.

Doctor Elder inserted a suction catheter to no avail. The hemorrhage was too massive for the apparatus to be effective.

Pushing his fingers under the arch of the aorta, Majorski located the two-centimeter tear. Repeated efforts of pinching it closed between his thumb and index finger failed due to the slick surface. Blood continued to cascade from the gash, filling the chest cavity and spilling out of the wound onto the surrounding surgical drapes. The warm liquid soaked through his surgical gown, scrub suit and dripped onto the floor. The familiar smell of blood penetrated his mask and his nostrils; a smell he would remember forever.

Together he and Elder attempted to clamp the great vessel and suture the gaping rent to no avail. Within minutes the patient bled out. Majorski's shoulders slumped when Elder pulled the sheet up over the *patient and he heard the ventilator shut down. He had lost his patient on the surgical table. It would never happen again—he would make sure of that.*

Majorski jerked his head upright, staring at the bank of lights before him. Drenched in sweat, he wrapped his arms around his chest, squeezing to ease the pressure. Gradually his mind cleared and he returned to the present.

His thoughts of the hostages represented only a part of the things rushing through his mind. He pictured images of the "brain trust" whining about the difficult decision forced upon them. He imagined the suited men, and maybe some women, gathered around a table or on a conference phone call, reviewing different scenarios; not debating how to save as many of the hostages as possible—no, how best to cover their asses.

"I hate fucking bureaucrats," he screamed into the black void behind the barricades.

* * *

Inside the store things were unraveling, especially for Jayco. He paced the floor, shouting obscenities at all the hostages, cursing God for His role in the botched robbery. "God has always been against me. I've never gotten a break. Not once."

The words flew out of Tracy's mouth before she realized it. "God is not inclined to help scumbags who shoot defenseless people."

Jayco spun around to locate the person who uttered the words. His eyes locked on Tracy and he could tell from her grim expression she was the culprit. He sprinted toward her, knocking over a stacked display of antifreeze, sending the metal cans crashing across the floor.

Tracy held Luke to her chest and turned away from the mad man charging at her. The fact she had a baby in her arms would probably not affect the psychopath. She was right.

Jayco grabbed Tracy by her hair and slung her into a wooden counter. Maintaining his grip, he dragged her across the floor toward the coolers.

Tracy screamed, "Don't hurt my baby. Please don't hurt my baby."

Her pleas fell on deaf ears. Jayco jerked her head around by the hair and bashed her face into the glass of the floor to ceiling coolers. He seemed oblivious to the blood pouring from Tracy's nose and mouth.

Wild with rage, he jerked the SIG SAUER from his belt, grabbed it by the barrel and raised it to bash the head of his hapless victim.

With the speed of a mongoose striking a cobra, the lanky frame of Jimmy Harris plowed into Jayco, knocking him off his feet. Both skidded across the floor with Jimmy on top.

The SIG SAUER clattered against the bottom of the cooler.

Physically stronger, Jayco reversed the positions in seconds and filled his hands with the straggly hair of the young boy. He lifted the boy's head and smashed it against the concrete floor. By the third time the boy could no longer defend himself, his head flopping on his neck like a broken doll. Jayco raised his fist to inflict damage to the face but before he completed his action he was stopped by the same soft voice that had infuriated him earlier.

"Get off him."

Jayco turned his head toward the voice and stared into the business end of the SIG SAUER. His eyes looked up from the automatic into Tracy's fiercely burning eyes. "Well, lookie here. Annie Oakley is drawing down on me. Ooh, I'm so afraid. Hell, you can't shoot anybody, Bible-thumper."

"If you don't get off him in five seconds, you will find out."

Jayco didn't move.

Tracy's finger tightened on the trigger.

"Put it down, little lady. Now," Charlie shouted.

Tracy maintained the pressure on the trigger. She looked to her left at the assault rifle aimed at her head. Afraid for her baby she lowered the gun and placed it on the floor. She wrapped both arms around Luke, pulling him to her face, breathing in his baby scent.

Jayco started toward the SIG SAUER but Charlie beat him to it. It only took one look at Charlie's face to see he wanted the crisis to stop. Slowly, Jayco got to his feet and walked back to his perch. He didn't look back at Tracy, or the young boy lying prostrate on the floor.

Tracy listened to the deep rumble coming from Charlie's mouth. She didn't understand all the words, but the message was clear. Don't antagonize Jayco.

Samantha held Luke while Tracy wrapped Jimmy's bloody head with strips she tore from a package of disposable dish cloths. They both repeatedly questioned Jimmy until they were satisfied his brain was functioning on a normal level.

Tracy leaned forward, wrapping her arms around Jimmy's neck. "Thank you. You saved my life. I think that mad man would have killed me if you hadn't intervened."

Jimmy simply nodded. Speaking at the moment was out of the question.

Outside, Majorski was unaware of the chaos that had taken place inside the store. He continued to pace, occasionally slinging lewd remarks toward the barricades.

Twenty minutes later, as if his outburst magically stimulated action, several uniformed officers marched toward him, moving the aluminum barriers as they approached. Behind them two EMTs, dressed in their standard white shirts and blue trousers, pushed a gurney loaded with large, heavily wrapped bundles.

Majorski hurried to meet them, a scowl on his face. "Those better be the surgical trays and instruments. Where's the surgical lamp?"

The EMT in the lead answered. "You've got it; also got IV meds for sedation, antibiotics, IV poles, cardiac monitors and a defibrillator. Everything you asked for and more. The portable surgical lamp is right behind us. Whatever you said to Walker got everybody's attention."

Majorski fixed his gaze on the EMT. "There's nothing on the gurney we didn't ask for, like a wire or mike or any of those tricks?"

The taller of the two emergency medical techs shook his head. "Not to my knowledge and I personally loaded most of the supplies. I'm also a trained surgical tech. If 'Billy Badass' gives us permission, I'll help you with the surgery."

A smile spread across Majorski's face at the first good news of the day. "Let's get the equipment inside before the idiots in charge have second thoughts." He pointed to the EMT who volunteered his services. "When the surgical lamp gets here, tap on the door and I'll let you in. Are you sure you want to get involved in this?"

"It's my job, sir."

Majorski opened the door a couple of inches in response to a tap on the glass. After identifying the EMT, he opened the door wider to allow the surgical light to be pushed into the store. The unit contained twin halogen lamps mounted in elliptical reflectors with an extension arm. The lamp heads were on top of a steel pole with a heavy base mounted on four wheels. He helped the EMT get it inside, quickly closed the door and keyed the bolt in place. His head slammed forward, bouncing off the glass door, from the impact of Jayco's rifle stock. His knees buckled from the intense pain coursing through his head.

"What the fuck is this guy doing here?" Jayco screeched, pointing at the EMT. "Who said you could bring someone in with the equipment?"

Jayco swung the AK-47 toward the EMT. "You've fucked up. Get on the floor, on your face."

The EMT was a head taller than Jayco and his muscular arms stretched the fabric of the uniform short sleeves. The rifle pointed at him didn't frighten him; he had faced the business end of a weapon before. He kept his cool, dropping to a prone position as instructed. It wasn't his job to trigger a blood bath by this nut case holding the rifle.

Jayco straddled the prone figure, giving him a thorough pat-down. Still crouched over, he raised the AK-47 to smash the butt of the weapon into the unsuspecting man's head. The downward swing didn't occur.

Majorski wobbled, trying to maintain his balance in spite of the spinning room. His right hand firmly gripped the barrel of Jayco's rifle. "He's a trained surgical tech. He volunteered to help me operate on Tupac and Mrs. Dixon. I need him."

Jayco's eyes blazed. Hatred was obvious in the tone of his voice. "Take your damn hands off my rifle." He stared at Majorski's glassy eyes, the jerky motion of his neck, and tried frantically to back away. His movement was not quick enough to avoid the gush of puke that showered his jacket, pants and shoes.

"Goddamn you, Doc. I ought to shoot your ass." He backed away from Majorski and the EMT. He accepted a roll of paper towels from Charlie who had rushed to the fracas to get Jayco under control.

Jayco fumed over the situation. He glared at Majorski and the EMT. "Get to work on Tupac. He ain't looking so good."

The EMT reached for the doctor, taking him by the arm and easing him to the floor. "I'm Tony Satillo. Are you okay?"

Majorski leaned forward, resting his head in his hands. "I'll be okay in a minute. Too many head shots from the butt of that asshole's rifle. Get a bottle of water from the cooler and pour it over my neck. It should help me bounce back."

After resting for a few minutes Majorski sat upright, normal color back in his face. "Thank you for the water and for staying. I'll need all the help I can get."

Satillo helped Majorski to his feet, refusing to turn loose until satisfied Majorski could remain upright. "I'm glad I was allowed to stay, although I doubt my own sanity after witnessing the actions of that psycho. I'll do the best I can to help you."

Ed took Satillo's hand in his own. "You're a brave man. You've put yourself in harm's way as you've already learned. The man is unstable and may eventually try to kill us all. I hope your department rewards you well."

"Like I said earlier, it's my job. Are you up to performing surgery?"

"I don't have much choice. If I refuse, Jayco might go 'postal' and open fire on all of us. Every word and action has to be carefully weighed against his possible reaction. I'm feeling better. Let's get to work."

The tension in the store was like static electricity—stable at the moment, but any movement could set off a shock. The hostages jockeyed for a vantage point to watch the doc work on Tupac, taking care not to raise Jayco's ire.

Samantha remained with her mother, caressing her cheeks and whispering encouraging words in her ear. She checked Lucille's pulse often, following the procedure exactly as Majorski had taught her. Jimmy stayed with her until the point when the doctor needed him to move a table.

Majorski made a slit in the heavy plastic overwrap covering a disposable thoracotomy tray. Wearing sterile gloves, he placed the items on a sterile drape on a display counter previously cleared to serve as an instrument table.

"Tony. We don't have wall suction. We'll have to create our own water seal barrier; an archaic method, but still effective. Start by filling the plastic bottles with sterile saline. First bottle should be half full to create a water seal. Attach the connector to the rubber cap and feed it to the second bottle, which should be only a fourth full so it can catch the blood overflowing from the first bottle."

He looked up to see if Tony understood the instructions and was surprised to see the EMT was not procuring the container of saline. Instead, he was on his knees sliding the defibrillator from the bottom rack.

"Tony. We won't need that," Majorski began. He fell silent when he saw the EMT assume a shooter's stance behind the table with both arms extended, his hands gripping a .357 SIG Pro pistol with the barrel aimed at Jayco. Two loud booms followed in quick succession.

Majorski dropped to one knee, pushing the gurney to the side. He heard a scream and felt certain it was Samantha. Please God, don't let this become a massacre. He saw Tony scramble forward, firing the weapon rapidly as he advanced toward Jayco's position. Tony dived for the floor, rolled over behind a counter, ejecting the empty clip and slamming a full one in its place. He peered around the wooden barrier spotting a splatter of blood on the wall behind where Jayco previously sat. The leader was no longer in sight. Tony scanned the front of the store, and then the large mirror mounted on the right rear wall. He was unable to locate the madman.

Majorski, as evidently did Satillo, assumed Jayco had fallen behind the stack of boxes. Before he could caution Satillo to maintain cover, Satillo left his place of concealment and sprinted toward the blood-splattered wall. Halfway to his intended target, his body was violently thrown backwards in a hail of bullets. His lifeless hand released the grip on the gun, which clattered across the floor and came to rest at Majorski's feet.

Jayco popped up from his hiding place, blood streaming across his face and neck from a pencil-sized crease in his scalp. He raved at Majorski. "Pick up the gun, Doc. Please. I want you to pick it up. I'll kill all you lying bastards."

Majorski yelled back, "I didn't know. They must have planned this outside. I didn't know the EMT intended to stay, remember?"

Jayco's stared back, his eyes wild with hatred. Again he commanded, "Pick up the damn gun, Doc. Now's your chance; just you and me, like the old west."

"No," Majorski stammered. "I won't give you a reason to kill me and I refuse to accept the opportunity to kill you."

Jayco walked forward and shoved the barrel of the AK-47 hard against Majorski's neck. He grabbed the gun from the floor, slipping it behind his belt. He swung Majorski around and pushed him toward the front door. "You don't have the balls to kill anyone." He handed a cell phone to Majorski.

"Call the fucking negotiator. Use any excuse to get him to the door, and then step out of the way. I'm going to blow his ass to hell."

Majorski stopped, pushing back against Jayco. "No. That would be insane. If you shoot him, they'll storm the place and we'll all die. Think about the situation. They've made a bad tactical error. Now they'll do whatever you ask to make up for it. If they lose control after what they attempted, the media will crucify them, and the politicians."

Jayco hesitated, glancing around the room at the fear-stricken hostages. He slammed the barrel of the rifle against Majorski's chest, shoving him toward the front door. "Get the negotiator to the door. Tell him if there are any more tricks, everyone dies and he can live with that."

Majorski took five steps toward the door, suddenly bent over and vomited again. He went down to one knee to keep from falling; the room whirled rapidly around him. He heard Tracy cry out and attempt to come to him, but she stopped when Jayco threatened her and Luke. Majorski forced himself upright and continued to the door. The situation had changed and not in his favor.

CHAPTER NINE

Noon

Thirty yards behind the barricades was parked Glynn County's latest addition to the fight against crime; a 2000 Prevost Marathon XLV motor coach. It was custom made in Canada for a country-and-western singer, who had used it as a traveling home for himself and his family. He had donated the motor coach to the county in gratitude for quick action by the members of the sheriff's office who prevented a kidnapping of the star's son. Along with the coach came a sizable cash donation which paid for a complete conversion to a traveling office for the sheriff's department.

The fifty-two-foot behemoth contained a bathroom complete with shower, a bedroom, kitchen, computer stations, wall monitors, wireless fax, blackboards and every electronic gadget available to the law enforcement, including access to the FBI's data base. The unit was completely self-contained with twin twenty-kilowatt generators, in-motion satellite dishes, and underbelly storage for weapons and crime scene investigation equipment. The silver-and-black beauty was immediately named the Crime Bus by the media.

Tension in the bus mounted quickly, with much the same atmosphere as the White House War Room during a crisis. Grant Watkins and Buddy Spalding sat across from each other at a six-by-four oak table. The wooden barrier prevented them from tearing into one another.

Watkins tilted his chair forward, his knuckles pale from the pressure exerted on the table. His voice cracked, the words spat out, more than spoken. "If you ever pull a stunt like that again, I will snap off your pointy head and shove it up your ample ass."

Spalding struggled to answer, wanting to explain how the idea had come from sources much higher. Passing the buck wasn't his style; the words stuck in his throat. He knew it wouldn't make any difference to Watkins, but the attempt to take out the leader of the perps and the subsequent failure would have dire consequences for him. His superiors needed a scapegoat and now, if the hostage situation resulted in more deaths, the media would never learn of the mayor's involvement. Spalding realized he was expendable and would be hung out to dry.

"I apologize for keeping you out of the loop," Spalding said. "I knew you wouldn't go for the idea and, to be honest, my superiors had my ass in a sling. Hell, it might have worked if the EMT had been a better shot."

"You mean he was a real EMT and not one of your officers?"

"Unfortunately he was not a policeman. That's the part I didn't like, but I was overruled. Someone really had a hard-on for the guy; ex-Special Forces and accustomed to tight situations. Evidently he hadn't been to the firing range in a while. Hell, I hate to be critical of him. He put his life on the line to try to help and got whacked for it."

The scowl on Watkins' face disappeared. "You're right. I would like a few minutes with the asshole who dreamed up the stunt. You aren't going to tell me his name, are you?"

"It wouldn't do any good. My ass will be canned no matter what happens. Sometimes it's just bad luck to be the ranking officer at the scene."

Watkins empathized with his friend. Besides, part of the blame was on his shoulders as well since it took him so long to get to the scene. Spending Christmas Day with an elderly uncle in a nursing home in Savannah had seemed a Christian thing to do. But no good deed goes unpunished. Fate reared its ugly head. A defective cell phone, the department's difficulty in locating Kathleen who was visiting children at the hospital and the time it took to get him back to Brunswick by helicopter may have resulted in the death of a courageous young man. Now he was already behind the eight ball and hadn't taken a shot.

"Bring me up to speed. How many perps? How many hostages and do you have floor plans for the building? Were any of the hostages injured?"

Spalding crooked a finger toward Trooper Ginn. "Get me that list of information I wrote out for Lieutenant Watkins." He turned back to the negotiator. "We've worked together so many times; I anticipated some of the questions you would have. Unfortunately things moved too fast and I couldn't keep a handle on it."

Watkins studied the list, impressed with the details present. "You think there's possibly a fourth perp but no way to tell?"

"Not so far. There's been a lot of confusion in that regard,"

Spalding said.

"What are their demands?"

"The hostage-takers haven't issued any demands. I think these guys are small time hoods who are now in way over their heads. We don't have any identification yet but we've taken fingerprints from all the cars parked in front of the store and they are being run for possible matches."

Watkins took his eyes off the list and stared at the ceiling. "The fact they allowed the medical supplies into the store is a good sign. Well, at least it was initially. It meant they were willing to work with us. Not sure about their willingness to cooperate at this point.

"What about covert monitoring—anything in place?"

Spalding shook his head. "Too much time wasted on the attempted take-down. I got people working on it."

Watkins sank deeper in his chair, staring at the intricate design on the ceiling. "You know, it's not too late to rescue the hostages and our respective asses. Doctor Majorski may be just the guy to save the wounded hostages and the rest as well. I'm going to the entrance of the store and try again to talk to that Jayco fellow. He's obviously a total psycho. The misery that human beings are capable of inflicting on one another never ceases to amaze me.

"If I can get the maniac calmed down, I can replace any supplies the doc needs and let him try again to treat the wounded. One thing for sure, he'll have to do it alone. The crazy fucker calling the shots won't let anyone else in there to help the doc."

"Grant, don't do anything stupid, like swapping yourself for a hostage. Kathleen is on the scene and I would not want to face her if you get killed."

"I read you. I just hope we don't lose a couple of innocent people who could have been saved. Now, let's see what the doc can do if we give him time in the spotlight."

* * *

Ten minutes later, Majorski, waving a single sheet of paper, approached Jayco. "I need to get this list of replacement supplies to the negotiator. I can't start on Tupac without them. Too many vital items were destroyed in the 'OK Corral' shootout."

"Don't be a wise-ass, Doc. I'm not in the mood for it."

Majorski put on his best I'm-sorry face. "I don't imagine you would change your mind and let them come get Mrs. Dixon. I'm sure I can help Tupac. Mrs. Dixon's injuries appear much worse. I won't know the extent of the damage until I explore her wound more thoroughly. I'm not sure I have the equipment or the skills to do the surgery she needs to survive."

"In your dreams, Doc. She's not leaving this building. Take the phone and call the honchos. Tell them to hurry up. If they try another stunt like before, I'll personally toss a body out for the media to capture with their cameras."

Majorski punched the speed dial button previously programmed in the phone by Jimmy Harris. The kid was an electronic whiz.

Watkins answered immediately, listening without comment while Majorski read off the list of needed items. "Are you finished with the list?"

"Yes. I can't think of anything else at this point. I may have forgotten something, if so I will call back. Please have an officer standing by at the hospital to transport anything I need later on."

"Hold on, Doc. I'll be right back with you." Watkins clicked off to prevent the doctor from hearing the conversation going on in the background.

Majorski's heart rate increased dramatically. Something was going on and he was sure he wouldn't like it. He kept the phone to his ear, praying Jayco wouldn't realize he had been put on hold. The charade didn't work.

"What's taking so long?"

"He told me to wait, so I'm waiting." Majorski held up his hand to interrupt Jayco's anticipated verbal barrage and turned his attention back to the phone. "Yes, okay, I'm listening." He spent the next minute in a one-sided conversation, his face becoming flushed as he shook his head in silent frustration. He flipped the cell phone closed with a grim look on his face. He remained silent, staring at Jayco, afraid of what the next few minutes would bring.

"They issued a new demand. You must release a hostage before they'll give us the supplies."

Jayco hurled a half-full can of Budweiser toward the front of the building. It bounded off the glass spewing foam while it spun on the floor. "Get the bastard back on the phone. NOW! Tell him I'm releasing a hostage in about two minutes. He won't be too happy, 'cause it'll be a dead one." He glanced around the room and his eyes locked on Jimmy and Samantha. He heard the girl's whimpering voice and a cruel grin spread across his face.

He crossed the room in four long strides and grabbed the frightened boy by the hair, snatching him up while jamming the hand gun against the back of Jimmy's skull. "Let's you and me take a walk to the entrance. You're going to deliver a personal message for me." He jerked forward the hapless boy, who struggled to remain on his feet.

A sudden resistance pulled Jimmy free from Jayco's grasp. He whirled around to renew his grip and discovered Samantha clinging to Jimmy's legs.

In a rage, Jayco struck the boy repeatedly across the head and shoulders with the barrel of the gun. He knocked Jimmy to his knees and placed the muzzle of the gun on his forehead.

"Don't do it, Jayco." The words were amazingly clear and strong coming from a man who was barely breathing. Tupac looked directly at Jayco. "Do what they say or I'm not going to make it."

Majorski stepped in front of Jayco, anticipating a bullet for his action. His heart pounded against his sternum from near panic. "Look, don't stress the cops any more than they are. They are so uptight now they can't make a decision unless it's scripted for them. For your friend's sake, let them have a hostage so we can get the things we need to save his life. I personally guarantee there will be no funny stuff. I will make sure no one else comes in and I will turn over anything I find in the packs that doesn't belong there."

There was silence, giving Majorski hope that Jayco was considering his plea.

"Who will I send out?"

The simple statement spoke volumes. Majorski realized the man was near exhaustion and incapable of thinking rationally. The combination made him even more dangerous.

A soft voice came from behind them. "Release my baby," Tracy said, tears streaming from her eyes. She had moved up alongside when Jayco grabbed Jimmy. Neither of the men had noticed her.

Majorski saw the pain in her face and understood how hard it would be for her to be separated from her baby. He turned to face Jayco. "She's right. It's the most logical thing to do. The negotiator will get his hostage, we get the supplies and Tracy will be free to help me with the surgery. I won't need any outside help."

Jayco's shoulders slumped. "Okay, tell them we'll swap the baby for the supplies. If anybody else comes in the store, I'm killing her." He pointed his weapon at Tracy.

CHAPTER TEN

1:00 p.m.

A leg of the eight-foot table snagged the metal frame of the door when Jimmy helped Majorski transfer it from the storage room to a place in front of the large coolers. The area provided the best light in the store, supplemented by the portable surgical lamp.

Majorski noticed the fatigue and frustration in Jimmy's face. The kid demonstrated guts and held up well despite all the stress; now was not the time to cave in. "Jimmy, flip the table on its side," he said. "Don't try to hold it up, just slide it along the floor. Once we get it in position, we'll turn it upright and cover it with the sterile drapes."

The two of them worked quickly. Majorski nodded his approval at Tracy, pleased she had cleared a display from a smaller table and positioned it to serve as an instrument table. She showed the instincts of a good operating room nurse, anticipating the surgeon's needs.

He placed a large surgical pack on the improvised table. When he began to tear open the tape securing the bundle, he was startled when Charlie grabbed his arm and reached for the pack. Majorski jerked his arm free and shoved Charlie away. "Don't touch anything in these sterile wraps," he demanded.

"He's following my orders," Jayco said. "He's going to search each one before you get to it.

"Don't touch a damn thing," Majorski shouted with more fervor. "You'll contaminate the entire thing. Can't you see the bundles are wrapped with a heat-sensitive tape? See these black stripes on the tape? That indicates the pack has been in an autoclave, subjected to intense pressure and heat. There's no way a weapon is in there. If you contaminate the equipment, you might as well shoot Tupac now and save him from an agonizing death from infection."

Jayco's facial muscles twitched and he murmured something inaudible before motioning Charlie to back away. "Okay, Doc, have it your way. We're watching you. If there's a gun hidden in there and you come out with it, playing James Bond like that other asshole, I'm putting the first bullet through this pretty lady's head." He pointed the rifle at Tracy to emphasize his point.

"Don't worry," Majorski said. "Even if they were crazy enough to put a gun in with the instruments, I'm not so stupid to fire anything that's been through the sterilization process."

Majorski positioned the two replacement bottles under the table to make it easier to attach the long plastic tubing to them once he got the tube inserted in Tupac's chest.

Motioning for Jimmy to follow him, he approached Tupac, gently touching his arm to prevent startling him. "I need you to stand and walk over to the table. I won't kid you, it'll hurt like hell. We'll help you all we can without putting pressure on your wounds. Once we get there, we can use leverage to get you up on the table. I'm sorry we can't carry you."

Tupac nodded his understanding. Groaning in pain, he pushed up from his sitting position while Jimmy and Majorski helped without touching his back or chest. When they reached the table, they eased Tupac up and into a sitting position.

With a pair of bandage scissors, Majorski cut away the blood-soaked gauze applied earlier and threw it into a box Tracy had placed near the table.

"Okay, now I need you to lie on your left side. I'll support your head and Jimmy will lift your legs."

Tupac did as instructed with help from his caretakers. In the new position no more than two seconds, he immediately rolled onto his back, coughing and gasping.

"No way. No way. I can't lie like that. I can't get air into my lungs. Feels like someone sitting on my chest."

Jayco leaped off his perch and stormed toward the trio, the gun pointed at Majorski. "What the hell you doing to him, Doc?"

"Calm down. Everything is under control. The change of position momentarily made it hard for Tupac to breathe, but he's doing okay now."

"That true, Tupac? You okay?" Jayco muttered.

Tupac didn't attempt to speak, instead nodded his head affirmatively.

Majorski placed his hands under Tupac's neck, lifting it to ease his struggle. "Don't panic. You will feel breathless initially; after the fluid shifts, it will be better. I'll give you an injection to relax you. I've got to put a tube in the right side of your chest to allow your right lung to re-expand. If we're lucky you won't start bleeding again."

A grimace formed on the black man's face. "What's this 'we' shit, white boy? I'm the one doing the bleeding."

Majorski ignored the sick humor and helped Tupac turn on his left side.

Tupac gasped and his eyes bulged in fear, but to his credit, he remained in position while Majorski injected a small quantity of morphine sulfate into the IV tubing.

He accepted a basin of surgical scrub from Tracy and poured it slowly onto the exposed chest wall. With sterile gauze pads, he scrubbed the area from the clavicle to the lower rib margin. Changing to a new pair of sterile gloves, he quickly applied the sterile drapes, cautioning Tupac to keep his right arm above his head.

"Before I insert the chest tube, I'll numb up the skin and the muscle layers. Later, when I instruct you, hold your breath and remain as still as possible. Do your best not to cough."

Tupac nodded that he understood.

Majorski explored the imaginary right anterior axillary line on the chest to a location between the fourth and fifth ribs. The less than ideal surgical setup distressed him, but he figured the chances of these guys getting out of the store alive negated any concerns over infection. He chuckled to himself at the macabre irony.

Tracy handed him a syringe containing Xylocaine, a local anesthetic. After warning Tupac to prepare for the stick, he pushed the needle through the skin and muscle until it touched the fourth rib. Withdrawing the needle a few millimeters, he worked it under the rib where each intercostal nerve coursed around the chest wall. He injected half the contents of the syringe before repeating the procedure under the fifth rib. As he extracted the needle he injected the remainder of the solution under the skin.

Next he made a one-half-inch surgical incision, extending it through the subcutaneous tissue and muscle. Taking the chest tube from Tracy, he clamped the middle of the tube with a large hemostat. Using the scalpel again, he made a stab wound through the parietal pleura, the outer lining of the chest cavity. A torrent of blood, mixed with frothy air bubbles, gushed from the wound.

Tupac grunted and he tried to get off the table. It took all of the combined strength of Majorski and Jimmy to hold him in place. He coughed violently in spite of the earlier warnings to resist it.

"You're okay," Majorski said. "The lung is re-expanding and creates the urge to cough."

He grasped the tip of the chest tube with another large clamp and prepared to thrust it through the pleura.

A nightmarish screech halted his motion and he jerked his head in the direction of the sound, searching for the source. He saw Samantha crawling toward him, her movements so disjointed she could barely raise herself to a crouching position. She crashed into the table, causing Tupac to cry out in pain.

"What's wrong?" Majorski yelled at her. "I'm in the middle of a procedure. Are you crazy?"

"I'm sorry. I … I'm scared. Mother is having a convulsion or something. She's white as a ghost and shaking all over. I think she's dying."

"Jesus, this is bad timing. Give me a break." Majorski placed a Vaseline-coated gauze pad over the stab wound and directed Tracy to hold it in place. He ripped off his gloves and ran around the end of the table to Lucille Dixon. He quickly assessed her vital signs, checked her pupils and listened to her chest. Her pulse was thready; the blood pressure lower and wet-sounding crackles were present in both lung bases.

"She's going into shock—heart failure from lack of blood volume," he spoke out loud. Cursing himself for allowing Jayco to bully him into not attending to Lucille's immediate needs before starting the procedure on Tupac, Majorski scurried across the floor to the supplies. He knelt by the box, filling his arms with two bags of Ringers Lactate, IV tubing and two large bore needles with plastic sheaths.

Balancing the items in his arms he twisted as he rose from the floor, and was immediately slammed onto his back by a boot to his chest. He ignored his assailant; instead he collected and inspected the supplies for damage. Satisfied everything was still intact he laid the materials on the floor, rose to a crouch and launched himself at the pair of legs before him. Driving his shoulders into Jayco's torso he sent the two of them skidding across the tile into a metal rack scattering packages of chips.

Stunned by the unexpected response, Jayco flailed at Majorski with his left arm, keeping a firm grip on the rifle with his right. Majorski saw the rifle coming at his head and blocked the weak and ineffective motion with his arm. Jayco lost his grip on the rifle and it clattered away on the concrete floor.

Majorski threw his full weight on Jayco, pinning him to the floor, his furor allowing him to overcome the weight disadvantage. He placed both hands around Jayco's throat, his thumbs pressed firmly against the trachea. He fought against Jayco's effort to pull his hands away. He let up briefly when Jayco's hands fell away, a mistake soon recognized when the butt of the hand gun slammed against his ear. Rocked by the impact Majorski released his grip and slumped forward, just enough for Jayco to shove him off.

"I'll kill you," Jayco screamed and placed the muzzle against Majorski's forehead. Whether he really would have pulled the trigger became a mute point when he flew backwards and landed flat on his back.

Tracy, screaming like a banshee, pummeled her small fist into Jayco's face.

The blows caused more damage to Jayco's ego than to his body. He grabbed Tracy by the shoulders, bucked her up with a thrust of his legs and slung her off like ridding himself of an irritating puppy.

Tracy bounced against the side of a counter, shook her head to clear the cobwebs and launched herself again at Jayco. Her motion was interrupted by Charlie's solid body standing over Jayco and helping him to his feet.

"Stop it!" Everyone in the room, including Jayco, was shocked by Charlie's sudden display of emotion. "Let the doc do his work so we can get out of here. The longer we stay the less chance we have to get out."

Jayco got to his feet, retrieved his weapons and stood glaring. He turned to walk away but was stopped by Majorski's grip on his arm

"Don't misjudge me, Jayco. I don't purposely take someone's life, but by God, if you interfere with my attempts to help these people again, I will give up my own life to end yours."

He released his grip, gathered up the materials on the floor and returned to Lucille's side. He motioned for Tracy to join him.

Charlie led his stunned, crazed friend back to his perch on the boxes.

The men outside the store were unaware of the drama unfolding within the building. Thanks to usual communication snafu the parabolic microphones were not in place. Spalding had requested the mikes along with infra-red heat sensors. Neither of the objects had arrived.

Within two minutes Majorski had intravenous fluids running in each of Lucille's arms. He opened the stopcocks wide open and instructed Samantha to let him know when the bags were empty. Lucille needed blood replacement, which obviously was unavailable. Majorski had learned from medical journals and from discussions with doctors and medics who previously served in Vietnam how critically injured troops were kept alive by massive infusions of Ringers Lactate to support the cardiac circulation. It served as a temporary measure and bought time until blood was available. He now faced a similar situation. Different types of combat with a different enemy but gunshot wounds were devastating no matter how they occurred. Time was a critical factor and definitely not on his side. Satisfied he had done all he could for Lucille, he moved back to Tupac.

"Sorry for the interruption. I couldn't delay starting the intravenous fluids any longer."

Tupac spoke through tight lips, masking his pain. "How is she doing?"

"Not well. She's lost a lot of blood internally. I can try to keep up her volume but the fluid replacement isn't adequate for long. She needs to be in a surgical suite where they can replace the blood loss and open her up to stop the bleeding."

"I'm sorry she's so bad off. Jayco gets crazy at times. Still, I don't think he intentionally shot her. We didn't intend to hurt anyone. In and out, that was our plan. Things just got all screwed up."

"Sorry, if you're trying to get me to join your friend's fan club, it won't work. My pounding head refuses to believe anything decent about the man. What you can do is help me convince him to let the authorities come get Mrs. Dixon and take her to a hospital before she dies."

"I'll try," Tupac said.

Majorski rinsed his hands in alcohol, dried them on a sterile towel and re-gloved. He instructed Tracy to remove the gauze and swab the previous incision with Betadine surgical scrub. Picking up the perforated catheter, he grasped it at the distal end with the large clamp, and then pushed the catheter tip into the wound, advancing it about six inches. He visually checked to make sure the end of the tube was connected to the water seal before releasing the middle clamp. Dark blood and air bubbles rushed through the tube into the first bottle, filling it before spilling over into the second bottle.

With coaxing, Tupac took several shallow breaths, which gradually became deeper when the effort of breathing lessened.

Tracy observed the procedure, fascinated at Majorski's skill and purposeful movements. "You did great, Doctor. It is obvious you've done this a few times before."

Majorski didn't answer. He picked up a needle holder and grasped a cutting needle pre-threaded with 2-0 silk suture. He took a deep bite through the skin and subcutaneous tissue on each side of the small incision. After tying several knots, he looped the suture material around the tube to anchor it in position and prevent it from sliding in and out of the wound.

After he finished he looked up at Tracy with a painful expression. "I completed four years of a general surgery residency and two years in thoracic surgery before I began working in the emergency room."

Tracy looked puzzled. "Why didn't you stay in thoracic surgery?"

Majorski checked the tubing, relieved to see the oscillation of the bloody fluid in the tube with each inspiration and expiration. A good sign Tupac's lung was re-expanding.

"It's a long story. Basically, I lost my confidence."

Tupac tried to laugh, which set off another spasm of coughing. "Damn, Doc. I'm glad you waited until you finished working on me before you made that comment." The smile left his face and he continued in a sincere voice. "This is a screwed-up mess and I thank you for saving my life. I don't think I could have had a better doctor." With effort he raised his arm, grasping Majorski's hand.

CHAPTER ELEVEN

1:00 p.m.

Doctor Thomas Elder made his way through the myriad of official vehicles until stopped by a young policeman posted at the periphery of the chaotic scene. He smiled at the officer, turning on his best Southern gentleman charm. "Excuse me, officer. You must be one of the people in charge."

The words worked on the young officer just as they did on neophyte medical students. The officer visually stood more erect, at the immediate service of Elder. "Not exactly in charge, sir. How may I help you?"

Elder leaned toward the officer, his voice dropping to a conspiratory whisper. "I was told there's a negotiator here. For the life of me, I can't recall his name. It's very important I talk to him. I have vital information to share regarding this situation."

The rookie cop didn't inquire about the details, instead pointed Elder in the direction of the Crime Bus parked behind the barricades. "When you get to the bus, ask for Lieutenant Buddy Spalding. He's my superior. He'll take you to Lieutenant Grant Watkins, the negotiator on scene."

"Thank you, officer. The citizens of Glynn County are fortunate to have courteous young men like you on the force."

Elder was dressed in his usual attire of gray dress slacks, a blue sports coat, a heavily starched white shirt and a red bow tie. A pair of Rockport shoes completed his wardrobe, which was a part of the folk lore at the Medical College of Georgia. The patients and staff on the thoracic surgery wing would have been blown away if he ever showed up for work in anything different. His obsessive-compulsive personality was a plus in his line of work and helped make him one of the top thoracic and cardiovascular surgeons in the country.

Approaching the bus, he saw another officer standing guard just outside the entrance. The officer appeared to be a veteran so Elder used a different tactic. "I've been directed here to see Lieutenant Spalding."

The police sergeant responded promptly, "May I see some ID, please?"

Elder presented the MCG photo ID he wore every day at the hospital.

The sergeant glanced at it briefly and returned it. "Just one minute, sir." He stepped up to the entrance and rapped three times. A face appeared in the doorway and the sergeant announced the arrival of Doctor Elder. The door closed for a moment, then reopened.

Spalding stood at the top of the step, his face registering puzzlement. "Doctor Elder, I'm Lieutenant Spalding. Welcome to the Crime Bus. I am familiar with your reputation at the Medical College of Georgia How may I help you?"

Elder made a sweeping gesture with his hands. "May I come in? I can explain the reason for my presence."

Spalding stepped aside, allowing Elder to precede him into the bus.

Once inside Elder offered his hand to Spalding. "I am the Chief of Thoracic Surgery at the Medical College of Georgia," the doctor said in a melodious voice. "I was a preceptor for Doctor Majorski during his thoracic surgery residency. According to the media, he is the physician caught up in the hostage crisis."

Spalding hesitated. "I can confirm that. Our negotiator has conferred with Doctor Majorski and is satisfied as to his identification. How does this involve you?"

Elder made another gesture toward an empty chair. "May I sit down? A friend was kind enough to fly me here on short notice in his private plane and my legs are still a little shaky from the experience."

Smiling, Spalding nodded his permission and took a seat as well.

"Doctor Majorski is an excellent, well-trained, caring physician. Unfortunately, he is probably the worst medical person to be in this situation. As you know, he is an emergency room physician at the local hospital. Prior to his present service, he completed six years in a grueling residency program at the medical college."

Spalding was impatient and confused. "Sounds to me we're lucky he's the man at the site."

"Ordinarily, you would be correct. How fortunate a doctor with so much training happened to be in position at a shootout and hostage situation? But, there are other circumstances. Doctor Majorski went through the emotional trauma of losing a patient on the operating table near the end of his second year in thoracic surgery training. Not an uncommon event for any surgeon, but the mitigating factor has been his inability to separate himself from the emotional setback. He blamed himself for the death of the patient although a thorough review by the surgical committee cleared him of any surgical error. I was part of that committee because I was the assisting surgeon on the case.

"In spite of the findings by the medical college, Dr. Majorski could not put aside the fear that he would harm another patient. Because he was unable to do so, he chose not to continue his residency. I'm privy to what has gone on here today through the hospital grapevine, which rivals CNN for speed and accuracy. I feel in my heart, Ed... uh ... Doctor Majorski would sacrifice himself rather than lose another 'patient.'"

"Go on," Spalding said, leaning forward in the chair, his forearms resting on his knees.

"You must take in consideration everything I've told you, in planning any action to rescue the hostages. I assure you Doctor Majorski will not cooperate if it endangers those inside the store, whether hostages or the men involved in the attempted robbery. In other words, don't plan any scenarios that require him to give you help on the inside, if it puts anyone at risk."

Spalding rubbed the stubble on his chin, pondering the new information. "I need to introduce you to Lieutenant Watkins, our negotiator on site. Please repeat to him everything you just told me."

He led the doctor toward the center of the bus where several men were clustered around video monitors and radios.

Grant Watkins placed his hand on the shoulder of Sergeant Dale Simpson for support as he maneuvered closer to the monitor capturing both men's attention. With his free hand, Watkins adjusted the brightness of the screen, enhancing the view of the subject inside the store. The scene was provided by a small flexible scope snaked through the rear ceiling air duct by a member of the SWAT team. It had required two hours to get the equipment in place, position the scope in the proper vent and maneuvered to an angle that allowed the authorities to see the perps.

"How many do you see?" Watkins asked the sergeant.

"Only two so far. The leader is obvious. He's perched on top of several boxes like he's sitting on a throne. A chunky guy carrying a weapon conferred with him a few minutes ago, but hasn't been in the picture since. According to Spalding, the doc told the 911 operator there were three suspects with guns."

Watkins stretched his neck and head back, trying to ease the muscular tension. "I recall Spalding giving out the information. He also mentioned the doc had tried to say something else, but was interrupted."

"You think there's a fourth?"

"I have no idea. Another may be hidden away with a hostage. If so, any attempt to storm the place will result in the death of the hostage without any hope of rescue."

Simpson got up from his seat and offered it to Watkins. "My vision is getting blurred from staring at the screen so long. Maybe you can pick up something I've missed."

"Any news on the parabolic microphones?"

Simpson shrugged before realizing Watkins couldn't see his movement. "Not a word."

Watkins adjusted the contrast on the screen again and observed the man suspected to be the leader issuing orders to Doctor Majorski. "Too bad we don't have the technology to fire a bullet through the scope," Watkins murmured to Simpson.

"Don't get me wrong. I'm thankful for the remote video feed. I'm getting too old to scale walls of a building to look through a scope."

Simpson laughed at the imagined sight of Watkins hauling his butt over the Mansard roof to get to the scope. "You know, the technology is probably available. The hostage rescue teams probably have it in their arsenal. 'Small fish' like us will never get it."

At the moment Watkins wished he had a reason to call in the HRT of the FBI. It would take the pressure off him and the local police. Their jobs were on the line and subject to the whims of the politicians, who never got their hands dirty. The politicians took the credit if things went well and shifted the blame to the underlings, if it went bad. The premise hadn't changed since Eve blamed the Serpent.

"Grant?"

Watkins straightened up, twisting his head in the direction of the voice. He saw Spalding approaching with an older, distinguished-looking gentleman in tow.

"Grant, this is Doctor Thomas Elder from the Medical College of Georgia. He is familiar with Doctor Majorski and he's got information you definitely need to hear."

CHAPTER TWELVE

2:00 p.m.

Majorski left the table, striding directly to Jayco's elevated perch. "Okay. I helped your friend, now let me do what I can for Mrs. Dixon—without any interference."

Jayco glared back, still fuming over their recent encounter. He dropped down to the floor, strolled over to the makeshift surgical table and conferred with Tupac. After a few minutes, he nodded his approval to the doc.

Majorski wasted little time in getting started. Too much precious time had passed already. With Jimmy's help and with Tracy guarding the chest tube, they moved Tupac from the table, propping him up against a display.

Tracy washed off the table with Lysol, as instructed, and dried it thoroughly with sterile towels packed separately from the surgical packs. She spread clean drapes before she helped Jimmy and Majorski lift the unconscious woman and place her on the table.

Both bags of the intravenous fluids were almost empty. Majorski rechecked his patient's pulse and blood pressure. Satisfied with the improvement; he replaced the bags, reduced the drip rate and moved the intravenous bags and poles further away from the wounded woman to allow Tracy to get closer. The surgical light was in position, with a sterile cover on the handle of the lamp to allow adjustment of the light beam during surgery.

He attached a pulse oximeter to Lucille's index finger to allow a constant readout of her oxygen level. He took a stat reading—ninety-five percent—not too bad considering her blood loss and shock. He inserted a needle attached to a piggyback bag of morphine into the IV tubing, and adjusted the rate, praying the continuous drip of the powerful narcotic would be enough to keep her unconscious during the procedure.

After gowning and putting on sterile gloves, Majorski palpated the entrance wound. He had previously discovered the absence of an exit wound. "This is bad," he said quietly to Tracy, not wanting to be overheard. "The entire area is spongy. She's losing a lot of blood into the retroperitoneal space. I was hoping the area would tamponade itself off. Evidently the bullet hit the renal artery and it's still pumping blood. I doubt I can help her. I've never done the procedure she needs. Hell, she needs the kidney removed and I certainly can't do it. I need to talk to someone for guidance."

He backed away, stripped off the gloves and motioned for Jayco.

"What the hell do you want now?"

"I need to talk to a urologist … uh … a kidney surgeon. Her injuries are far worse than I suspected. Let me use the cell phone to call the hospital and discuss the situation with the surgeon on call?"

Jayco's face remained a mask of hatred. After a quick glance at Tupac, who gave a thumbs-up, he again nodded his approval.

Majorski caught the phone thrown at him. He punched in the hospital number from memory and notified the operator who he needed. Within minutes he was conversing with the on-call urological surgeon. After explaining the situation, Majorski ceased talking and listened to the reply. His face fell when he heard the information he had expected and feared. He thanked the surgeon, closed the phone and tossed it back to Jayco.

He turned to face Tracy, taking care his voice didn't carry to Samantha, sitting ten feet away. "The only thing we can do is pack off the wound as tightly as possible. The surgeon said if we try to explore the wound blindly to find the artery, we run the risk of perforating the aorta. If that happens, I can tell you from personal experience, she would bleed out in a matter of seconds."

Tracy noted the pain in Majorski's expression. She reasoned it was more from a terrible memory than from any physical injury. "So, doctor. What do we do first?"

Majorski snapped out of his morbid thoughts, taking charge of the moment. "Start opening the sterile eight-inch surgical pads. I'll extend the wound to allow us better access. We'll pack the pads close to the source of bleeding. Then we pray."

* * *

3:00 p.m.

The room was eerily silent except for the steady hum of the refrigerated compartments. Samantha, curled up on the floor several feet from the table, whispered a continuous litany of prayers for Lucille. From her position it was impossible to observe what the doc was doing so she listened intently to his curt instructions to Tracy.

A large box lined with plastic garbage bags rested on the floor beside the table. It was the target for multiple bloody gauze pads Majorski used to scoop out large blood clots from the wound. The pads gradually became less saturated and fewer in number, a hopeful sign for the doctor and his assistant.

Majorski looked up from the open wound, attempting to focus on Tracy's face. His vision was blurred and he prayed it was from the intense concentrated effort of searching for bleeders. Several times it took repeated attempts before he was able to clamp and tie off small arteries which steadily pumped blood into the wound. The clumsiness wasn't from lack of skill or practice. He did laceration repair almost every shift in the ER. He recognized his visual changes for what they were—another sign of brain trauma. He waited until his vision improved, stretching his back and neck muscles as a ruse for the delay. He returned to work without Tracy noticing his discomfort.

He paused again, taking the time to study Lucille's face. Her nostrils flared with each breath, a sign of increased respiratory effort. The blood pressure readings called out by Jimmy, who was pressed into service, were encouraging as the pressure continued to rise and the pulse rate fell. Without blood replacement, Lucille's status was still precarious. The volume replacement with Ringers Lactate improved her cardiac status only temporarily. Without whole blood, it was only a matter of time before her status began to deteriorate.

"Jimmy, turn up the oxygen to three liters per minute."

Jimmy quickly complied and also adjusted the nasal prongs in Lucille's nose. Anxious, more than frightened, he had shown a willingness to do anything he could to help Samantha's mother.

Majorski packed the last layer of abdominal surgical pads on top and held them in place while Tracy applied two-inch-wide strips of adhesive tape to anchor them. "We've got the bleeding under control, now infection becomes a concern." Finished with his effort, he backed away from the table and felt a soft pressure against his back. He heard a soft, trembling voice.

"Thank you, Doctor, for saving my mother's life," Samantha said, tears streaming from her crystal blue eyes.

Majorski's chin dropped to his chest. It seemed forever since he last heard those words regarding one of his surgical patients. His voice, reduced to a whisper, acknowledged Samantha's grateful praise. "I appreciate your words more than you can know, but your mom is not out of the woods yet."

He focused his attention on his patient and pulled a sterile drape over the taped pads and up around her neck. After applying a double layer of blankets from the remaining pack, he adjusted the flow of the intravenous fluids and reduced the rate of the morphine drip. Satisfied he had done all he could do at the moment, he walked over to Jayco's perch. The tone of his voice revealed none of the anger he felt toward Jayco.

"What's the purpose of keeping her here? You've scored points by letting us attempt to save her life. Now continue to show good will by letting the EMTs come and take her to the hospital."

Jayco's scornful laugh echoed in the room. "Right, so the bastards can slip another hero in here to take me out. No way. She stays."

Fatigue, jangled nerves and a loaded gun made for a lethal combination. In spite of it all, Majorski' wall of reserve collapsed. His face flushed and his eyes widened in fury. Without regard for his life, he charged Jayco, knocking him from his lofty seat. The two of them crashed to the floor with Majorski on top. Completely ignoring the presence of the gun, he repeatedly pummeled the sadistic man in the face. Maybe if the beating had gone on for much longer, Jayco would have used his weapon. It became a moot point when Charlie raced to the two men, dragging Majorski away and pinning him to the floor.

Jayco jumped to his feet, wiping the blood streaming from his nose on his shirt sleeve. He looked around the room, where the hostages stood watching him. This seemed to add to his rage. "Touch me again, Doc, and I'll kill you, no matter the situation."

Majorski fought against Charlie's physical restraint, finding he was no match against the man's superior strength. "Go ahead. Kill me. I've done all I can do here. I'm of no use to you anymore. Listen carefully to what I say. I promise you, if you attempt to harm anyone else, I will take any opportunity I can to kill YOU."

Jayco glared back at him. "Goes against the oath you take as a doctor, doesn't it?"

"It goes against the Hippocratic Oath and the teaching of the Bible, but I believe Hippocrates and God would grant allowances to rid the earth of scum like you."

Tracy quickly grabbed Majorski by his arm, shaking it hard to get his attention. "Let it go. You're tired and frustrated. Don't get yourself killed. He may not need you, but we do."

Majorski's face fell, his anger dissipating. He rubbed the side of his head, attempting to massage away the pounding headache. "Okay. Let me rest for a minute and I'll check Tupac again."

When Charlie released his hold, Majorski allowed Tracy to take him by the arm and lead him to the back of the store. Their eyes met briefly when they passed Jimmy and Samantha, cuddled in each other's arms at Lucille's side.

Majorski located a place in the back corner of the room where he could partially recline. His eyelids were heavy and he was almost asleep when he heard Tracy's voice.

"Okay, Doctor Miracle Worker. I'm going to search the shelves in these coolers and find something to make you a sandwich. What would you like to drink?"

"A fifth of Jack Daniels Black Label would do nicely."

"Sorry, not available. Got beer and wine."

Majorski smiled, grateful for a break from the tension and violence. "Never mind. A bottle of spring water will do fine. I'd just finished a twelve-hour shift in the ER before I got caught up in this madness. Anything stronger than water will put me down for the count."

As he watched Tracy walk away, Majorski thought about her and the others in the store. At daybreak this morning, they were all strangers; now, they were kindred souls in hell.

Tracy returned with a paper plate loaded with turkey on rye and potato chips. She found Majorski asleep, snoring quietly. "Hey, wake up. You need food in you. There's a coffee station over by the checkout. I'll get fresh coffee after you eat. I've got good news as well. Jayco let Charlie pass out food and drink. Maybe your action got to him and he's softening up some."

Majorski took the plate and with half the sandwich crammed in his mouth, he mumbled his thanks. "Don't get your hopes up about that one. There's more to him than his jolly personality."

"Smart ass," Tracy replied. She retrieved several bottles of spring water from the cooler and passed one to Majorski before she flopped down beside him. She slid across the tile until their bodies were touching, hip to hip and shoulder to shoulder. The warm feeling from the contact swept away some of the horror of their plight.

They munched on the sandwiches in silence. Several times Tracy punched Majorski preventing him from drifting off to sleep with food hanging out of his mouth. "Finish your food. I promise I will let you sleep," she said.

The eyes of the exhausted surgeon reminded her of a begging puppy. The pitiful look stole Tracy's heart. The corners of her mouth turned up in the beginning of a smile, and then the look on her face changed to one of concern. Something was different about his eyes, more than the result of fatigue.

Majorski resumed chewing and with each bite his eyelids grew heavier. When he swallowed the last bite, he leaned toward Tracy, his head coming to rest on her lap. Within seconds, he was asleep.

Tracy gazed at him with increasing worry. She gently stroked his hair, tousled from wearing the surgical cap. She brushed the hair with her fingers, and became alarmed when her caress outlined the multiple lumps on Ed's scalp. "Like I told you, Doctor Majorski, God works in mysterious ways. *He* put us in this predicament for a reason. Please don't try to be a hero and get hurt."

She pulled herself more erect to allow better flexibility. She leaned down, placing her lips against those of the sleeping doctor. When she raised her head, her eyes locked on the smiling faces of Samantha and Jimmy.

Majorski awoke with a jerk, his eyes darting quickly around him. Several seconds passed before the brain fog cleared and he regained his awareness. He stared up at Tracy, who was stroking his face.

"You're okay. You were so exhausted you fell into a deep sleep."

"What time is it?"

"Eight o'clock," she answered.

"I need to check on my patients."

Tracy held him tightly against her lap. "They are fine. Jimmy and Samantha are watching Lucille with fervent attention. Jimmy checks on Tupac frequently. It appears they have developed a bond between them, as strange as that might be."

They both became silent again, lost in their own thoughts.

Several minutes passed before Tracy spoke. "Tell me about Ed Majorski. It's obvious you are a good doctor. What about the boy and the man before medicine? Where did you grow up?"

Majorski glanced at his hands, noticing she had interlocked her fingers with his own. He rarely spoke of himself to anyone, much less to a total stranger. For some reason he felt at ease talking to Tracy. "I'm a native Georgian. I grew up in Social Circle, a little dot on the map in northeast Georgia. My parents could be subjects for a Norman Rockwell painting; just everyday folks. I was an only child so they doted on me. Made sure I got a good education at the University of Georgia—I mean, where else could I have gone? My dad is a diehard Georgia Bulldog fan."

He smiled for the first time in many hours. "I wasn't a nerd even though half my friends thought so. I stayed near the top of my class in high school and college, mainly as a way of thanking my folks for their sacrifices. I went to the Medical College of Georgia on a Ty Cobb scholarship and a student loan."

Tracy looked at him with admiration. "You must have been smart to get a scholarship. Who is Ty Cobb?"

"Most people remember him as a famous baseball player. What they don't know is how much he did for the people in the state of Georgia. He established a scholarship fund for students who couldn't afford tuition at the medical college. He also provided the money to build a hospital in his hometown of Royston."

Tracy's eyes sparkled as she listened. The story was interesting, and it helped take her mind off Luke. Even though she was relieved he was out of danger, she missed him terribly.

"Did you grow up wanting to be a doctor?" she asked.

"For as long as I can remember. When I was a child, a few doctors still made house calls. I remember Doctor Randolph making trips to our house to check on my dad, who has a bad heart. I watched him use his stethoscope to listen to my dad's heart and lungs and occasionally he would let me do the same. He would always stay around and talk to my parents in the kitchen over coffee and pie. That's the image I developed about all doctors. Unfortunately, it's changed a lot since those days. In my mind, he was the epitome of a gentle, caring country doctor."

Tracy cleared her throat, unsure if she should ask her next question. "You mentioned earlier that you lost your confidence. Why did that happen? You look so competent when you were performing the procedures on Lucille and Tupac."

At first Majorski was hesitant to reveal that part of his life. Sensing

Tracy's genuine concern he spent the next thirty minutes telling her everything about his residency days up to and including the fateful event in the OR. They both were emotionally spent by the time he finished.

Tracy found herself wanting to reassure this man who only a few hours earlier had been a total stranger. "God uses adversity to prepare us, so He can use us in a way to benefit others," she said. "He put you here in this store, at this time, because He knows you are the one person who can save us. Don't doubt Him. Ask for the strength you need, and He will grant it."

"Tracy, I wish my faith was as strong as yours."

"It might be. Maybe you haven't exercised it enough lately. It's like a muscle. If you don't work it hard, it will grow weak and useless. I don't see any flab on your body. I doubt there's much on your faith, either."

Majorski's eyes filled with tears. He turned away, quickly wiping the moisture from his face with his shirt sleeve. He kept his head in Tracy's lap and within minutes both were asleep.

CHAPTER THIRTEEN

8:00 p.m.

Grant Watkins inhaled deeply on a cigarette, stubbed it out on the heel of his shoe, field-stripped it and put the filter butt in his pocket. The routine had been developed in his ROTC days at North Georgia College. At times like the present, he longed for the days when his greatest worries centered on spit-polished shoes and crisp khaki uniforms. Located in the foothills of the Blue Ridge Mountains, the campus was noted for its pristine beauty and echoes of drill cadence reverberating off the buildings surrounding the sunken drill field. In addition to being Georgia's Senior Military College, it also ranked high on the national "best education value" list.

He easily recalled those days after morning chow when the cadets lined up abreast of each other and covered the campus, picking up cigarette butts, pieces of paper, or anything detracting from the exquisiteness of the college grounds. At the time, it seemed like slave labor, but now when he returned to the campus and absorbed the elegance of the site, he was proud of his contribution and agreed the scheduled duty was a good one.

Remembering those days gave him a respite from the pressure-packed atmosphere in which he now found himself.

Returning to the bus, Watkins realized the time away from the other officers was exactly what he needed. Grabbing a smoke made a good excuse to get outside. The days of cops gathered in smoke-filled rooms were history, replaced instead by the stale odor of partially consumed cups of coffee and body odor of men and women under stress. Deep in thought, he ambled back to duty, almost colliding with someone hastily exiting the bus.

Spalding grabbed him by the arm. "Hold up a minute, Grant. I need to talk to you."

Still irate over the senseless death of the EMT, Watkins responded in a harsh tone. "Make it quick. I've been away from my desk too long already."

"How long we been working together?" Spalding questioned.

Watkins stuffed his hands deep into his pockets, a crooked grin spreading across his face. "Long enough to know I'm about to hear something I won't like."

A crimson line spread up around Spalding's ears, but he continued. "Come off it, Grant. We've always been straight with each other and worked toward the best outcome. I'll admit I fouled up earlier when I went along with that 'Rambo' stunt by the EMT. You have no idea how much pressure was on me, and still is.

"You've got to help me out here. I'm catching hell from the mayor's office. I was just reamed out by Victor Lynch in proxy for the mayor. They want this 'situation' resolved *now* before it attracts the national media. The buzzards aren't circling yet but they've definitely left the roost and are heading this way. We've been lucky only local media vans have showed up. Once CNN gets the word and brings their vast electronic toys, the pressure will ratchet up considerably."

Watkins laughed. "That's almost poetic coming from you. But it doesn't hold much water with me. I'm not interested in the mayor's public relations problems."

"Well, damn all, you better get interested. I know you've got political relationships enough to insulate you, but the rest of us serve at the whim of the politicians. The mayor understands one thing; the public has a short memory. He knows the majority of the people will eventually forget if a few people are killed in a rescue attempt. They will remember all the way until election time if this thing becomes a media circus and our fair city takes a bath in a tub of national media crap."

Watkins reached for another cigarette, thought better of it and nodded to Spalding. "Okay, I'll hear you out."

"Thanks. First of all, we got the parabolic microphones in place, and from what we've been able to pick up, we're pretty sure one of the suspects is also one of the wounded. Unfortunately, we still don't know the total number of suspects or hostages. They might have one or more of the hostages squirreled away in the store, like in a walk-in cooler."

Watkins began to pace, his hands deep in his pockets. "Okay, now tell me what you have planned, although I'm sure I'm not going to like it."

Spalding hesitated, trying to organize his thoughts. He had to sell Watkins on the idea right off or it would be a no go. "Have you wondered why three men would hit such a dump as this store appears to be on a Christmas morning? What's the expected take? Couple of thousand? Split three ways—that's nothing. There's something else in the store they were after and they failed. Why else would they have hung around as long as they did? We've got to change their thinking. Get their minds on a bigger prize—enough to tempt them to leave the store without their sought after bonanza."

Initially disinterested in anything Spalding planned to say, Watkins was now tuned in and ready to hear more. "What do you think they were after in the holdup?"

"I don't know for certain. One of my officers has a buddy on the drug force. He mentioned this place has been staked out before as a suspected site for money laundering or at least a drop site."

"So, you're thinking they got word of a big cash cow just waiting in there for them to pick up. Then snafu occurred. Makes sense, but what can we do to entice them to leave?"

"Offer enough money to get their attention and—this is the kicker—unimpeded escape in a vehicle of their choice. But only if they leave all the hostages in the store unharmed."

Watkins responded with a funny noise in his throat. "Your superiors will never sign off on it."

"My superiors, and I use the term loosely, will learn of it after it's over."

"Are you nuts? You'll be busted off the force and will lose everything."

"They are going to hang me anyway over the EMT's death, even though it wasn't my idea. I can't prove I wasn't the one who dreamed it up and approved it."

The two men remained silent—each awaiting the response of the other.

Spalding blinked first. "If the perps buy into it, will you support me?"

"I'll do better than that. As negotiator I'll deal with the perps directly and later if there's any heat—I'll take half."

"Noble, but not necessary," Spalding replied.

"It is to me. Up to this point, I haven't contributed much to bring this crisis to an end. Let's see what we can get accomplished without all the city hall brainpower."

CHAPTER FOURTEEN

10:00 p.m.

The interior of the store was darker than normal. Charlie had discovered the bank of electrical switches and selectively turned off all the overhead fluorescent bulbs except those over the front and rear exits. The reflected light from the coolers gave off enough illumination for observation of the wounded. Standing watch near Jayco, Charlie noticed everyone was asleep except him and Tupac, who waved and held a thumb up.

A sudden loud ring jarred Jayco awake. Instinctively, he grabbed for his rifle but was restrained by Charlie's hand.

"Just the phone. In your jacket."

Jayco opened the flip phone, frowning at the "unknown ID." He knew the caller. The cell phone was the only link of communication since he had jerked the land line from the wall in his anger with the doc. He also had refused the direct line and the special phone from the negotiator. He reasoned those were methods the officials used to dictate their superiority over him.

"What you want?"

"Is this ... uh ... Jayco?"

"Who the hell did you expect, President Bush? Does this place look like the fucking White House?"

Watkins paused, allowing the tension to dissipate. One of the earliest lessons he learned as a negotiator was to avoid an adversarial relationship with the hostage takers. He might want to stomp the bastard to death but he couldn't let it be revealed it in his voice. "I request your permission to speak to Doctor Majorski again. The people in charge need to confirm the wounded are okay."

Jayco grinned. "I'm 'the people in charge,' asshole, and I'm telling you they are fine and will stay that way if you give us what we want."

Bingo, thought Watkins. "And just what do you want? You haven't given us any specifics."

"We want the fuck out of here," Jayco screamed, awakening

everyone in the room except Lucille, who slept peacefully in a narcotic stupor.

Watkins purposely remained silent for fifteen seconds before he spoke again. "Take it easy. I know you're getting tired. So are we. All of us have to stay calm to work this out. Why don't you let the doc meet me at the front door? Tell him exactly what you want us to do and he can relay it to me."

"I don't trust you."

"I understand why you have such an opinion. Let me make it clear to you that I had no part in what took place earlier. We've got to develop some trust between us or this will turn into a no-win situation for everyone. Think about it. Give me a shot at doing the right thing."

"No fucking tricks?"

"No tricks. You have my word. We want this resolved without anyone getting killed. Let me work it out with the doc. He can relay what you want and can tell me about the wounded at the same time. We'll do our best to accommodate your desires. You do trust the doc, right?"

"More than I trust you bastards and that's not saying much."

"Okay. We can work together on this. Have the doc meet me outside the front door in ten minutes."

Jayco closed the cell phone, returning it to his jacket pocket before ambling over to the coolers. He looked down at Majorski and Tracy nestled together on the floor. "Now, ain't this cozy? Get off the floor, Doc. Nap time is over. The negotiator wants to talk to you outside in ten minutes." He turned his back to them, hesitated and spoke over his shoulder to Majorski.

"They don't know about the old man so don't mention it. Got me? While you are out there, I will be standing close enough to the door to hear you and my rifle will be aimed at your pretty assistant's head." He placed the end of the barrel at Tracy's temple to emphasize his point. "Be back in the store in exactly ten minutes or the first shot goes through her blond hair."

Majorski tried to speak. The moisture in his mouth had dried up and his tongue stuck to the roof of his mouth. Finally he croaked, "Don't do it. You have my word I won't help them in any cockeyed plans. I'll tell you if they attempt to do anything."

Jayco's mouth twisted in an evil grin. "Go ahead, Doc. Just keep her pretty face in your mind."

"I will and you remember my face. If you hurt her, my face will be the last thing you see on this earth."

Majorski raised his head from Tracy's lap and was immediately assaulted by a wave of nausea and vertigo. He closed his eyes for a few seconds willing the attack to end. He had to get himself together for Tracy and the others.

"Are you okay?" Tracy asked, her concern evident. She pulled Majorski back down to her lap.

"Too little sleep I guess," Majorski said, knowing Tracy wasn't buying it for a second. "I've got to do this. Help me stand up and I'll be okay."

Together they got him to his feet and after a minute or so Majorski felt steady enough to walk. "Stay here by the coolers. Keep away from that psychopath."

Tracy clung to his arm, her eyes pleading. "Please don't get more involved. You've done enough."

"I would like nothing better than to sit with you on the floor until it's all over. Like it or not, I am involved. Jayco is like a grenade with the pin already pulled. Somehow I need to make sure the 'spoon' isn't released."

Majorski opened the door just wide enough to squeeze through and quickly closed it. Behind him he heard the bolt slam home. Charlie must have followed him to the door.

Watkins, standing to the left of the door, took a drag on his cigarette. Showing consideration, he blew the smoke out of the corner of his mouth and away from the doc. "I've got to quit these damn things before they kill me—what the hell, if I don't smoke, the tension will get me."

Majorski managed a chuckle at Watkins' macabre attempt at humor. The smile quickly left his face, remembering the threat to Tracy. "What's up?"

Watkins coughed and tossed the cigarette away—the act a result of the unnerving situation. His face registered his uneasiness and finally his shoulders slumped in resignation. "Doctor Majorski. I'm not going to bullshit you. To be honest, I was sent here to grab you and haul you away from the building. It is completely surrounded by SWAT teams. The mayor's office decided they could take the risk of injury to some of their good citizens inside, but they aren't willing to take the heat from the media if they lose the city's hero doctor."

Majorski backed away, staring in disbelief at Watkins. "Don't let them do this. Tell them to be patient. The wounded are stable and if you'll buy me more time, I think I can talk Jayco into letting the EMTs come get the wounded."

Watkins shook his head. "Time is the one thing I can't give you. The mayor is scared shitless the national media is going to pick up on this. CNN would have a field day showing the rest of the nation what a bunch of country bumpkins we are. His office wants this over, now!"

Majorski slammed his hand against the steel frame of the front door. He immediately regretted the action when the throbbing in his head started again. "We're talking about real people here, not some academic scenario the cops dream up for practice. Are you like them? Are you so anxious to see blood flowing in the streets?"

"Cut me some slack, Doc. You know better than that. If I thought like they do, I wouldn't be working in this job. Don't forget, I didn't have to say a word to you. I could've cold-cocked you and hauled your ass away from the store while they charged in mass. The men downtown will hang my ass out to dry for not following orders."

Majorski leaned against the door, his head gripped between his hands. Waves of nausea rolled over him and the ground tilted unnaturally. He fought back the bitter taste of bile in his throat. After a few moments the episode passed and he straightened up, locking eyes with Watkins. He spoke quietly, but firmly.

"Look, I don't care what you have to do, just give me another chance with Jayco. All three of those guys are in way over their heads. They are nothing more than small time bandits. This thing ballooned on them before they could get away. They don't know a damn thing about how to use hostages."

Watkins's face took on a puzzled expression. He stared at the curious appearance of the doc's eyes. "Doc, are you okay?"

"I'm fine. Just tension and lack of sleep."

Watkins suspected Majorski was holding something back. He decided not to push it. "You're telling me only three perps are involved."

"That's right. Don't speak too loudly. The leader is behind the front door and might hear us. One of them is seriously wounded. He's stable at present. That could change for him and Mrs. Dixon if this goes on much longer. She probably will die in the next few hours unless we get a resolution of some kind real soon."

Watkins felt squeezed between his orders and the right thing to do. "You got a suggestion?"

"If I can convince Jayco and his compatriots to leave, will you guarantee them a car and unimpeded escape?"

Watkins managed a wry smile. "Actually Lieutenant Spalding and I have discussed such a scenario. Have the perps spent much time attempting to get into the safe?"

Majorski cocked his head to one side. That same thought had occurred to him earlier. Why was Jayco spending so much time trying to open the safe when he should have been hauling ass? "Yes, they have."

"We suspect there is a lot of cash in the safe—drug money. That's why they weren't in such a hurry to leave. Spalding and I decided to offer the men a hundred thousand in cash and unimpeded escape if they leave the hostages unharmed in the store."

Majorski snorted in disbelief. "You forgetting these men killed an EMT?"

"No, we haven't forgotten it. The vehicle we provide will have a tracking device planted in an inaccessible spot. When the perps have cleared the city we will follow them with a helicopter until they reach a less populated area and then we'll take them down."

Majorski fought through the brain fog in an attempt to remember all the facts. He decided to withhold the information about the storeowner. To release it now would only make the decision harder to make. "These guys are exhausted and strung out on Sudafed and every other stimulant they can find behind the counter. Don't bullshit me."

He looked at his watch. Nine minutes had passed. "Come on, Watkins. I've got one minute to get back inside."

"One minute or what?"

Majorski screamed at him. "Give me an answer now or it won't matter."

Watkins took a leap of faith. "Okay. Okay. Tell Jayco we can have a vehicle parked in front of the store in thirty minutes, with a briefcase containing one hundred grand. That should satisfy him. That's a lot more than he was going to get from this robbery. But—and I emphasize this point—he cannot take a hostage with him. We will not impede his escape nor will we immediately pursue him, if he does not take a hostage."

Sweat rolled off Majorski's brow when he checked his watch again. Fifteen seconds. He spun toward the building, hammering on the front door. When he heard the bolt slide back, he turned toward Watkins. "Thank you," he said, and he disappeared inside.

Watkins remained in position, staring at the closed door. "Don't thank me, Doc;" he said to the empty space, "You're the man who keeps returning to hell. What on earth makes you do it?"

CHAPTER FIFTEEN

11:15 p.m.

Majorski guzzled his third bottle of spring water. He was bone dry from hyperventilating and the constant pleading with Jayco over the past hour. He presented every scenario possible, attempting to convince Jayco to accept the deal offered. "It's the best chance you've got. Take it. Even Charlie agrees."

Charlie nodded his head.

Jayco sneered. "We walk out of this building without a hostage; they'll shoot all three of us dead before we get out of the parking lot."

"Listen to me, Jayco. The negotiator is trying hard for us. I can see the tension in his face. He's losing the battle with the politicians who want this over with, no matter how many people get killed. It's a sure bet if the SWAT team storms this place, a lot of people are going to get killed, especially you, Charlie and Tupac. If you aren't killed in the initial assault, they'll gun you down even if you try to give up. I can read it in Watkins' face. Take the deal, it's the only chance you have."

Jayco looked at Charlie, then Tupac. Both nodded that they agreed. "Okay. We'll accept the deal. But in addition to the money, I want food, medical supplies and a SUV with four-wheel drive and heavy duty suspension. When I see it parked outside, we'll leave. When we do, the blond teen and your girl friend go with us."

"That's not going to happen." Majorski replied. "They will never allow you to leave if you take a hostage. Don't be so stupid. Take the offer."

"Easy for you to say, Doc. Your ass won't be out there hoping some cop will keep his word. I'm taking a hostage and if the cops open fire then the hostage goes down with me."

Majorski made eye contact with those surrounding him. He turned back to face Jayco. "If you insist on taking a hostage, it'll have to be me."

Jayco's eyebrows arched. A grin that would have made the Joker proud spread across his face. "Fucking-A, Doc. Nothing could make me happier. You're my date." He pitched the cell phone to Majorski. "Call 'em. Just don't give away our little secret."

* * *

11:35 p.m.

Spalding squeezed the handset of the phone, fantasizing it was Victor Lynch's throat. Sitting impatiently in the bus, waiting for the prick to pick up was not helping his disposition. After multiple attempts to contact the mayor had failed, it became obvious his only option was to talk to Lynch—an event he likened to a root canal without anesthesia.

"Lynch, here."

"What took you so damn long, Lynch? I don't have time to sit here and hold a phone."

"Who is this?"

Spalding shouted into the phone. "You know goddamn well who it is. I identified myself to your butler when he answered."

"Harbin is not my butler. He's a very competent aide."

"Not too damn competent if he didn't tell you who was calling."

"Humph," answered Lynch. "Why are you calling me at midnight? It's possible you have awakened my entire family."

Spalding slammed the handset against the counter top three times. "I hope your family heard that, you insensitive prick. While you're getting your beauty sleep, we are dealing with a situation in which a lot of innocent people may die. Where the hell is the mayor?"

Lynch paused. "The mayor is unavailable. I have assumed the responsibility of the office."

"That's great. You can take this message for His Honor. In about an hour we are releasing the hostage takers. We have consented to their demands including no immediate pursuit in exchange for their assurance no hostages will be harmed or taken with them."

"What? You … you … can't authorize any such thing!"

"Fuck you, Lynch. I already have. You're the ass wipe who dreamed up the scheme that resulted in the death of a brave young man and has jeopardized the lives of all the hostages. Don't tell me what I can't authorize. It's my show, good or bad. And let me tell you something else. If a single word of this conversation is leaked to the media, I'll hunt you down and beat your sorry ass senseless. Do you understand?" Spalding heard a click followed by a dial tone.

"I guess he does," Spalding said out loud to himself with a chuckle. He walked with a strut to the front of the bus, proud he had found his balls.

CHAPTER SIXTEEN

December 26, 2007

12:45 a.m.

Spalding looked away from the monitor when he heard exasperated voices coming from the entrance to the bus. The scene at the convenience store was stable at the moment so he hurried toward the voices to check on the commotion.

Kathleen Quick was inside the bus and waging an intense verbal battle with the young trooper, Hank Ginn. Though she was a head shorter, she stood toe to toe with him. Her green eyes flared with as much fire as her red hair.

Spalding hurried across the room and stepped in to rescue Ginn, who appeared to be torn between saying "yes, ma'am" or physically throwing her ass out of the bus. "Kathleen, you know the media is not allowed in the Crime Bus. The rule applies to everyone, even family members."

Kathleen turned her wrath on Spalding. "Buddy, I'm not here representing the media. Do you see a microphone or a camera? I'm asking for information about my husband. As a concerned wife, I have that right. What is going on? Grant hasn't called me since this situation started."

The last thing Spalding needed was involvement in a domestic situation. "Look, Kathleen. He's been occupied doing his job, and you've been doing yours. The time wasn't available for chit-chat. He's talking with the hostage takers as we speak. I'll tell you something on the promise you won't use it. We're allowing the suspects to leave unimpeded. They've agreed not to take a hostage and we've promised not to make immediate chase."

"My God, Buddy! Did the mayor's office agree with the compromise?"

The corners of Spalding's mouth turned up in a sly grin. "Well, let's just say they didn't strongly oppose."

"Buddy, please don't let Grant do anything stupid. With his heart condition he shouldn't be working these long hours. Please make sure he doesn't extend himself too far."

Spalding put his arm around her and gave her a reassuring hug. "I'll do my best. Grant has a mind of his own. You know that better than anyone."

"Thank you, Buddy." She turned to Ginn who had remained at her side. "You've got backbone, Trooper Ginn. They should promote anyone who'll stand up to me." With an impish smile she turned toward the door leaving the flabbergasted trooper in her wake.

* * *

1:00 a.m.

The exterior of the convenience store was lit up like Macy's at Christmas. Banks of portable spotlights were placed at strategic points behind the barriers; no shadows remained in which someone could lurk. The area behind the lights was a different scene. All the flashing lights of the official vehicles were turned off. The windows in the bus were blacked out with thick cloth. In the darkness behind the barriers, three expert marksmen lay motionless on elevated platforms at strategic locations. Each man trained the powerful scopes of their CZ 750 Tactical Sniper Rifles on the front entrance awaiting targets and the "go" signal to fire.

Watkins balked on the plan to take down the perps and relented only when Spalding promised no shots would be fired unless each marksman had a clear head shot on each man at the same time.

Inside the building things were more chaotic. Majorski moved repeatedly from Lucille to Tupac checking them for unforeseen complications. He gave instructions to Tracy, who wrote everything down through a veil of tears.

Jimmy and Samantha stood beside Lucille, whose hand was firmly in Samantha's grasp. They both focused their anxious looks toward Majorski as he helped Tupac sit on a stool placed near the front.

He glanced up when Jayco and Charlie approached. "I guess it's time to go?"

"Not quite," Jayco answered, "we got one more thing to do."

* * *

Watkins parked the black Ford Expedition as close to the store front as possible, making sure there were no other vehicles blocking the SUV. From the driver's seat he electronically raised all the darkened windows before exiting the car. Following Jayco's instructions, he left the vehicle's engine running and the driver's door open. Walking toward the rear of the vehicle, he glared at the police bus. He didn't trust Spalding's cohorts and half-expected to be cut down in a hail of fire, along with the men trying to escape.

Spalding appeared to have second thoughts about the arrangement and for the past hour, he had been much too silent. The short hairs on the back of Watkins' neck bristled when he opened the passenger and right rear doors. He shook his head in disbelief at the array of items on the back seat and rear compartment. Blankets, pillows, jugs of water, food and an assortment of prescription pain pills and antibiotics were stacked up like a mobile hospital. On the floor of the front passenger seat was a small gym bag containing the one hundred thousand dollars in small denominations. He had been assured there were no explosive dye markers.

Watkins had done his part with the procurement of the vehicle and the supplies. The GPS tracking device installed beneath the engine mount would allow the police helicopter to follow the SUV and once the vehicle was in a less densely populated area, the police could take it down with less collateral damage.

The plan was solid—as solid as they could make it—right up to the moment the front door opened.

CHAPTER SEVENTEEN

Majorski stepped out of the store with the business end of a Mossberg shotgun firmly attached to his head with duct tape. The stock and trigger assembly were taped to Jayco's hand, arm and trigger finger.

Watkins spun toward the bus and the barricades, his arms raised and palms out. "Stand down. All weapons down, now!" He heard Spalding repeat the command and the order echoed around the perimeter of the building. He turned to face the two men bound together.

"What the hell? You said no hostages would be taken."

Jayco gave Majorski a shove toward the SUV. "I lied."

Keeping his eyes on Watkins, Jayco addressed Charlie, who was standing just inside the door. "Help Tupac move outside and into the rear compartment."

Thirty seconds later, Charlie reappeared. "Tupac ain't coming. He don't like it, you taking the doc. He also said he would just slow us down."

"Okay, if that's what he wants." Jayco grimaced. "I wish he'd come, though. We've always been a team."

Majorski made a play on the emotional moment. "Tupac's right and you know it. You and Charlie would be better off giving up now rather than face death on the road. Do you really want to be on the run from the law for the rest of your life?"

Jayco spat a wad of mucus on the ground. "Spoken like a man who's never been caged in a five-by-eight cell. I'd rather be dead than spend the rest of my life cooped up like an animal."

Majorski responded quickly, afraid he would lose the moment. "You won't get life for this."

"Don't try to bullshit me, Doc. A murder rap is no five- to ten-year sentence."

Watkins head came up abruptly. "Murder—what murder? Are you talking about the EMT? There's extenuating circumstances that will be taken in account. It wasn't premeditated; a charge of manslaughter at the worse. Doctor Majorski, you holding out on me?"

Majorski avoided eye contact with Watkins. "There's more. I didn't mention it because I thought the police would nut up and overreact. The store owner was also killed. The shooting was sort of self-defense. The store owner shot the man who has elected to remain in the store. Jayco's action was a natural reflex when the owner turned his gun on him."

Watkins thought about it for a moment. He and Spalding were doomed. When the politicians learned they had let three murderers leave the scene unscathed, even if they did have a hostage, nothing would save them from a public "hanging." He immediately went into a damage control mode. The doc was right. Get the men to surrender now. It was too late to stop them physically without getting the doc's head blown off on national television. "Probably a charge of manslaughter and coupled with armed robbery, you are looking at ten to fifteen years. Less with good behavior."

Majorski pleaded with Jayco. "Think about it. This mess wasn't your intention. The situation got out of hand. You've demonstrated compassion by allowing me to help the wounded. The jury will take your action in consideration. Give it up. Serve your time and get on with your life."

Jayco remained silent for a moment. When he spoke it was one word. "Charlie?"

Majorski saw movement out of the corner of his eye. Charlie stepped past him, slamming the stock of the AK-47 into Watkins' belly.

"There's your answer," Jayco said. "Get your ass back to the barricade or we might take you along for the ride."

"You're making a big mistake," wheezed Watkins. He did as ordered and walked toward the barricade, bent over at the waist, his hands cupped over his gut.

Jayco's response was lost in the wind. "My whole fucking life is a mistake."

Spalding spoke into the mouthpiece of his headset. "Spotter One and Spotter Two, do you have them in sight?

"Affirmative," both answered.

"Can your shooters take them out, both at once?"

"Shooter One. Negative. I have sight on the suspect in the back seat with the hostage but my line of fire is partially blocked by the hostage. If either one moves I can't guarantee a perfect head shot."

"Shooter Two. What do you have?" Spalding was practically pleading.

"If Shooter One can take out the suspect in the driver's seat then I can get a cross shot to the head of the suspect in the back seat. There's an additional problem. I can see through my scope the suspect's trigger finger is taped so that if his head or body moves uncontrolled, the gun will fire. His finger could twitch from reflex."

"Anyone. Let me hear some suggestions," Spalding said.

"Shooter Two, here. My spotter has my fifty-caliber rifle here as well. If I can get the angle, I can take off the suspect's arm at the shoulder. Still no guarantee there won't be a twitch but less likely than a head shot."

"Hold one," Spalding said. He was sweating, his heart pounding. The bastards had outwitted him. He turned up the volume on his mike.

"Don't try it," snapped Watkins, who had moved up behind Spalding.

"I wasn't. No way would I risk injuring the doc. We'll still get a chance at them."

"Snipers. Stand down. All weapons on safe and locked. SWAT, as soon as the vehicle clears, breach the store. No firing unless fired upon. One wounded suspect is still in the store."

Spalding turned to Watkins. "You okay?"

Watkins stared back, pain and guilt in his eyes. "No, but it doesn't have anything to do with the blow I took. We've got to talk."

Inside the store the remaining hostages held their breath. Jimmy ran to the front door, peered through the slits in the paper and gave a running account of the activities outside. "Charlie gave a whack to some dude and sent him away. Evidently didn't like something he said. Jayco and the doc are getting into the back seat." He paused to catch his breath. "Charlie is now climbing behind the wheel. Okay. They're driving away and no one is trying to stop them."

The moment the tail lights of the SUV disappeared from sight, the SWAT teams rushed the building. A heavy battering ram crashed through the back door followed by two men in full gear, who entered crouched over through the remains of the shattered door. Their weapons were leveled and only a last-minute order from Spalding prevented them from using the flash bang grenades. The front door was spared a similar fate since Jimmy saw the black clad men coming and slid back the bolt and swung the door open before the teams could breach the entrance.

The team members were stunned by the silence. No cries of relief, or loud prayers or pleas for protection. The hostages were huddled together around a middle-aged woman and a young black man, both obviously wounded.

Tracy raised her hands, drawing attention to herself. "Everyone is okay. We have two wounded, but both are stable, thanks to Doctor Majorski. He was the hostage taken away with the shotgun taped to his head."

The bodies of the owner and the EMT were discovered in a matter of seconds. A crime scene investigator scurried around snapping shots with his camera before ordering the body positions to be chalked. Additional investigators placed the dead men in separate body bags, tagged them and moved them out of the store.

One of the men removed his face shield and began issuing orders to those around him. "Sergeant Stewart, notify the bus all is secure. Sergeant Poole, I want the EMTs in here, now. Have them check on these people and get the wounded to the hospital. I want ID from everyone in this room. Assign a team member to stay with each person while they are transferred. Keep them separated, and keep the press away from them."

The men, all dressed alike in black jumpsuits, black helmets and clear face shields, spread throughout the room. Four men went to the aid of the EMTs, two assigned to each stretcher, to help transport Lucille Dixon and Tupac to the awaiting ambulances. Other men began securing yellow CSI tape around the outside of the store.

"Lieutenant." One of the men called out as he approached the tall, ramrod-straight man standing in the center of the action. "Sir, this is Samantha Dixon." The team member placed his hand gently on Samantha's arm, urging her toward his commander. "Samantha is the daughter of the wounded lady and wants permission to remain with her when she's transferred to the hospital."

Lieutenant Sam Lochner shook the small hand offered as he studied the youngster. So much stress visible on the face of someone so young and pretty, he thought. "Hello, Samantha. I'm Lieutenant Lochner. I know you've been through a lot and we're not here to add to your misery. You may go with your mother. I must insist on avoidance of the media and please do not leave the hospital until one of my men has an opportunity to talk with you."

Samantha smiled at him, shook his hand again and ran after the stretcher transporting her mother to the ambulance.

"Pretty girl," the SWAT team member said.

"Right on," answered Lochner. "I pray to God my children never have to endure something like this."

* * *

2 a.m.

Tupac lay quietly on the gurney anchored securely to the floor of the speeding ambulance. He closed his eyes, marveling at the wonderful sensation of the cool oxygen flowing through the tubes placed in his nostrils. He kept his eyes shut, his brain adrift in the morphine-induced fog, relaxing to the sway of the box-shaped vehicle.

None of the hostages had fingered him in the convenience store. A nice gesture on their part, though he couldn't reason why. It didn't matter. Sooner or later, his part in the robbery would be found out and he would be moved to a prison hospital. Then he would be staring through prison bars for the rest of his life. At the moment he didn't care. In his mind-numbing haze, he thought only of the doc. The man had saved his life and kept the situation from totally blowing up. A man like that deserved to live. He feared for the doc's safety. Jayco was unpredictable and dangerous; if cornered, he would go berserk and Charlie couldn't control him.

"I should have gone," he muttered to himself, "even if it killed me."

Tears flowed from the corners of his eyes and down across his cheeks.

The EMT in attendance heard the muttering and saw the tears. Concerned his patient was in pain, he increased the flow of the morphine drip.

Tupac sensed he was sliding into a black void. He could do nothing to stop it; nor did he care.

CHAPTER EIGHTEEN

2:00 a.m.

Jayco peered out the rear window of the Expedition, half-expecting to see a procession of police cars in pursuit. The absence of blue flashing lights did little to relieve his anxiety.

"I'm not a genius, but I ain't stupid. I know they put a tracking device somewhere on this SUV. Goddamn pricks! We ain't wasting time looking for it." He fell silent, considering his options.

"Charlie, at the next intersection make a U-turn and head back north on Highway 17. When you get to Spur 25, turn left and follow it until you intersect I-95. Take the interstate south toward Jacksonville. Keep plenty of space between us and other cars."

Jayco leaned back against the seat, which allowed his hostage to do the same. His arm ached from the strain of holding the shotgun in place, even though the tape lightened the burden. "Doc, when we get to our destination, I'll cut this gun loose from your head."

With a grim expression on his face, Majorski responded with a sarcastic laugh. "I hope we don't hit a bump and you accidentally blow my head off before then. I'm sure such an accident would upset you."

Jayco snorted. "Don't worry 'bout it, Doc. The gun ain't loaded. I couldn't tell you before we left. It had to be convincing and the look on your face was perfect."

"If you mean a look of total fear, you are one hundred percent correct. I'm sure I shit my pants."

The threesome rode in silence as the SUV crossed the bridges over the South Brunswick and Turtle Rivers that emptied into the Atlantic. Majorski inhaled deeply, enjoying the smell of the brackish marshes. He had always loved the sight and smell of the marshes, one of the reasons he chose to come to Brunswick to do ER work. Enjoy them now, he thought, it'll probably be the last time.

Several minutes passed before Jayco spoke again. "Charlie, Highway 82 is coming up. Take the exit ramp and turn west on the four-lane. Once you are on 82, stay in the right lane. I don't want anybody passing us on my blind side. It's about twenty miles to

Atkinson. When you get there, turn left onto Highway 110. There's a Chevron station at the turn. A sign should be there indicating the road to Waverly. I'm going to rest my eyes for a few minutes. Wake me up after you turn. Doc, don't try no funny stuff."

Majorski's eyes were already closed and the last thing on his mind was attempting a heroic act. He didn't buy the story about the gun not being loaded.

* * *

2:30 a.m.

The driver of the Crime Bus, following his instructions to the letter, maintained a steady fifty-five miles per hour in the right lane of I-95. He called out each exit number as he approached it. He glanced at the outside mirror noting the single patrol car following them. Spalding had made it clear for all units to remain in Brunswick except for one which would follow the bus and without flashing lights.

Spalding yelled out from the computer console. "The tracking monitor shows they've turned west on Highway 82. Take the same exit west and maintain the present speed unless I tell you differently."

Watkins sat in a folding chair behind and to the right of Spalding. His eyes were fixed on the green screen. The GPS monitor was superimposed over a roadmap. Watkins watched as the blip they followed continued west. "They've passed the turnoff to Highway 99 so they obviously aren't circling back to Brunswick."

Spalding shifted forward in his chair and made a fine adjustment to the monitor. The screen changed to a map defining a larger area. "If they plan to return to Brunswick, they can take Highway 110 east at Atkinson, swing north to Highway 32, then back to Sterling and Brunswick."

Watkins shook his head in disagreement. "No, it would have been easier to take Highway 99 straight to Sterling."

Spalding rubbed the top of his head, something he often did when deep in thought. "They might stay on 82 until Nahunta, and take 301 south to Florida. But hell, if they plan to go to Florida, why didn't they stay on I-95?"

Watkins laughed while watching Spalding switch the screen back to the close up view. "We're calling out numbers like we're in a game of bingo."

"That might be," replied Spalding. "So far our playing card is empty."

Watkins didn't respond immediately and when he spoke his speech had taken on a serious tone. "Are you sure you don't want to put out a blocking screen in front of them?"

"About as sure as I was with the plan we hatched. We're in deep and we need to capture them soon. Once the media starts applying pressure on the mayor, he'll call the governor and request an all-out dragnet. That would certainly result in the deaths of the perps and Majorski. Let's string this out for awhile and pray for a break. As long as that shotgun is taped to his head we can't do anything."

"If we lose contact with them he's probably as good as dead anyway," Watkins replied.

"With the tracking device in place and the helicopter overhead, we can bide our time."

Watkins had another nightmarish thought. "We might not be the force that spooks them. If John Q. Citizen gets involved, there will be more bloodshed."

"I know," Spalding said, shaking his head. "From the time we left the store every new victim will be on our consciences forever."

* * *

3:00 a.m.

Charlie gave a shrill whistle through his teeth, startling Jayco awake. "I've turned off 82 and I'm in the parking area of the Chevron station you mentioned. There's a big sign out front. Paige's mini-market. Everything is closed up. I'm going to run around behind the store and take a leak. I'm about to bust."

Jayco rubbed the sleep from his eyes with the back of his left hand. He was anxious to get the damn shotgun off his right hand. No way could he risk it until he got rid of the SUV. He leaned forward toward Charlie, dragging the doc's head along.

"Make it quick; until we get rid of this SUV, we're hooked to them like a leash on a dog."

Charlie did his business in record time and soon was standing at the driver's door, shaking his pant leg to get rid of the last few drops that never come until you zip up.

Jayco became impatient. "Get in the damn truck and let's go. Stay on Highway 110 until you get to the Brantley/Camden county line. About two miles after you get into Camden County, there's a dirt road across from where the Little Satilla River turns back east. Follow the dirt road to Tarboro. Been a while since I traveled on the road. It should be passable."

"What are we going to do in Tarboro?"

"Find a damn truck and get rid of this one. Try to find one with four-wheel drive."

He collapsed back against the seat, turning his eyes toward the doctor, who had dropped off to sleep again. "How the hell can he go to sleep so fast?"

* * *

3:00 a.m.

Tracy's body was exhausted yet her mind was in warp speed. She had been examined and released by the doctors at the Brunswick Hospital ER and now was waiting for one of the officers to question her. She and the other hostages were assured the questions would be brief and they would be allowed to go home to sleep. The authorities informed them of possible further contact if additional information was needed.

Her body sagged, her head nodding forward. She felt she could sleep for a week. She thought of the people with whom she had spent Christmas Day. Virtual strangers when the day had begun and now their lives would be interlocked forever. She knew Lucille was already in surgery and possibly the young black man as well. She hadn't seen Samantha or Jimmy since they all arrived within minutes of each other at the hospital. She was concerned about them and missed them already.

But another soul filled her heart and her mind. Doctor Ed Majorski. Was he still alive and if so, what hell was he going through at the moment. Another of God's angels who appeared at the right time and in the right place to care for others. The man had spent the majority of his short life so far in preparing himself to ease the suffering of others. She was certain he never dreamed his role in life would be to sacrifice himself in this way. Was it love or intense gratitude that made her heart feel so full and yet empty at the same time?

Her spirits improved immediately when a young lady wearing a uniform that identified her as a member of the Glynn County Sheriff's Department brought Luke to her. She thanked the woman and hugged Luke, kissing him on the face and neck. She inhaled deeply, enjoying his smell. Evidently someone had recently changed him and applied a liberal amount of baby powder. Tears filled her eyes, from joy and from pain.

She was relieved Luke was so young he would never remember any of the nightmares they had endured. At the same time she couldn't get Majorski out of her mind. Meeting the nurses and doctors he worked with in the ER seemed to bond her to Majorski even more. All of them spoke highly of his professionalism and his concern for his patients. Their concern for his safety was evident in their voices and facial expressions. They recognized a special bond had developed between Tracy and Majorski and told her they would be praying for him. Her own prayers for his safety were in her heart and were ongoing and she knew God would hear them. Surely He wouldn't put someone like Majorski in her life and then take him away so quickly.

Luke began to squirm and made the funny faces that usually indicated he was hungry. She walked to the receptionist desk, waited for someone to notice her and then cleared her throat to attract attention. "Excuse me. I know you're busy and I hate to interrupt. Is there a place where I can have some privacy to nurse my baby?"

A nurse standing nearby recognized Tracy as one of the hostages brought into the ER earlier. She took Tracy by the arm and directed her to the chapel. "I'll make sure you are not disturbed and I'll inform the investigating officer of your location. If they need you, they can just wait until Luke is finished."

After the nurse left, Tracy settled on a padded pew and opened her blouse. She smiled as she watched her beautiful son's mouth root around on her breast until he located the nipple. He began nursing immediately and appeared undisturbed by the tears dropping onto his little face.

CHAPTER NINETEEN

3:30 a.m.

Charlie maneuvered the Expedition along the narrow dirt road taking the bumps in stride. Low hanging clouds reached down through the tree tops, mating with the foggy mist spreading out from the river. Combined with the darkness, the elements made the SUV almost invisible. The area was foreign to Charlie, yet he drove without lights through the blackness as if aided by night vision goggles.

Several times he heard the whine of a helicopter back across the river, cutting circles in the night sky, well east of their location. He chuckled over the cat-and-mouse game; for the moment, the mouse was winning.

The passengers in the back seat were jarred awake by the sudden swerving of the vehicle, followed by a loud crunch. "What the hell you doing, Charlie? You falling asleep up there?"

"No. I think I hit a deer. Wasn't my fault. It came right out of the bushes. Pitch black out there. I wish I could have missed it."

Now awake, Jayco leaned forward to question Charlie about their location. He suddenly screamed. "My arm is on fire. It feels like it's being jabbed by a thousand needles. How long we been on this road?"

"About thirty minutes," Charlie replied, glancing at the illuminated clock on the instrument panel.

"We should be close to Tarboro. My arm is killing me. First car or truck you see on the outside of town, stop somewhere near it."

Majorski, struggling to stay awake, heard the exchange. "My head doesn't feel so great either. Take the shotgun off or pull the damn trigger? At this point I don't care either way." His captors ignored him.

Fifteen bone-jarring minutes later, Charlie eased the SUV onto a blacktop road. The area was far more desolate than any place he had ever seen. A faint light slicing through the black void farther down the isolated road offered some hope. Ten minutes later, he was out of the vehicle, investigating a possible new form of transportation parked on a hard-packed dirt yard of a farm house.

Jayco and Majorski, working in tandem, managed to maneuver out of the back seat and now stood at the rear of the SUV, parked deep in high brush. They silently watched Charlie crabbing back across the road to their position.

Jayco spoke in a whisper, his voice tight with impatience. "How 'bout it, Charlie? Can you hot-wire it?"

"No problem. The truck is parked beside an open window. Looks like a bedroom. Got fancy curtains in the window. We got to push it down the road a piece or find another truck."

Jayco considered the options for no more than a second before succumbing to the pain. "Take your knife and cut this damn tape or my arm will be totally useless. I'm not waiting until we find another truck."

Jayco and Majorski remained rigidly still, more afraid of being cut by the knife than being heard by the family in the house. He ordered Charlie to cut the tape from his hand and arm. He kept his arm elevated and steadied the shotgun while Charlie cut the tape from around Majorski's head and neck.

Jayco lowered his arm, immediately regretting the sudden move. "My arm is burning and my fingers won't work. We got to wait a few minutes before I can help push the truck."

Recognizing Jayco had symptoms of nerve compression, Majorski knew the discomfort was temporary; however, he wasn't in a hurry to allay his kidnapper's apprehension. He had problems of his own; taut neck muscles momentarily prevented him from flexing his neck or turning his head to the right.

Jayco moaned and groaned in between strings of prison-polished profanity. Flexing and extending his arm, he worked to restore normal function. Several minutes later, he whispered to the others. "Okay, enough of the pity party. Let's get the truck moved so Charlie can get it started. We've got to put more distance between us and Brunswick."

He spat his words at Majorski. "Don't try anything, Doc. Even with a bad arm, I'm still a damn good shooter."

* * *

4:45 a.m.

An hour later, the stolen pickup, with the three men crammed into the small cab, was parked in a vacant lot on the outskirts of Burnt Fort.

Jayco and Charlie were deep in discussion over the next phase of their plans, ignoring Majorski who was wedged between the two men and appeared to be asleep.

Opening the passenger door, Jayco checked out the area before he stepped out of the truck. "Keep an eye on the doc. I'm going to dig through the supplies the nice people of Brunswick gave us. There's a bottle of pain tablets in there somewhere. My damn arm is driving me nuts."

"Don't take too many," warned Charlie. "I can't drive and watch the doc by myself. I need you to tell me where to make turns. I've heard 'bout the backwoods of Georgia before, but this place is spooky."

Jayco retrieved a package and three bottles of water from the supplies stacked in the rear of the truck. With his booty in hand, he slid back into the seat. "Don't sweat it, Charlie. Found some Vicodin. They make me hyper instead of drowsy. And we don't have far to go."

Charlie accepted a bottle of water, finishing it in one continuous gulp. He pitched the empty out the window. "Where are we going? You haven't told me anything except where to make turns."

Jayco ran his hand across his mouth, an attempt to wipe away spilled water on his chin. A speck of white residue from the tablets clung to his bottom lip. "I've been thinking about our options. I think our best shot is to take Highway 252 into Folkston. We can get breakfast at a fast-food place and then take 23 south to the Suwannee Canal Park road. It's practically deserted this time of year; shouldn't be any problem getting around the entrance gate. We'll drive down to the recreational area, steal a boat and go into the Okefenokee Swamp."

Ashen-faced, Charlie stared back with a wide-eyed expression of disbelief. "I don't know about getting in a boat in the swamp. I can't swim. I've never been in a swamp."

Jayco answered with a snort of scorn. "Damn, Charlie. You don't have to swim. You can stand up in most of the places. Don't you keep up with the news? Global warming, man. There's a drought and the swamps are drying up. It'll work out good for us. We got enough supplies to last for weeks and we can wait out the police in the swamps while they look for us on the roads. After a few days, the manhunt will peter out and we can make our way northwest to intersect the Suwannee River."

Charlie's voice revealed his continued doubt. "How 'bout the river? Bet its deep?"

"Don't worry. I won't let you drown. Anyway, once we get on the river, we can take it down to Fargo or stay on it until we get to White Springs. Down in Florida. Either way, the cops won't have a clue where we are."

Majorski spoke, startling the men who thought he was asleep. "It's almost daylight. Most rangers are up early and tourists usually get to the recreational area at opening time to take the tours before the heat of the day." He prayed his bluff would work. His knowledge of the park was limited at best.

"I suggest you find a place to spend the day and get some rest. I've slept more than you two combined, and I still feel like crap."

"You taking over as leader?" Jayco gave Majorski a hard shot to his ribs.

"No. Only a suggestion."

"And a good one," echoed Jayco. "There's an old farm not too far from here. Been deserted for years; least it was last time I was down this way. Maybe it still is. If so, we can park in the barn and eat and sleep."

* * *

3:45 a.m.

"Where did they go?" Spalding moved the cursor on the screen, double-clicked the mouse and closely studied the enhanced view. The tracking blip was at a forty-five-degree angle to the direction the bus was presently traveling. It appeared the blip was traversing an area not indicated as a road on the map.

"Sergeant Kimble. Find a place to turn this beast around. We've missed a turn not shown on this damn map."

Spalding picked up the radio handset on the table. "Trooper Hill, are you still at our rear?"

"Yes, sir."

"Turn around. Drive slowly back toward Atkinson. Use your spotlight to locate any turnoffs to the west, somewhere within five to eight miles. It probably won't be an improved road."

A double click came over the speaker in response.

Sergeant Kimble drove almost to Waverly before he found an area large enough to turn the modified bus back in the direction they had come.

Virtually at the same instant, Hill came back on the air. "Sir, I found a dirt road just south of the Brantley-Camden county line. I'm not sure the bus can maneuver on it."

"Hit your flashers and wait there," Spalding said. He twisted in his seat, giving Watkins a questioning look. "What do you think?"

Watkins shrugged his shoulders. "Obviously they're driving without headlights on, or the helicopter would have picked them up when they left the highway."

"So much for modern technology in high pursuit," Spalding said. "We haven't heard a word from the helicopter because they don't want to admit they don't have a clue where the damn SUV went."

Watkins, ignoring the remark, continued to speak his thoughts out loud. "They won't go to ground this close to Brunswick. They know we can canvass this entire area in a short time."

Spalding spotted the flashing lights of the patrol car and picked up the headset. "Hill, lead the way and we'll follow. If the bus can't make it on the road, we'll leave it and continue with you." Spalding punctuated his remarks by slamming the hand piece on the table in frustration.

CHAPTER EIGHTEEN

6:00 a.m.

The soft-hued light of dawn revealed a chaotic scene in the front yard of the Williams family. A police helicopter sat idle in the yard, the long blades overhead motionless and sagging from their weight. Loud pops came sporadically from the cooling engine. The noise was loud enough to attract attention from those nearby.

The number of official vehicles parked in and around the yard gave the appearance of an ongoing police convention. A Glynn County Sheriff's car was parked in front of the chopper, along with a Georgia State Trooper cruiser, and additional police cars from Charlton, Brantley and Camden counties. Adjacent to them was the large Crime Bus, with a scratched and muddy exterior.

Scott Williams sat on the top step of the front porch with his nine-year-old son. The boy appeared mesmerized by the number of vehicles and uniforms. Williams patiently answered the questions offered by two professionally dressed men.

Spalding jotted something in a small spiral notebook and turned his attention back to the man and his son. "Mr. Williams, you stated you weren't aware anything was amiss until the helicopter landed in your yard. Is that correct?"

"Yes, sir. I'm a pretty heavy sleeper. That helicopter sure woke me up. I didn't hear anything during the night. I don't have a clue what time my truck was taken."

Spalding nodded, referring again to the notebook in his hand. "And you're positive you didn't leave the keys in the truck?"

Williams gave the boy a goose in the ribs. "Jake, check and make sure my keys are on the peg in the kitchen."

The boy jumped up, dashing into the house. He was back with a large key ring attached to a leather strap before the front screen door closed. He gave the key ring to his father who fingered the keys and held up the key to the truck.

Spalding stared at the key. "Most likely they hot-wired the truck or punched out the lock on the steering column. Was the ignition switch on the column?"

Before Williams could answer, Watkins touched Spalding on the shoulder and motioned for Spalding to follow him a few feet away from the steps. Turning his back to the family, he said, "I'm not questioning your ability to do your job, but what damn difference does it make how they got the truck? We are convinced they took it since the Expedition is parked less than a hundred feet from the house.

"We know what time we lost them in the chase and approximately the time it took to get to this point. What we need to be working on is where the hell did they go?"

A pink flush crept up the sides of Spalding's neck. Realizing Watkins was right, he kept his cool, responding in a calm manner. "You're right. Old habits are hard to break." He returned to the porch. "Thank you for your help. We'll let you know the moment we recover your truck."

Watkins followed Spalding to the bus. Neither man spoke. When they entered the bus they discovered Sergeant Kimble on the computer searching Google Earth. They watched him alter the view from long range to local.

Kimble moved the cursor on the screen. "There are several options available. Most likely they took Highway 252 to Folkston, near the Florida line."

Spalding made eye contact with Watkins. "Makes sense. That's why they didn't go straight down I-95 to Florida. They used the back roads to ditch the Expedition before they headed for Florida. They obviously suspected we had a tracker on the SUV."

"I agree," Watkins said. "Something doesn't sit right with me." He touched Kimble on the shoulder. "Sergeant, pull back on the view so we can see all the roads out of Folkston." He waited while his instructions were carried out, and then pointed at the screen with his pen.

"Look at the limited options they have out of Folkston. They can take Highway 1 due south into Florida or follow 23 south along the St. Mary's River and stay in Georgia a lot longer. The other option is to take Highway 40 east back toward 95; however, I think we can eliminate the last option. It doesn't make sense. So, we have two roads we can easily cover. They aren't dumb. What are we missing?"

Kimble sat quietly for a moment, deep in thought. "Something else bothers me. There are a lot of places to dump a body. We might not have a hostage situation any longer."

The look on Watkins' face was not kind; nor was his response. "I don't want to hear any more talk like that. Until we actually see the doc's body, we will assume he is alive and is still a hostage, and we will approach the suspects with that reasoning in mind."

Spalding cleared his throat, anxious to change the subject, saving Kimble from further embarrassment. "Let's not forget about the northern routes out of Folkston. If the suspects feel trapped by the roadblocks on the southern escape routes, they might decide to head north."

"Buddy, we're thin on personnel. We've got offers of help from Charlton, Camden and Brantley counties, but even with the people they can spare, we still can't cover all the exits from Folkston."

The subject had tormented Spalding's mind since his earlier comments. "We can if we eliminate the northern routes. I mean, think about it. Why would they turn north again? US Highway 1 to Waycross and 301 to Nahunta are their only options north. That puts them squarely back in the hunt. No, I think we can eliminate those routes and concentrate on the southern routes, especially Highway 1 south. That would take them through farm country to Jacksonville. It would be almost impossible to find them there."

The two men settled back in their chairs. The room remained silent and they stared at the map on the monitor as if waiting for a sign from God.

God apparently wasn't inclined to offer help so they both called out Kimble's name at the same time.

"What? Now you want my advice? Okay, I'll tell you what I've been thinking. I would concentrate on Highway 1 because it's a major highway and they could move quickly in whatever vehicle they are driving. It's a sure bet they've changed cars again by now. I'd put some men on Highway 23 that parallels the St. Mary's River down into Florida. Just after 23 crosses the Georgia-Florida line it intersects with both Highway 90 east and Interstate 10 east. Both would take them to Jacksonville, and I agree with you, if we don't get them leaving Folkston, we won't get them at all. Not with our limited manpower."

"You're right," Watkins said. "But once we have evidence they've crossed the state line with Doctor Majorski, we can call in the FBI."

"I can't see them doing that," Spalding said. "These guys may act like country bumpkins but they are smart as hell. That Jayco fellow—he's been in and out of prison enough times to have a doctorate degree in crime. He'll know not to cross the state line with his kidnapped victim. If the doc is still alive at that point, they'll let him go or stash him somewhere."

Kimble couldn't let it pass. "Doesn't say much for their intelligence, botching the robbery the way they did."

"Just call it bad luck or bad timing," Spalding said. "Think about it. How many people would you normally expect to be in a convenience store early on Christmas morning? The three of them entered the store thinking there would be the owner, who was old, and them. I'm sure they expected to be in and out within two minutes but the shootout blew their plan all to hell."

Watkins had remained quiet during the discussion until now. "I think you're giving credit to the wrong people. I believe Majorski is the only reason this hasn't resulted in total carnage," he said. "So far, the only death resulting from the robbery was the store owner. We have to assume some responsibility for the death of the EMT. If the doc hadn't been there to stabilize things, the situation would have deteriorated rapidly."

"You think he's helping them escape—you know, helping them stay one step ahead of us?" Kimble asked.

"Not exactly, but remember what Doctor Elder said. He felt the doc's mental state was such, he didn't want anyone to die, good guys or bad guys."

Spalding brought the debate to an end. "We're wasting time. We need to make a decision on our next course of action and get started, right or wrong."

"I agree," Watkins sighed. "We are exhausted and they won't be much better off. Why don't you post what personnel you have available on the southern escape routes while we take a nap? I'm sure the perps are smart enough not to travel in daylight with a bound hostage."

Spalding nodded. "Kimble, let's get going. Drive us to Folkston, find a place to park and you can sleep in the bedroom. I'm going to radio dispatch and disperse the teams. I'll crash on the sofa. Watkins, you can share the bed with Kimble. No funny stuff."

"Don't worry," Watkins said, "I'm so tired it wouldn't matter even if it was Ms. Kimble."

* * *

7:00 a.m.

How ironic, Tracy thought. *Here I am riding in a deputy's car and violating the law.* She looked down at Luke who was cradled in her arms as she rode in the passenger seat. Not too many law enforcement vehicles came equipped with car seats for infants.

"Deputy Brown, I really appreciate you driving me home."

"I told you to call me Patsy. You and Luke are like family to the Sheriff's Department now. It's the least we can do to take you home after what you've been through. Later today I'll take one of the officers to the impounded vehicle area and we'll pick up your car and drive it to your house. Do you have a garage?"

"No, I live in a small apartment. Just park it on the street and put the keys under the mat."

"You sure you don't need me to get anything else for you?"

"We'll be fine. I do appreciate the Pampers you got for Luke. That's why we were at the convenience store on Christmas morning. I had forgotten to get them when I was at the grocery store earlier in the week. God, it seems like it's been a week instead of one day."

"Forgive me for saying it but you look like you've been up for a week. You and Luke get to bed and sleep for a couple of days."

Tracy laughed at the suggestion. "You have any children, Patsy?"

"I haven't found a husband yet. I plan to have a bunch someday. Kids, I mean. Not husbands."

"When you have children I want you to remember what you just suggested I do. You'll find out you sleep when the baby sleeps and that's it."

Deputy Brown, following the instructions from the GPS, pulled up in front of Tracy's apartment. "Bless your heart, honey. You still thinking about the doctor, aren't you?"

Tracy's surprise kept her silent for a moment, and then she shook her head. "It's that obvious, huh."

"Yep. Everybody's talking about the two of you. You can blame that boy and girl who were in the store for it. They said you and the doc got real close in a short time."

"Closer than I've ever been to anyone. It's hard to believe I could feel this way about someone so quickly."

"Don't take long when it's the right person. If it feels right, then it probably is. Don't you worry. We got a good department and they're going to find your man for you. Now, you call me if you need anything and I promise I'll be here before you know it."

Tracy leaned over the center instrument panel and hugged Patsy Brown. It seemed God had suddenly put all kind of good people in her path.

* * *

8:00 a.m.

Spalding changed positions on the sofa, his light sleep interrupted by a persistent buzzing. No matter which way he turned the annoying sound continued and finally awakened him completely. He sat up, looked at his watch, realizing he had been asleep less than an hour. He stared at the phone on his desk some four feet away. It would make a good target for his automatic. The buzzing noise from the phone continued, evidence the caller wasn't giving up.

Spalding rubbed the sleep from his eyes and lurched toward the offending object. "Lieutenant Spalding here. This had better be important."

"Lieutenant Spalding. This is Mayor Theodore Swanson and my calls are always important."

"Yes, sir. Sorry for the unpleasant greeting. I've had little sleep in the past twenty-four hours."

"I understand you have been quite busy. Victor filled me in on your escapades and I must say I'm more than a little displeased over your assumption that you can ignore your superiors and create half-baked ideas on your own, which have placed the citizens of this community and state in jeopardy."

Fuck a duck, thought Spalding. *I really need this crap so early in the morning.* "Your Honor, our plan was well thought out and discussed amongst men who have been in hostage situations before. We did what we thought was best to avoid needless bloodshed."

"I don't see it that way," the mayor said. "If those men kill anyone outside our area, we will be blamed and possibly subject to civil lawsuits from aggrieved families."

Spalding switched the handset to his left hand. The muscles in his right hand were cramping from the tight grip maintained on the receiver during the conversation. "I wish it was the bastard's neck," he murmured.

"What's that, Spalding? I didn't hear what you said."

Spalding ignored the question.

The long pause was broken by Mayor Swanson' instructions. "I'm sending a helicopter for you. Give me a location where they can pick you up. I want you back here and I anticipate a full explanation as to why you proceeded with a plan not approved by me or Victor Lynch."

"With all due respect to the office you represent—go to hell. I'm not leaving my post. If you want my badge, then contact the police commissioner. If he agrees with your assessment, then you'll have it."

"Are you implying you will ignore my direct order?"

"Mr. Mayor. There's a doctor out there somewhere who's at the mercy of killers. He put his life on the line to save a bunch of people he didn't even know. He's worth more than ten of you. I don't give a rat's ass about your direct orders or what you do to my career after this is over. I'm going to give my all to save the doc. Now unless you plan to send storm troopers to arrest me and pull me off my job, don't bother me again."

A sigh of disbelief was audible over the speaker. "You are finished, Spalding."

"Probably so, but not before I do everything I can to save the doc."

* * *

9:00 a.m.

Victor Lynch replaced the phone in the cradle with a more gentle motion than he felt. The points he had scored with the mayor were rapidly dissipating, demonstrated by the ass chewing he just received. It could have been worse. The mayor's office was only three doors away and had he been summoned to the office everyone in the outer offices would have noticed. The mayor spared him the humiliation by expelling his furor over the phone in a moderately controlled tone.

It wasn't all peaches and cream. The mayor also informed him that Kathleen Quick was waiting at the main receptionist desk and the task of dealing with her was passed to him. An escaped prisoner in a murderous rage would be easier to handle. Kathleen Quick lived up to her name. She was quick in thought and action. Lynch admitted to himself that he was frightened by her presence even when he wasn't her primary target. God help him. He knew the office of the mayor was on her list today and he was going to be the sacrificial lamb. Blasted media! You couldn't survive in politics without them but it would be fantastic if you could.

Lynch pulled himself upright in his leather covered chair, finger-combed his hair and made sure his tie was snug. He pushed a button on the phone console to alert his secretary. "Doris, please escort Ms. Quick into my office." He picked up a pen and began scribbling on the top sheet of a stack of papers on his desk. He was no fool. His attempt to appear busy would not delay the verbal barrage expected from Quick.

He stood behind his desk with his hand outstretched when the lady entered. "Ms. Quick, the office of the mayor is honored by your visit."

Kathleen ignored the hand and without prompt sat in a chair in front of Lynch's desk. "Let's skip the pleasantries, Victor. I know you don't want me here; however, your boss doesn't have the guts to face me, so you're it."

Lynch sat in his chair, staring over the teepee formed by the fingertips of his hands pressed together. "Kathleen, I don't understand why you attack this office as you do. We've always been open with the media, especially with you."

Kathleen leaned back in the visitor's chair, crossing her long shapely legs at the knee. She watched Lynch's eyes lock in on her legs and then back up to her face, his cheeks crimson.

"I have my sources, Lynch. I know what took place earlier with the attempted take-down by the EMT. A total hare-brained idea culminating in the death of a brave, if misguided young man. That scheme has your name written all over it. You've always been aggressive with other people's lives."

Lynch placed his hands flat on the desk, pushing himself erect from his chair. "You have no right coming to my office and making such accusations. If I see or hear anything about this in the media, I will sue you for slander."

Kathleen stood as well. Her point had been made. "I don't have to come at you directly. I can end your career in such a way you won't see it coming. But let me tell you this—lay off Spalding. He's not political. He's a cop and a damn good one. He's doing his best in an impossible situation. You and this office are damn lucky a blood bath didn't erupt from your nonsensical antics. I suggest you get on your knees and thank God that men such as Spalding, my husband and Doctor

Majorski live in our fair city. They are the only reason I'm not going for your head right now."

Lynch plopped down in his chair, his face ashen from the verbal beating. He didn't look up when he heard the door close.

CHAPTER TWENTY-ONE

9:50 a.m.

The sun climbed in the sky, past the tops of the tall pines, casting shadows on a long-neglected field. A weather-beaten barn some three hundred yards from the road accepted and stored the early morning heat like a clay oven. Rays of sunlight pierced the ancient building through missing sections of the tin roof, casting bizarre shadows over the hay covered floor. An odor prevailed in the old barn, not unpleasant, more of a sour smell of wet, decayed hay. The empty interior of the structure revealed no evidence of recent use, other than a truck parked in the center.

When the exhausted trio had arrived earlier, dawn peeked from over the horizon providing enough light to see a ramshackle house nearby, as dilapidated as the barn. The nearest neighbor appeared to be miles away, making it unlikely they were seen.

Giving in to the oppressive heat and his pounding headache, Majorski sat up and gazed around at his surroundings. He saw feet protruding from the truck window; the cab was Jayco's selection for a few hours of rest. Charlie lay stretched out in the bed of the pickup, his feet crossed on the flattened tailgate.

Majorski licked his lips, his mouth as parched as a sun-dried apricot. He made an effort to stand before remembering he was tethered with duct tape to a floor-to-ceiling support pole. "Hey, Charlie, wake up. I'm thirsty."

Charlie sat up, rubbing his eyes and the top of his head. He continued the mannerisms for several minutes before fully awake. "Man, I was sleeping good. I even forgot we was in a barn."

Majorski chuckled. "Not exactly a five-star hotel. But I'm not sure I've slept better anywhere else. I'm thirsty and I need to take a whiz. How about cutting me loose?"

"Promise you won't run. Jayco will give me hell if I let you get away."

"I won't run. I don't want to be the one to get you in trouble."

Charlie replied with a snort, not fully understanding the play on words.

After answering nature's call, the two men sat on the tailgate sipping bottled water and downing granola bars.

Charlie was the first to break the silence. "My momma's cornbread and pinto beans sure would taste good right now. Never have been one for sweet stuff early in the morning. Before me and Daddy went to the fields, we always loaded up on the beans and cornbread, and sometimes Momma fried salt-cured ham and put big chunks in with the beans. Food like that will stay with you in the fields until supper time. Me and Daddy would have farting contests while we hoed the corn rows. Daddy always won."

"What about school? Didn't you go?" Majorski asked.

"Of course, I went. I ain't a dummy. I went to a lot of different schools 'cause we moved a lot. When we moved to southwest Georgia, my daddy got some land from a man for near nothing. I was fourteen and still in the fifth grade. The kids at all the other schools would tease me because I was so much bigger than them and I didn't know as much. Daddy and Momma decided I didn't have to go to school no more. Nobody knew any different. I just stayed at home and helped Daddy with the crops. We grew everything—corn, peas, butterbeans, tomatoes, okra, and squash. We had a bunch of yard chickens and layers and a couple of hogs. Never did want for food."

"You sound fond of the place. Are your parents still there?"

"No," Charlie answered with a slight choke. "My daddy made extra money by delivering stuff for the man what owned the land. One night he didn't come home. Me and Momma waited on the front porch all night. Didn't have a telephone. The next morning we saw a trail of dust headed toward our house. When Momma recognized the sheriff's car, she knew right away it would be bad news. She started praying right then for Jesus to take my daddy into His bosom. The sheriff told us a drunk hit my daddy's truck head on. Killed them both right off."

"How did you and your mother manage the farm?"

"Didn't. My momma sat down in her big chair with her Bible and she didn't get up. No amount of begging made any difference. She just sat there in that chair and one morning when I woke up, she was dead."

"God, Charlie. I'm sorry. You really loved your folks, didn't you?"

"Got that right. They was good people. They wouldn't be too proud of me, if they could see me now."

"What did you do when your mother died?"

Charlie stared at the big barn door as if reviewing his past on a video screen. "I walked to town and told the sheriff. I don't remember much after that. I know the people in town paid to bury Momma next to Daddy, and a preacher and his wife took me in their house. I heard him tell his wife, the judge over at the courthouse would decide where they would place me. That night I sneaked out of the house and I've been on my own ever since."

A question had been in Majorski's mind since he first observed Charlie in the convenience store. The gentle man didn't appear the type to associate with people like Jayco. "How did you end up in prison?"

Charlie paused for a moment, took another swig of water and continued. "Never did nothing bad. Just stealing. Sometimes it was the only way I could make it. Once I went to prison the first time, it seemed to get easier. I'd serve a couple of years, get out, bum around, couldn't find a job so I'd steal and end up in prison again.

"The last time, I got lucky. I met Jayco. He told me a lot of things. Said we was going to pull one last job and then head to Mexico. He said we could live like kings on just a little bit of money in Mexico. Don't look like we're gonna make it."

* * *

Robert McDaniel drove his vintage pickup truck the two and a half miles to Edward's Grocery Store every morning except Sundays. He and Sheila, his Labrador retriever, made the trip to have coffee with Zach Edwards, the owner of the store. Both men were widowers, and having coffee together while Zach opened the store for business seemed a natural thing to do. There weren't many customers so Zach never opened before ten.

Robert rarely drove more than thirty-five miles an hour. Being in his mid-eighties, his reflexes weren't as good as in his younger days. He drove with the windows down, and Sheila lay across his lap with her head out the window biting at the rushing air.

Something looked out of place this morning and caused Robert to slow his truck. He stared at the field next to the abandoned Miller place. He knew every foot of the terrain on his daily round trip so when things were different, it stood out.

"There's a bunch of tire tracks going across that field to the barn," he said to Sheila in normal conversational tones. It wasn't unusual for him to carry on a one-sided conversation with his pet. He reached over and rubbed the dog's long black hair. "Those tracks weren't there yesterday. We may have to check on it on the way back. Can't be late for coffee."

He rubbed the dog's head, quite sure the dog understood every word he said. He loved the dog as much as his grown children, who never called or visited. He loved the dog's name about as much. He never forgot the first time he'd heard the name from an Aussie when he was in the Pacific in World War II. The man kept talking about going home to see his "Sheila." Curiosity finally got to him and he had to ask the Aussie just what in the hell a "Sheila" was. He was flabbergasted to learn it meant a girl—a favorite girl.

Well, there was no doubt that "Sheila" was his favorite girl, actually his only girl since Geraldine died. Nine years now. That's a long time for an old codger like him to be alone. Wouldn't have made it this long without Sheila.

* * *

The heat built up much faster in the cab of the truck than in the rest of the barn. Sweat rolled off Jayco's face; some ran into his eyes. He awoke rubbing his eyes and cursing. "Damn, it's hot in here." He kicked at the door, which didn't budge until he pulled up on the handle. When he got out he stretched, trying to relieve the cramps in his back and leg muscles. He walked stiffly to the back of the truck, where Charlie and Majorski were sitting on the tailgate drinking water.

"Charlie, get me one of those waters." He stared at Majorski. "What the hell are you doing untied?"

Majorski couldn't pass up the opportunity to needle Jayco. "Oh, I'm hauling ass out of here. Can't you see me running?"

Jayco made a face, accepted the water from Charlie and didn't comment further. He walked to the rear of the barn, opened a small door and peeked out. "I need to take a dump." He returned to the truck, got his rifle and left the barn.

Charlie grinned. "He's in a 'shitty' mood."

Both men started laughing, enjoying the joke at Jayco's expense like longtime friends. They were still cracking jokes when the front door to the barn opened.

Charlie jumped from the tailgate when he saw the elderly man enter the barn. He looked back at Majorski, who remained seated.

"What are you fellows doing here in Miller's barn?" Robert McDaniel asked.

Charlie, stunned by the sudden intrusion, remained speechless.

Majorski, aware he had to do something to protect the old man, held up his bottle of water in a friendly sign of greeting. "Just taking a break from the heat. We've been traveling around these parts looking for old barns. A lot of them have virgin timber used for support beams. We scout 'em out, make notes, then contact the owners to see if they are willing to sell. We tear down the building and salvage the valuable timber. There are quite a number of people who are willing to pay top dollar so they can build those fancy houses with exposed beams. You'd be surprised how much money old beams will bring."

McDaniel stared suspiciously at him. "I'd be more surprised if that bullshit story of yours turned out to be true. If it is, you have no problem. I think I'll let the sheriff decide." He turned for the door, finding it blocked by a man pointing a rifle at him. "I think I know now your story is totally bullshit."

Majorski eased off the tailgate and moved toward the old man, while keeping his eyes on Jayco. "Things are okay here, Jayco. No need for the gun. I was just explaining to Mr.—uh …"

"McDaniel, Robert McDaniel."

"I was just explaining to Mr. McDaniel how we check out old abandoned barns for good timber."

"Don't waste your time, sonny," McDaniel said. "I've been around a long time. Survived Saipan and Okinawa. Knocked around the states for a few years before I settled down. I know a mean son of a bitch when I see one and I'm looking directly at him now. He ain't a timber buyer."

Jayco twisted his lips into a narrow smile. "If you're so smart, you should have kept your ass in your truck and minded your own business. Now it's too late."

"Don't try to scare me, sonny. I ain't been scared a single day since I left Saipan. Figured if I could survive the Japs without shitting my pants, nothing else would do it."

Majorski took advantage of the brief pause as the old man and Jayco stared at each other. "Why don't we pack up and get out of Mr. McDaniel's way. There are other barns we can look at."

McDaniel ignored the remark and stepped around Jayco, pushing the rifle out of the way. "You boys get out of here before I get back with the sheriff and you won't have any problems."

Majorski heaved a big sigh as he watched McDaniel walk out the door. The relief of his anxiety was short-lived.

Jayco followed the old man out the door, reversed the rifle and struck him in the back of the head with the rifle butt. He switched the gun to his left hand and reached down to check the man's pulse. "He's alive. I didn't hit him hard."

With his back to McDaniel's truck, Jayco was unaware of the charging dog until it hit him at a full gallop, knocking him to the ground.

The retriever was thrown off balance as well but quickly scurried to her feet, renewing the attack on her master's assailant again, snarling with her teeth bared and going for Jayco's neck.

Jayco kicked out at the dog, at the same time doing a backward crawl toward the barn. "Get the dog off me!"

Majorski remained still as Charlie flashed by. He watched Charlie grab the dog, wrapping his large arms around the animal's body.

The dog ignored the intruder, her attention locked on Jayco. Her teeth grazed Jayco's neck. Snarling, she lunged again, her jaws clamping down on the collar of his shirt. She shook Jayco's head from side to side, dragging him away from McDaniel.

Charlie set his legs and heaved, pulling the animal away. A large portion of Jayco's shirt remained in the retriever's mouth. Both Charlie and the dog went over backward from the sudden release of the big retriever's purchase.

Jayco scrambled away, rose up on his knees and lifted the rifle in firing position.

"No," screamed Majorski, failing to reach Jayco in time to prevent him from firing. The bullet missed Charlie and struck the dog in the side, knocking her to the ground.

Jayco was now on his feet, panting hard, a scowl on his face. "Majorski, drag the old man inside the barn while I finish off this damn dog."

"Don't shoot again," Charlie pleaded. "Let me get her in the barn and I'll tie her to a post. I don't think the dog can hurt you anymore."

"Shut up, Charlie. Help the doc get the old man in the barn. I'm going to finish off this dog."

Majorski grabbed the rifle. "Think about it, Jayco. One gunshot might not attract attention; two shots might cause someone to be curious enough to call the police. Let Charlie tie the dog up."

The amount of time passed since the attack more than Majorski's words allowed Jayco to settle down. "Okay, Charlie. Get the dog in the barn and make damn sure it's tied up real good. If it moves toward me again—I'll kill it."

•

Majorski knelt beside the wounded animal, speaking in a low voice to prevent movement and further damage. He had a lot of respect for veterinarians who were forced to practice their art without the benefit of taking a history from their patient. The retriever showed no sign of respiratory distress. Though a small miracle, the bullet had missed the lung. The dog whimpered in protest to pressure on the abdomen. The bullet probably pierced the gut. Majorski applied a thick dressing of gauze and tape and with Charlie's help positioned the dog beside McDaniel. The two of them could comfort each other.

Charlie walked back to the road and drove McDaniel's truck down to and behind the barn while Jayco stood guard.

McDaniel finally spoke, the first time since awakening from the blow to his head. He looked at Jayco. "Mister, I don't know what you're up to, but it ain't worth letting my Sheila die. She's all I got in the world. Let me go so I can take her to the vet. I'll tell him I accidentally shot her. I won't say a word about you people. I'm begging you. Please let me get her some help."

Jayco snarled back. "You can blame my soft-hearted partner and the doc for your dog's suffering. I would have put her out of her misery. They stopped me. Sorry, I ain't letting you go anywhere. I don't believe you won't tell the cops."

"I believe him," Charlie said, just before he hit Jayco in the back of the head with a piece of lumber from an old stall. He had entered the back of the barn just as Jayco raised his rifle. "I'm sure Jayco will get me back for this, but I ain't letting him kill the old man and his dog."

He dropped the wood and picked Jayco up from the ground with little effort. "Help me get him in the cab of the truck. We need to get out of here."

After everything was loaded and the doors to the barn were open, Charlie approached McDaniel. "I'm sorry 'bout your dog. I hope she makes it." He dropped a knife beside the old man. "Give us thirty minutes, then cut yourself free. I trust you won't say anything. Even if you do, it probably won't matter." Charlie knelt beside the dog and stroked the silky coat of black hair. "Sheila, I like your name."

CHAPTER TWENTY-TWO

8:00 p.m.

The first thing Tupac noticed on awakening was an agonizing itch of his nose. He moved his right hand toward his face and was surprised when the action was halted after a couple of inches. Fighting against the narcotic fog, he turned his head and saw a plastic restraint securing his arm to the bed rail. Looking to his left he found his left arm similarly restrained and taped to a long arm board. Above him, attached to a tall metal pole, a plastic bag of blood dripped via an intravenous tube to a needle buried in his arm.

He struggled to keep his eyes open and between heavy blinks he made out a figure standing at the foot of the bed.

The figure spoke. "About time you woke up. That well-meaning EMT almost did you in with the morphine. I'm Detective Mark Daniels. My partner, Rodney Smith, is downstairs scrounging up some food and coffee. The doctor called us an hour ago and told us you were showing signs of waking up. Damn obvious you don't do drugs. You were out big time from a simple morphine drip."

Tupac heard about every third word of the man's rapid discourse. He understood little of what he did hear. He ignored the man and closed his eyes. Something hard struck the bottom of his right foot. The jar from the blow radiated up to his chest; the searing pain jerked him awake.

"Wake up, Tupac—if that's your real name? The hostages told us your buddies called you that when you were in the store. It took forever to get that much out of them. For some reason they all wanted to protect you. We couldn't find any ID on you; so what is your name?"

Tupac shook his head, attempting to clear his thoughts. "That's my name. Tupac Garcia. You should have my prints by now. It won't take long to get my history. I've spent time in Reidsville." He paused for a few seconds. "Is the doc okay?"

Detective Daniels started to speak, stopping short, puzzled by the question. He noticed Smith had entered the room in time to hear the question as well. They looked at each other. Strange the man would inquire about the doc rather than his friends.

"Can't answer you there," Daniels responded. "We haven't been in touch with the search team for the past few hours. We've been waiting for you to wake up. We need you to tell us the names of the men with you and where they are going."

Tupac closed his eyes, more to concentrate than from drowsiness. "Jayco Dubois and Charlie Williams. We were all in Reidsville together. Believe me, man, if I had any idea where they plan to go, I'd tell you. Jayco and I are tight. I don't want him to get hurt. I'd rather be back in prison with him, than learn he's been killed. He may not feel the same. Prison 'bout broke him the last time. I'm scared he might do anything to keep from going back. I don't want the doc to get hurt."

Daniels took a sip of his coffee. "Why would you care if something happened to the doc?"

Tupac choked up, straining to answer. "The man saved my life. He saved all our lives. He stayed so cool when everything was going to hell. You should've seen him when he was operating on the lady. Blood was squirting everywhere, yet he was as cool as Marshall Dillon in a shootout on Main Street. Sure hope the lady makes it."

The corner of Daniels' lip curled. "What's this? You getting religious? Why do you give a damn if she lives?"

Tupac was unable to look at Daniels when he answered. "I know you won't believe it. I didn't want anybody to get hurt. Jayco promised me there'd be no shooting. Things just got screwed up when the old man pulled out his gun and shot me."

Daniels wrote a few words in a pocket-size notebook before he turned his attention to the sandwich brought by Detective Smith. He sat on a straight-back chair near the bed and turned over the questioning to his partner.

"My name is Detective Rodney Smith. I've got a few questions also. I guess the main one is why did you stay? Your buddies got all those supplies, plus took the doc. You probably would have survived the run."

Tupac shook his head. "Maybe. I would've slowed them down though. I wish now I had gone so I could keep Jayco calm. Charlie won't be able to do it."

Daniels wiped mustard from his mouth with the back of his hand and then raised a finger to interrupt the interview. "That the only reason?"

"No. The things Doc did for me got me thinking. I ain't ever laid it out on the line like that for anybody. Maybe someday I'll get the chance to help somebody. Maybe I can even keep some kid from taking the path I took. Like the doc told me, it really comes down to choices. All the ones I've made in life were bad ones."

Smith started to speak. "Uh ... what—"

"I ain't finished," Tupac said. "The doc had choices. Nobody in the store knew he was a doctor. He could've stayed on the floor and not got involved. But if he'd done that, me and the lady would have died for sure."

Smith made eye contact with his partner before he spoke. "The doctor may be wishing he made a different choice last night."

"He's in big trouble now and could get killed," Tupac said. "I got a feeling if you gave him a do-over, he'd do the same thing again. Some people are just that way, I guess. They do what's right, no matter what."

Smith nodded, peering across at the bed at Daniels, who had just poured himself a glass of cold water from the pitcher on the bedside stand.

"Yeah, let's get back to Jayco and uh ... Charlie," Daniels said. "You're saying, from your knowledge of Jayco, you don't have any idea where he's headed. Any family or friends around these parts he could turn to for help?"

Tupac closed his eyes, trying to recall anything Jayco might have told him in prison. He remembered him talking about growing up in Louisiana and working in the south during the short times he wasn't in prison. "Not that I can remember. He knows this area pretty good. Spent some years here before we met up. I never heard him speak of any kin 'round here. Back at the store, he didn't say much about his plans except get transportation and head south."

"Where to, I mean, exactly where south? Florida?"

"Like I said, he wasn't specific. He and Charlie talked about going to Mexico. I'm not sure he even knew where he thought he'd get to in the end. But that's Jayco. He just decides to do something and does it. Most of the time, he just wings it. I guess you can figure that out by the way we screwed up the robbery."

"Uh ... Mr. Garcia. A little late, but we need to read the Miranda rights to you."

"Couldn't care less. I ain't out to beat the rap. I take what's given to me. I deserve it. Something happens to the doc, I don't care what they do to me."

Detective Daniels' voice was cold when he responded. "If they kill the doc, I know where your friends' final destination will be—strapped to a gurney with fluids dripping in, just like yours, except the stuff they'll get won't make them feel better."

* * *

9:00 p.m.

The large room in the hospital reserved for families of surgical patients was nearly empty. Not unusual for the holiday season. Surgeons wanted to be with their families so elective surgery was not scheduled. However, there was nothing they could do to prevent emergencies from interrupting their plans.

Tracy cradled Luke to her exposed breast while she and Samantha watched him nurse. Jimmy had promptly made himself scarce on the pretense of looking for snacks.

Samantha picked up a knitted bootie that fell off Luke's foot. She smiled warmly at the infant, who was kicking his legs as if to provide energy for nursing. "Tracy ... thanks for coming. I know you must be as exhausted as I am; still, it means so much for you and Luke to be here. Jimmy has been great, never leaves my side. I'm sure he appreciates the opportunity to get away from my constant whining."

Tracy shifted her position to ease the strain on her back. Luke got heavier by the day and even though she enjoyed the bonding experience that came with nursing, the physical discomfort took its toll. It was ironic how a tragic event had brought her closer to more people in a couple of days than all the time since Luke was born.

"Don't be so hard on yourself. You have reason enough to be down. Almost losing your mom on Christmas Day and watching her struggle to stay alive would get to anyone. How long has she been in surgery?"

"About two hours. The doctors explained they couldn't start surgery until her vital signs were stable and the lost blood was replaced. That took most of the day. Then she was in the MRI unit for what seemed like forever. The surgeons wanted to know exactly what they'd face once they opened her up."

"She's lucky she made it this far," Tracy said. "Doctor Majorski did a great job keeping her alive—actually, he kept all of us alive."

Samantha blurted out, "You're in love with him, aren't you?"

A pink flush covered Tracy's face, making her smile more radiant when she answered. "Love is a strong word, but yes, I think I do love him. It seems so improbable to develop a bond so quickly. Maybe I'm not being realistic, but I sensed he had feelings for me as well."

Samantha grinned, delighted with her intuition. "I read something at school this year about things being stronger when they're forged in fire."

Tracy nodded and remained silent, her thoughts turning again to Majorski and the danger that still threatened his life.

CHAPTER TWENTY-THREE

10:00 p.m.

Jayco and Charlie hunkered down behind a large green dumpster in the rear of Big Croc's Sporting Goods store in Folkston. Jayco had taken inventory of their supplies while at the barn and was satisfied with the amount of food and water. The medical supplies were a plus for traveling in the swamps; however, they needed mosquito netting, sleeping bags and waterproof boots. Things they couldn't put on the list given to the authorities without tipping their hand.

"Jayco, you sure you're not mad at me for hitting you?"

"Damn, Charlie. Of course I'm mad. I don't like being cold-cocked by my own friend, but I understand why you did it so leave it be. We got other things to worry about."

Charlie seemed relieved, but then again he'd looked relieved the last time he asked Jayco the same question. "I've been thinking. We need one of those pump type water filters. Our water supply might run out and I ain't drinking that stuff in the swamp."

"Now that's what I'm talking about. Good thinking. We might better get a snake bite kit as well."

Charlie frowned. "I don't think we should. The doc said the kits cause more problems than most snakes."

Jayco curled his upper lip—a habit he picked up in prison when he wanted to show disgust, without saying something that would get his ass whipped. He ignored Charlie's comment. "I sure wish I could find an outside box for the burglar alarm. I know they've got one but damn if I can find it."

"You want to go look for another store?"

"No. We need to get moving on this thing. I'll bust in the little window high up on the back wall. It's probably over a bathroom. When I get inside, I'll unlock the door from the inside."

"You want me to follow you through the window into the store?"

"Charlie, listen to me. I told you I'd let you in when I unlock the door from the inside. When I break the window and crawl in, I want you to listen for an alarm and watch for cops. There might be a silent alarm. If you don't see a cop car within two minutes, then back the Jeep up to the back door and come inside to help me move the stuff we need to the door. Once we get everything together we'll load it all at one time."

"We should have stolen something bigger than a Jeep."

"Come on, Charlie. It's not like we can go shopping at a used car lot. We took what was easy picking."

Charlie remained rooted to the ground, his mind spinning with unanswered questions. "Are you getting equipment for the doc?"

"Don't worry about it. I got no immediate plans for the doc. He still might come in handy. Don't forget, he's still a bargaining chip. If he becomes more of a liability than an asset, we'll have to make some tough decisions. Now do what I told you to do."

Walking back to the Jeep, Charlie wrestled with Jayco's words. He knew his partner was sometimes crazy and could become violent if he was crossed. He wouldn't have killed the old man if the old codger hadn't shot Tupac. Now Jayco was talking about getting rid of the doc. There was bad blood between those two.

"Not right," he murmured to himself. The doc had saved Tupac and so far had been cooperative in their escape. It wouldn't be right to kill him just because they didn't need him anymore. He had gone against Jayco about the old man and the dog and he might have to do it again. That worried him; Jayco would be more alert now.

The rustic sporting goods store reminded Jayco of a hardware store in the town where he grew up. Visibility in the old store was always dim; the only light source a single one-hundred-watt bulb at the end of a long electric cord suspended from the center of the ceiling. The interior where he presently stood wasn't much better, with faint illumination from a street lamp outside the front door. He waited impatiently for his eyes to adjust to the minimum light before starting his scavenger hunt. It was too dark to read labels so he would rely on familiarity of shapes of the objects he needed.

"This will be fun," he said. "I feel like a kid in a toy store with an unlimited credit card." He felt foolish, realizing he was talking to himself. He opened the back store, motioning Charlie to enter. "Any sign of the cops?"

"Haven't heard or seen anything. I hope it's not wired with one of those silent alarms."

Jayco shrugged. "Doubt there's an alarm. No devices on the window or the door. Leave the Jeep where it is until we get what we want and then we'll load it."

Jayco pulled everything off the shelves that struck his fancy, stacking the items at the back door. As the mountain of supplies grew, he realized it would be impossible to get the stuff in the Jeep, much less carry it all on a boat. He worked through the supplies again, sorting the items into two piles—those absolutely needed and those which would make life more tolerable in the swamp.

When the stacks appeared manageable, he took inventory. Three sleeping bags with mosquito hoods, insect repellant, freeze-dried foods, water filter with hand pump, aluminum pot, plastic spoons and forks, spade with folding handle, reusable plastic plates, canteens, two Coleman lanterns with extra fuel, a small Coleman stove, waterproof matches in carrying case, roll of plastic drop cloth, and as a luxury item, a twelve-pack of toilet paper wrapped in plastic.

He looked at the pile again; though the list wasn't long, all the items were bulky. They would need a boat at least seventeen feet in length. God! The list of things they needed kept growing. Paddles, fuel cans ... they would have to get those when they stole the boat. Something had been in the back of his mind since he entered the store and he was unable to remember it. Then it hit him. A compass, they must have a compass. Luckily he found what he needed when he picked up a knife with a compass built into the end of the handle. It looked similar to the knife Rambo used in the movies.

Satisfied with the supplies, he helped Charlie load them into the Jeep. It took them thirty minutes and when they finished, Majorski was almost completely covered in the back seat.

"Sorry about the cramped space, Doc," Jayco said. "It won't be as bad on the boat. I promise to cut you loose before we board."

"Well, I thank you. I would be worried if you kept me bound up like a hog in the boat."

Majorski acted giddy, possibly going insane. He continued to ramble. "What a grand time we're having. How did I miss all this fun earlier in my life? I know. I was studying and working my ass off so I could help mankind. And I was missing all this?"

Jayco stared at him. "Take it easy, Doc. I know you feel confined. Try a five-by-eight cell for a few years and you'll understand the meaning of imprisonment."

Charlie cranked the Jeep, peering cautiously up and down the streets to make sure they were empty before he pulled out of the space behind the store. "I'm sure glad the owner of the store was too cheap to buy an alarm."

"Score one for our side," Jayco said.

The drive through Folkston was uneventful. It was almost midnight and the only vehicles seen were occupied by kids joy-riding on the main street. They didn't encounter an official car of any description.

Majorski had mixed feelings. On one hand he was grateful a curious officer hadn't stopped them, as it might have led to a bloody battle; on the other hand, being stopped by the police on a routine check might be his only chance for survival. He wouldn't want that—it would most likely cost the life of the officer. Not a religious person, Majorski was getting closer to God by the minute. His situation reminded him of something his grandfather once told him about World War II: "There were no atheists in foxholes."

CHAPTER TWENTY-FOUR

11:30 p.m.

Watkins felt drained of every ounce of energy. Guzzling multiple cups of black coffee no longer worked. He considered pouring the dry grounds inside his lower lip in imitation of the locals who used smokeless tobacco in such a manner. *Might give me a boost*, he thought, *if the sudden jolt didn't stop my heart*. He didn't get the opportunity to try it.

"Lieutenant Watkins," hailed Corporal Ginn. "I'm here to relieve you for a couple of hours. Lieutenant Spalding gave orders for you to go back to the bus and get some sleep."

"Yeah, I hear you. Where is Superman right now? He still feeling invincible or is he using something I haven't found to replace sleep?"

Ginn smiled at the retort, aware of the friendly competition between the two men. "Not that I'm aware. I mean he's not taking anything I know of, but I do know he just woke up from a nap. He was out on his feet a few hours ago and Kimble practically forced him to go back to the bus. Guess he thinks it's your turn."

"I welcome the opportunity. This roadblock business is boring as hell and personally I think it's a waste of time. They probably went through Folkston even before we got the men here to set up."

"More than likely you're right, but it's not my call. I just do what I'm told."

"What's your gut feeling, Ginn?

"I agree with you. Good chance they are in Florida, either heading for south Miami where they can get lost in the crowd of people or maybe they went west along the Panhandle. Lots of places to disappear in Alabama and Louisiana, 'specially down in the bayous. If they make it that far they won't need the doc anymore. I know how you feel about negative thinking, but it's a logical assumption."

"Let's pray you're wrong. Send someone for me in a couple of hours and make sure they have a supersized cup of coffee with them."

Watkins climbed into the back seat of the trooper's car and curled up in a fetal position. Physically, he was tired; mentally and emotionally he was totally spent. The decision to call in the Georgia State Patrol and the local sheriff's office had deflated him like jabbing a knife into a balloon. He and Spalding knew the decision would most likely result in the doc's death; if Jayco hadn't already killed him. If the doc was alive, a confrontation with the psychopath leader at a roadblock would be all it would take to get him killed. In spite of the agonizing thoughts he quickly drifted off to sleep.

CHAPTER TWENTY-FIVE

December 27, 2007

12:30 a.m.

Two miles south of Folkston on Highway 23, Charlie saw a long red glowing line about a half mile ahead. The line appeared motionless. He was almost upon the apparition before he realized the colors were the tail lights of stopped cars ahead in the southbound lane. The headlights of cars in the northbound lanes on the other side of the medium were moving unimpeded toward Folkston.

He punched Jayco to get his attention. "Roadblock ahead."

"Crap," Jayco exclaimed. "Get off this road. Find a side road or a driveway, but don't stop or turn around until we are out of sight of the highway. We'll stay out of sight until it's safe to drive back to Folkston without attracting attention. We'll find another way out of town."

Charlie fell in behind the line of cars and eased forward with them until he spotted an isolated mailbox. Adjacent to the rural postal box was a winding driveway that led into a heavily wooded area. He didn't see any other houses nearby so he pulled onto the hard packed dirt road, following it deep into the woods. Out of sight of the highway, he flipped off the headlights and continued on the road steering by starlight. Another hundred feet brought them to the house located at the end of the driveway. Charlie saw a single light in a window off the carport—probably a night light in the kitchen. Unless someone decided to leave or there was a late arrival to the home, the three of them would be safe.

After maneuvering the vehicle in a three-point turn, Charlie headed the Jeep back toward the highway. He killed the engine and leaned back against the seat. "Might as well take a nap while we wait."

The longer Jayco waited, the more apprehensive he became. He erupted from the Jeep and paced up and down the dirt road. "Somebody in the house might have seen us. They may have already called the cops. We are like sitting ducks out here."

"Relax," Charlie said. "The house is dark and quiet. It's after midnight. Everybody should be asleep."

"I can't relax. I've got to make sure."

"What are you going to do? Why don't we just leave?" Charlie pleaded.

Jayco reached in the passenger window and removed the automatic handgun from the glove compartment. "I've got to check out the house. Stay here and make sure the doc doesn't leave."

Charlie reached out and grabbed Jayco by the arm. "Don't do it. If you trigger an alarm the cops will be here before we can get out of this driveway. Don't you remember? They are just down the road. Why, Jayco? Why do you have to do these crazy things?"

"I'll be damn. Look who's calling someone crazy?"

"No—no—no, Jayco. I might be slow—I know that –but I'm not crazy. I don't do things like you do. Things that don't make sense."

"Shut up, Charlie. Get back in the Jeep and watch the doc like I told you."

Charlie's shoulders slumped and he got in the Jeep behind the wheel. He looked over his shoulder expecting the find the doc asleep. Instead he looked into the doc's wide awake eyes.

"Untie me, Charlie. We've got to stop him. If there are people awake in the house or if he wakes them up—he'll probably hurt them. Maybe even kill them. Whatever he does, won't be good for them or us."

"I can't do it, Doc. I've gone against him too many times already. I'm his friend but I'm scared of him. When he gets all crazy like this, nothing can stop him."

"Untie me, damn you. I'm afraid of him as well, but I'm more afraid of sitting here and letting him kill a house full of people, maybe even some children."

Charlie bit the inside of his cheek. He lowered his head in his hands. "I'll get him. He might shoot me, but you're right. We can't let him kill any children."

Majorski had squirmed and jerked at his bindings until his arms were bleeding. No matter how hard he tried he couldn't free himself. He attempted to get into the front seat so he could press his body against the horn. That failed as well. He couldn't get through all the supplies piled around and on top of him.

Minutes dragged by, seeming like hours. He neither saw nor heard anything. What had happened to Charlie? Had Jayco bushwhacked him when he entered the house? His head dropped forward. Never had he felt so useless. "God, please help those people inside the house. I'm sorry I'm so weak. I've failed you."

"Who you talking to?" Jayco asked.

Majorski jerked his head up. His eyes locked on the hard stare from Jayco. "No one you're familiar with," he replied. He searched the area behind Jayco. No sign of Charlie.

"What did you do with Charlie?"

His apprehension was relieved when he heard a husky voice coming from the opposite side of the Jeep.

"I'm here, Doc. There weren't any people in the house. We got some stuff from the kitchen to make sandwiches. Jayco found some maps in the truck parked in the carport. Got some cold Mountain Dew. A nice change from all that bottled water."

Majorski said a silent prayer of thanks that God had heard his plea. "Did it look like someone might come home tonight?"

Charlie appeared to ponder the question while sipping on the cold soda. He smacked his lips in satisfaction. "Doesn't look like anyone has been there in days but we better leave now. Don't want them to drive up while we are parked here."

An hour later, stuffed with sandwiches and sodas, Jayco felt better. Not so much from the food as from the information gleaned from the county map he had found. Data printed on the front cover of the map identified the owner of the house as a part-time volunteer fireman. The detailed map revealed every dirt road and goat path in the county.

"Okay, Charlie. Listen up. We'll start west through this subdivision here." He indicated the location on the map with his finger. "On the other side is a small unmarked county road. It wasn't on the other map I saw. We'll take the road south. It will eventually intersect with Highway 23 and will be far enough south to be beyond the roadblock. Once we reach the intersection, we switch back to our original plan. Do you remember the landmarks to find the turnoff to Suwannee Canal area?"

"Got 'em locked in my brain," Charlie answered.

Folding the map, Jayco stuffed it in the glove compartment. He turned to face the back seat. "Okay back there, doc?"

"Never been happier," answered Majorski in the most sarcastic tone he could muster.

Jayco laughed and gave Charlie a shot to the arm. "Doc's developing an attitude. Let's hit the road and find us a boat."

Charlie drove out of the vacant parking lot where they had parked. His stomach was in knots from the mention of a boat. He'd drive to Mexico if Jayco asked him, but he didn't think he could get in a boat going into a swamp.

* * *

2:00 a.m.

Charlie found the turnoff from Highway 23/121 into the east entrance of the Okefenokee National Refuge. The entrance was well marked, including a warning not to enter the park at night. A warning they chose to ignore. The distance from the turnoff to the visitors' gate was longer than Jayco had remembered. It had been years since his last trip to this area. But their luck held and no one else was on the road. The few houses on the desolate stretch of gravel were occupied by the wilderness rangers and as expected were dark.

Easily bypassing the gate, they drove using only the parking lights past the empty visitor center to the Okefenokee Adventures building. Jayco recalled from previous experience the boats used for swamp tours were kept in a small marina behind the building. The solar-powered lamps on tall aluminum poles supplied enough light for the men to make their way to the wooden porch around the building. A single light burned in the registration center.

Charlie swung the Jeep around in the vacant parking lot and, guided by hand signals from Jayco, backed the Jeep to the long dock where fifteen boats were anchored.

Jayco returned to the vehicle, opened the right back door and began removing supplies. When he finally uncovered his hostage, he pulled out the Rambo knife from the sheath in his boot and cut through the tape binding Ed's hands and feet. "Don't cause trouble, Doc. It would be a good idea if you helped us load the boats; you know, to keep you occupied."

* * *

2:00 a.m.

Stan Rutledge, muttering obscenities under his breath, swung his long legs out of bed for his second nocturnal trip to the bathroom. "Goddamn prostate. Need to get the new medicine so I can get some sleep at night."

He pulled the door closed between the bedroom and the bathroom as a courtesy to his wife though he suspected she was probably awake. All those years of listening out for the children when they were babies had conditioned Mildred to be a light sleeper. Now the children were grown and she had to put up with him and his enlarged prostate.

He sat on the commode, not trusting his aim in the middle of the night. Another thing, he thought, the urge to go was so bad it would wake him up but then it took forever to get started. He made himself relax, accomplished the task, pulled up his pajama bottoms, and as he turned to flush the commode he saw a flash of light outside the bathroom window. No thunderstorms were in the forecast; shouldn't be lightning. He pulled aside the white linen curtain in time to see a vehicle travel down the park road toward the information center.

"Now who the hell is out there tonight? Must have driven around the gate." He walked back to the bedroom and Mildred rolled over in bed to face him

"Come back to bed, Stan. What's taking you so long?"

"Saw a car or truck on the road while I was in the bathroom. There shouldn't be anyone on the park road this time of night. I think I'll slip on my clothes and take a look."

"That's nonsense. Get back in bed. It's probably some teenagers looking for a place to neck, like we used to do. You aren't so old you don't remember those days, are you?"

"No, I'm not that old. Matter of fact since you're awake we might pretend we are teenagers right now."

"You ain't that young, either. Just come back to bed and go to sleep. If the trespassers bother you so much you can't sleep, then call Al Carter and let him check it out. That's why you have younger assistants."

Stan slipped into his trousers, threw his US Park Ranger jacket over his pajama top and started for the door. "No. I might wake up his young kids. I'll just drive down to the boat ramp and check it out myself. You go back to sleep. I won't be long."

* * *

2:30 a.m.

Jayco walked the length of the long dock inspecting the watercraft. He selected a Carolina Skiff, a flat-bottomed fiberglass boat, eighteen feet in length and six feet in width. Four open flat seats, one each in the bow and stern and two in the center, gave ample space for sitting and for storage of their gear. They also served as supports for the lightweight vessel. A ten-horsepower Evinrude outboard motor was attached to the stern and appeared in good condition. The motors were probably serviced often since they appeared to be rentals.

While Charlie and Majorski transferred the supplies to a section of the dock adjacent to the boat, Jayco examined the rest of the boat. Ample space for the three of them and their supplies and the empty boat rode high in the water and appeared stable. He would feel more secure if he could perform a test run of the motor. Afraid the noise would attract unwanted attention, he decided to take the chance it would crank when they needed it. The plastic fuel container next to the motor was full. Satisfied, he crawled out and searched the other watercraft, returning with two additional five-gallon containers of fuel. His search for motors of higher horsepower was unsuccessful.

"Why don't we take an extra motor?" Charlie questioned.

"Too heavy and takes up too much room. We need the space for the supplies."

Charlie wrung his hands while pacing on the dock. "Why can't we use the big boat down at the end of the dock—the one with the top on it?"

Jayco scoffed at the suggestion. "That monstrosity is for tours in the open water. It won't work for us. We need to get into low areas and hide. The canopy would hang up on vines and would be too easy to spot from overhead. Don't worry, Charlie. I've got a big green tarp. We'll use it and the mosquito netting to cover us. We'll be dry and bug-free."

Charlie secured the extra gas cans with short bungee cords in both the bow and stern to distribute the weight. "How long we got to stay in the swamp?"

Jayco spun toward him. "For Christ sake, Charlie. Stop worrying about the fucking swamp. You're driving me nuts. We'll stay hunkered down for a few days, to give the cops time to get bored with the search. Remember, they'll be looking for us on the highways, not out here. When the time is right, we'll follow the channel to the northwest until it intersects the Suwannee River.

"It won't take us long to reach Fargo just north of the Georgia/Florida line. When we get well south of Fargo, we'll let the doc go. By the time he walks from the river back to Highway 441, we'll be long gone."

Unsatisfied, but silenced, Charlie busied himself loading the remaining supplies. As he shuffled along the dock searching for overlooked items, his vision locked onto a steel rod about six feet in length and thick as his thumb. A horseshoe-shaped grip had been welded on one end and the opposite end tapered to a sharp point.

"Looks like a gator gig," he laughed, "you know, like a frog gig but bigger." He glanced around, disappointed no one heard his attempt at humor. Returning to the boat, he twirled the rod in his hands; it might come in handy for something.

Charlie held up the rod when he stepped into the boat with Ed. "What you think of my gator gig?"

Before Majorski could answer a booming voice shattered the still night. "Are you two fellows planning on gator hunting tonight?"

Charlie spun around in his seat, realizing the voice didn't belong to Jayco. A tall man in olive green trousers and a dark jacket stood on the dock starring down at the men in the boat. "Where the hell did he come from?" Charlie whispered to himself.

Majorski saw a figure move out of the shadows behind the snack shop. Before he could shout a warning the tall man slumped forward, crumpled onto the deck and remained still.

Majorski leaped out of the boat, almost throwing Charlie into the black water. He ran the few feet to the man's side, felt the spongy mass that previously was the back of the man's skull and then checked for a pulse which he felt certain would not be present. It wasn't.

He looked up at Jayco who was still holding the heavy anchor in his hand.

Jayco dropped the anchor, pulled his handgun from behind his belt extending it toward Majorski. "Don't go nuts on me, Doc. I ain't through with you, yet. But if you move toward me, I'll put a bullet between your eyes."

"Go ahead," Majorski challenged. "You better kill me now. I warned you earlier, and if you give me half a chance I'm going to carry out my threat."

"I doubt it, Doc. You ain't got it in you to hurt anyone, much less kill them."

After finally getting out of the boat, Charlie rushed between the two men. "We got to get out of here. What are we going to do with the body?"

Jayco regained his composure, immediately taking charge again. "Put him in the boat. Find more anchors and put 'em in the boat. When we get out in deeper water we'll weight him down and sink him in the lily pads.

"Doc, you get back in the boat and stay in one position. If you move, I'll shoot, no matter how much noise it makes."

Majorski sensed this wasn't the moment to make a move. He climbed into the center of the boat and remained immobile as instructed. His mind, however, was racing. The man was dressed similar to a ranger and would be missed. When someone came looking for him, they would find his truck along with a Jeep that didn't belong in the parking lot. Put together with a missing boat, even an amateur would figure out what had happened. Majorski had mixed emotions. A search for the ranger could be his only chance to be rescued. But more deaths would most certainly occur.

CHAPTER TWENTY-SIX

3:30 a.m.

The skiff glided away from Okefenokee Adventures through the dark water, disturbed only by the stroke of the paddles, each dip of the blades creating small eddy currents. The small security light at the edge of the boat ramp faded behind them in the mix of the ink black night and the low mist over the water. Majorski thought of tourists who lined up and paid good money to enjoy the boat excursions. Their jaunts were in the daylight hours and with guides familiar with the swamp. At the moment, he would pay any amount of money to be off the boat.

He and Charlie made no effort to conceal their fear of the swamp at night. Jayco continued to play his role of "Billy Badass," afraid of naught, as he paddled the boat further into the swamp.

Time and again, Majorski felt the boat quiver from Charlie's sudden jerks when the flashlight beam was reflected back by shiny objects, some manmade, most not. Several times large eyes glowed in the light beam before disappearing under the water. In some areas, the water had a fluorescent sheen, likely from chemical decomposition of swamp vegetation.

The initial sounds of grunts and groans soon gave way to the rhythmic swish and gentle splash of the paddle, expertly wielded by Jayco. The repetitious sound was mesmerizing and mingled perfectly with the black night.

Majorski sat in the middle of the skiff, seemingly surrounded by more supplies than Lewis and Clark took on their excursion from St. Louis to the Pacific, discovering the Oregon Trail. It was somewhat comforting to see the items present were in triplicate. Maybe they didn't plan to sink him in the swamp along with the ranger. Majorski had little faith in Charlie's vision so he kept his eyes forward, following the beam from Charlie's flashlight, sweeping back and forth across the narrow channel.

After an hour of travel, he faced the stern when Jayco placed the paddle in the boat. He watched with curiosity as Jayco hooked up the line from the gas tank to the motor and pumped the priming bulb several times. The motor fired up on the second pull of the starter cord. Relief was apparent on all three faces.

Majorski didn't share in Jayco's confidence of night travel. He turned partially in the seat, speaking over his right shoulder. "We've been traveling by motor power for over an hour. Why don't we tie up and wait until daybreak before going further?"

"Relax, Doc. You're a passenger on this cruise. I'm the captain of this vessel and as ship commander, I'll decide when we stop. Upset me and I'll make you walk the plank." A sharp laugh punctuated his statement.

Majorski wasn't surprised by the negative response and grinned when he heard the groan coming from the front of the boat. Charlie wasn't enjoying the nocturnal journey at all.

Time passed at a snail's pace. Majorski had difficulty remaining upright on the middle seat, his head bobbing, and with each movement his headache intensified. He jerked his head to the left when he saw a second beam of light splash around the overhanging vines and brush. He saw what he thought was land but indeed was a false island of peat, held together by vegetation and small trees. He turned around on his seat to watch Jayco swing the large spotlight along the water, then in and out of several small tributaries. He released a deep sigh of relief when the watercraft swung left and the motor died. The skiff continued to drift forward into the brush.

"Be careful, Charlie," Jayco said. "Stay in your seat and grab those overhead vines and swing us around. I want the stern as far back in the brush as we can get it and the bow pointed toward the deep water. The sun will be up soon. We need to get tied up and covered."

"You think they're looking for us in the swamp already?"

"Not likely. I don't want a surprise by some fool on a canoe trip."

It took thirty minutes to get the boat positioned. After determining the water was deep enough between the floating islands, Jayco and Charlie wrapped the chain and anchors around the ranger and dropped him over the side. They didn't bother to ask Majorski for help.

Working together, the three of them got the tarp strung up and the mosquito netting hanging inside the tarp. By the time they finished, all three were exhausted; within minutes, they were asleep, each curled up in his own section of the boat.

Morning sounds in the swamp differed from those occurring at night; they were more exuberant, or so it seemed to Majorski. A different set of insects, birds, and other creatures added to the daybreak symphony.

One creature was far more vocal than others. This one was human. "Damn, I've got to piss," Jayco exclaimed, much louder than was necessary. This apparently was his crude method of a wakeup call. After relieving himself over the stern, he whacked the side of the boat with the paddle, just in case his previous noise-making efforts weren't sufficient.

"Wake up, Charlie. I'm hungry. No more pork and beans out of a can. Set up the Coleman stove and boil some water. We'll try some of those fancy freeze-dried meals."

Charlie mumbled something under his breath, pulled his legs closer to his chest and was promptly asleep again. He enjoyed the extra slumber for no more than five minutes before he was rudely awakened by a wet rag slammed against the side of his face.

"Did you hear me, Charlie? I'm hungry. Get up."

Charlie struggled to a sitting position in the floor of the boat, yawning and rubbing his eyes at the same time. "What's the hurry? We ain't got no schedule to follow. The sun ain't even up yet."

Jayco nodded toward the warm glow appearing to arise from the swamp. "It's light enough to cook. My stomach has a schedule and it's telling me we're behind time on eating."

Majorski watched Charlie reluctantly unpack the stove and the fuel container. He didn't appear overly excited or hungry. "Need some help?" Majorski offered.

"Not yet. I've used this type stove before. It won't take but a minute to get the water boiling. Takes longer to set everything up than it does to cook."

Majorski sat erect, his butt resting on a plastic-wrapped blanket and his back against the sidewall of the hull. The position gave him some relief from the pounding headache that worsened whenever he lowered his head. His vision, though still blurred, was somewhat better than the day before. A medical student in his junior year would recognize the symptoms and signs of a subdural hematoma. He hoped the bleeding in his brain had stopped and if he was able to avoid further head trauma, he might survive. Well, at least from the brain injury. Nothing would help him if he received a gunshot wound.

The just completed short nap reminded him of his residency days when a total of two hours in two days was welcomed. Without realizing he had fallen asleep again, he was rudely awakened when he felt a paddle shoved hard against his ribs.

"Second wakeup call. Everybody up. That means you too, Doc. Charlie has breakfast ready. Pass the 'bacon and eggs' to me. Better be over easy the way I like 'em." He snorted with laughter, accepting the plastic bowl of chicken and rice. "Oh, sweet Jesus, just like I ordered."

The three men wolfed down their food like starving dogs. Charlie had prepared the meals by pouring boiling water into six of the prepackaged containers. Meal times would be few and far between so they made the best of it by eating double portions of the carbohydrate-rich food.

Majorski passed his empty plate to Charlie and resumed his position of comfort. In different circumstances this would be a dream trip for a group of men who sought adventure to prolong their youth. He had missed the ritual of male camaraderie and bonding in his twenties, as the rigors of medical school and residency programs didn't allow time for such enjoyment. Born just after the Vietnam War and involved in medical training during Desert Storm, it had been his good fortune to avoid being in harm's way. Until now.

A splash behind him brought him out of his daydream. The sky took on a warm glow though the sun was still buried in the swamp. The previous night had been cool and with the tarp in place they were spared a soaking from brief showers and the morning dew. Now, with the tarp rolled up, he was able to view his surroundings better.

Beauty came in many different packages. He saw movement among the trees and watched as a white egret gracefully landed amongst the lily pads. The bird's excellent eyesight enabled it to pick out a solid surface isolated in the expanse of water. *I hope he's not on the back of a hungry alligator.* The beautiful bird appeared unconcerned. How well creatures of nature lived in cohabitation; much better than man, God's most fallible creation.

After the sun moved above the horizon and out of the swamp, the men reversed the previous night's work, rolling up and packing the tarp and netting between the seats.

With everyone back in their usual positions, Jayco primed and fired up the motor, easing the skiff out of the brush. Within minutes they were in open water, traveling with enough speed to create a wake which rolled toward the lily pads flanking the channel. The motor, though only ten-horsepower, was powerful enough to move them swiftly through the water. With the sun at their backs they churned further west for several hours before swinging northwest into a smaller tributary.

Majorski was clueless as to their location. He knew of the Okefenokee; he had read articles in *National Geographic* magazines and watched features on the Discovery Channel. But his overall knowledge was limited, making the familiarity of the waterways Jayco demonstrated even more amazing.

"Jayco, how come you know so much about this swamp?" Majorski asked, his curiosity finally winning out.

"I spent some time here when I was a boy and later, after I got out of prison the first time, I worked for a lumber company, cutting and pulling cypress out of the swamp. That was one bad job. The heat and the mosquitos made you forget all about snakes and gators."

"Did you stay in the swamp at night?" Charlie asked.

"Depended on where we were cutting. I remember camping out on Billy's Island a few times. Most of the time we traveled by boat to more permanent places. Still wasn't too fancy, but we had running water and out-houses. The wooden buildings were covered with tin roofs and screens were on the windows. That helped to keep out the insects. Sometimes it was so hot and humid, we had to get outside for a spell. But even outside the buildings the air felt too heavy to breathe."

"You must have made good money if you put up with all that," Charlie said.

"The money wasn't good at all. There weren't any jobs available anywhere else, especially for an ex-con. I didn't stay with it long. Got into it with the foreman on a hot day and when we went back to camp for the night, I took off."

"Is that why you ended up in prison again—parole violation?" Majorski asked.

"Not directly. I hadn't been reporting to a parole officer anyway. He knew where I was. Transportation was about as hard for him to get, as me. Anyway, when I went back to Waycross, I got drunk one night and let some guys talk me into standing lookout for them while they knocked off a bank. Hell of a thing, that was. They walked into the bank, saw a guard who recognized one of them and they took off. Didn't even ask for money or pull a gun or anything. Just ran and he chased them.

"They got away. Someone told the guard I was seen with them and he arrested me. That's all it took. They booked me for attempted bank robbery, and since I was out on parole and hadn't reported to my parole officer, they sentenced me to three to five years. I mean, that is a bunch of bullshit. I've probably killed at least five people and ain't ever been caught for it. Then I get sent to prison for some crap like that."

"How long were you in prison?"

"I met Tupac in prison. He made me play it straight. He saved my life so I owed him. I got out after twenty-eight months."

Majorski listened to the story with fascination. His own past hadn't brought him in contact with the element of society that produced people like Jayco and Charlie. The system obviously failed them, as it did so many others. He knew that the majority of men released from prison were back inside the walls within a few months.

"Where did you and Charlie meet?"

Charlie jumped into the conversation. "I knew Tupac before Jayco came in. We were in the same cell block and in the yard together during exercise time. I remembered he was good at basketball. I just watched. I couldn't keep up with those guys. They were fast. I stood on the side and threw the basketball back if it went out of bounds."

Jayco chuckled, the cruel grin on his face again. "See there, Charlie. There's always something for a dummy to do, even in sports."

Charlie spun his head around, his face flushed. His lips moved but for seconds nothing came out, then he sputtered, "Jay—Jayco, I'm not a dummy. You said you wouldn't call me names anymore."

"Okay, Charlie. Take it easy. I'm just kidding. I won't call you dummy anymore."

Majorski closed his eyes. The pounding in his head had increased again. *God must have a good reason for me to be here with these two. So far I don't have a clue exactly why he needs me.*

The trio remained silent, lost in their thoughts as the boat slid slowly through the channels that wove in and out of the prairies and cypress stands.

CHAPTER TWENTY-SEVEN

Jeff Rutledge finger-combed his long blond hair and headed for the kitchen. Deeply tanned with a muscular body on a six-foot frame was evidence enough that his life was spent outdoors as much as in a classroom. Since early childhood his dream had been to follow in the footsteps of his father and work in the forestry service. His eighteenth birthday was coming up in two weeks and he was chomping at the bit to graduate from high school and started college. His father had arranged a part-time job for him so he could get more experience while attending classes.

He removed a carton of orange juice from the refrigerator, turned it up and drank at least half directly from the carton. He smiled when he replaced the juice knowing his mother had witnessed his disgusting habit. It was his favorite way to get her riled up so he could tease her. He stepped behind his mom at the stove and placed a kiss on the back of her neck; his way of saying thanks for the ham and eggs she was preparing for him.

He glanced out the kitchen window and noticed his father's Range Rover was not in its usual parking place "Where's Dad gone to so early? I wanted to swap vehicles for today. My truck motor is skipping and I was hoping he would take a look at it."

Mildred scooped up the food from the pan, layered it on a plate and placed it on the kitchen table. She motioned for Jeff to be seated. "He saw some lights last night and went to the boat ramp to check things out."

Jeff paused with a fully loaded fork halfway to his mouth. "He hasn't been back? He didn't call you?"

Until that moment Mildred had not been concerned. It wasn't unusual for her husband to get busy with things and forget to call home. "He probably called Al in to help him check out the boats to make sure nothing was stolen. He should be home soon."

Jeff dropped his fork onto the plate as he pushed back from the table. "Save my breakfast for me. I have time to drive down and check on him before I have to leave. If I'm late picking up Carolyn, she won't mind. We're just going shopping for the after Christmas sales."

"Okay, but if you get caught up in whatever your father is doing give me a call. I'll let Carolyn know, so you won't be in trouble."

"Get real, Mom. This is the 21st century. Men aren't slaved to women like the old days. She won't mind waiting."

"Keep that attitude, young man and you'll find out the world hasn't changed as much as you think. Now go check on your father so you can get on with your plans." As she spoke her previous non-worried demeanor changed and a cold chill went up her spine.

Jeff parked adjacent to his father's Range Rover, immediately noticing that Al Carter's forestry truck was not present. A Jeep was parked at the lower end of the lot nearest the boat ramp. The absence of any official decals meant it belonged to a civilian. Jeff leaped out of his truck and ran across the parking lot shouting his father's name. He went to the boat ramp first, and then to the snack building that doubled as a souvenir shop. Unable to find him in either location, he ran to the welcome center, a hundred yards away. It was closed for the holiday season and there wouldn't be a reason for his dad to be there unless he had discovered something suspicious. If that was the case, police vehicles would be present.

Within minutes he had completely circled the building, checking all the outside doors. All were locked and no one answered his knocks. He ran back to the marina. This time he noticed one of the boats was missing. He was familiar with all the boats and knew exactly how many should be in the small docking area. He made extra money helping Chico Diaz maintain the boats and the motors and he knew Chico was on holiday, so he certainly didn't take the boat.

Jeff followed the rim of the basin to a small shed a couple hundred feet away. The lock was still in place. Peering through a crack in the wooden siding, he saw the inboard-outboard cruiser owned by the forestry service, was still present. His father and Al Carter were the only possessors of the keys to the boat. If his father had decided to go on the water for some reason, he wouldn't have taken the small tourist boat, unless he planned to travel a short distance.

Jeff selected a boat tied up nearby, checked the fuel tank and fired up the motor. He opened the throttle to the maximum and sped down the narrow channel. He had spent most of his life at the park and was familiar with the cypress knees lurking beneath the tea colored water. Rounding a bend in the channel, he remembered he had left his cell phone plugged into the charger in his truck. He throttled back for a brief moment, and then surged ahead. He shouldn't be gone too long.

CHAPTER TWENTY-EIGHT

5:00 p.m.

Twice during the day Jayco ordered Charlie to tie up in heavy brush. Each stop was brief, just long enough to eat saltine crackers and canned Beanie Weenies. He scanned the skies often, watching for helicopter search teams. But the blue canvas above was painted only with the white contrails of commercial jets passing miles high overhead.

He continued onward, putting miles between him and the authorities who most likely were still searching the highways. Though the plan was created on the run, it was a solid one. Years in prison provided him an unofficial "degree" in criminal activities and it certainly came in handy.

It was hard to hide his disappointment over the big score. Still the hundred grand from "Brunswick's finest" would go a long way in soothing his pain. Though they were unable to get to the drug money, he planned to make good on his promise to send money to the old lady, his former inmate's mother. He would have to send it from Mexico. His picture might be too prominent in post offices in the states. He grinned at the thought.

The late afternoon breezes brought a chill to the air as well as heavy cloud cover that blocked the usual warm rays of the sun. The men put on additional layers of clothing, including heavy jackets.

Charlie zipped his jacket closed and struggled to get his life jacket over it. He had not been without the vest since the boat left the dock. "My life vest won't fit over this thick jacket. What am I going to do?"

Jayco snickered at his friend's quandary. "Don't worry about it. Just keep your jacket close by. We ain't the Titanic. Not likely to hit any icebergs in the swamp."

Charlie tied the straps from the floatation device around his right leg to keep it close. Mollified with the temporary solution he settled down in the bow of the boat.

Jayco suddenly spoke in an exuberant tone, loud enough to be heard over the noise from the motor. "Tonight your benevolent captain has a surprise for his crew. I smell rain in the air. We'll tie up early, eat a big meal and then get everything in place for the night." He guided the skiff under a stand of cypress trees draped with long tentacles of Spanish moss hanging almost to the water.

The moment the skiff was secured, Charlie started working with the stove. The thought of a large meal helped him forget his anxiety about the surrounding water. There was ample daylight left to prepare a meal. He decided to open several cans of beans and corn as well as the prepackaged freeze dried foods. The canned goods would be filling and eating them would decrease the weight of the supplies. There would be time after they ate their meal to attend to the tarp and netting. As he stood to take the waterproof bag of prepackaged food from Majorski, a long black snake dropped from an overhead limb into the boat at Charlie's feet.

Reacting instinctively, he jumped away from the creature. In his panic, he tripped over the stove and fell backwards out of the boat. His head banged hard against a cypress knee under the surface and he sank out of sight.

"Charlie," Jayco screamed, plunging headlong out of the boat after his friend. The water closed over both of them like a grave. Jayco broke the surface a few feet away. "Do you see him?" he pleaded.

"No, he hasn't come up." Majorski answered, searching the water around the boat.

Treading water, Jayco repeatedly dived beneath the surface. Focused on his task, he drifted away from the boat. After several minutes it was apparent his efforts were futile. He grabbed a bush growing out of an island of peat to hold his head above water. When he looked back toward the skiff, it was gone.

Ed was stunned. He was alone in the boat. Those who had kept him captive were out of reach for the first time since the initial holdup attempt. He peered in the direction the men had entered the water. He saw neither of them. His mind became alert. *I'm free. Just start the engine and travel in the direction away from the setting sun. Get as far as I can before total darkness and tie up for the night. I can get through one more night. Tomorrow, I'll travel east until I find others on the water—kayakers or tour-guided boats, I don't care.*

He started the engine without difficulty. That was the easy part. He untied the rope anchoring the stern to a tree and eased the skiff into the narrow channel. He had traveled less than fifty feet before he slowed the engine, turned the boat and sped in the direction of the lost men.

His difficult job became more so with a loud clap of thunder and flashes of lightning announcing the oncoming storm. A curtain of rain swept across the swamp, reducing visibility to near zero. Accompanying wind churned the waterway making navigation virtually impossible, especially for a novice at the controls. The skiff was blown sideways down the channel, the gale force wind overpowering the puny outboard motor and his attempts to keep the bow pointed to the middle of the channel.

"Jayco. Charlie." He called out for the men until his voice was reduced to a raspy bellow. The only reply to his repeated calls was the cacophony of the wind and rain. The gusty winds pushed the boat faster down the channel, banging off cypress trees, throwing Majorski about in the boat. In desperation he pointed the skiff directly at a large clump of vegetation, and at full throttle drove the boat in as deep as it would go. He grabbed the hanging vines and lashed them with rope to the motor.

Exhausted and terrified, he collapsed in the bottom of the boat. He reached out in the near darkness and located a flap of the tarp, dragging it over his head and chest. Then he prayed.

***

Jeff was caught off guard by the sudden change in the weather. He was familiar with the swamp and the reduced light brought on by the storm did little to dampen his determination to find his father. He shivered as he drove his small skiff deeper into the swamp. His light weight jacket was no match for the driving rain and wind. Once he thought he heard the voices of men. A sense of hope drove him on in spite of the elements. After another hour of searching he determined the wind had played a trick on him.

Finally, disheartened by his inability to locate his father, he reduced the throttle and allowed the boat to drift. He buried his face in his hands and sobbed. He couldn't accept his failure. Instead he convinced himself that his journey had been a foolish gesture and his dad was safe and sound back home. His impetuous action might be the cause of unnecessary worry for his mother and father. Neither his mind nor his heart would believe it. Somehow he knew his father was in trouble and he was unable to do anything to help him. He revved up the engine and turned the boat for home.

***

After what seemed an eternity, but in reality only thirty minutes, Majorski flipped back the corner of the tarp. Though the rain and the wind had let up, he was soaked from head to toe and shivering so violently the skiff vibrated. He crawled over the middle seat toward the bow where additional supplies were stored. He remembered there was a wool blanket wrapped in plastic.

After moving the small burner and other supplies, he located the blanket and was tearing open the wrap when a hand emerged from the black water, latching onto the side of the boat. Startled, Majorski crabbed backwards away from the sudden appearance of the hand. Recovering from the shock, he reached out to grab the hand.

He stood upright, his legs spread and braced between the seat and the side of the boat. His muscles ached as he pulled with all his strength to the owner of the hand out of the water. Without shame, he murmured a prayer. "Please let it be Charlie."

After minutes of herculean effort, he hauled the water-soaked man into the boat. Both men collapsed in exhaustion.

Majorski was on all fours in the bottom of the boat, gasping for air. When his breathing slowed and some of his strength returned, he lifted his head.

He stared directly into the hard features of Jayco Dubois.

Jayco lay spent, his head propped against a pile of supplies. His labored breathing has subsided. He opened his eyes, staring at Majorski for a long moment. He suddenly spoke, accompanied by crazed animated movements. "We got to find Charlie." He stumbled to the stern, freed the rope from the vines and cranked the motor. He blasted the skiff through the remaining vegetation back into the channel.

Majorski huddled in the bottom of the boat, covering his head with his arms. The constant crisscross maneuver of the skiff, back and forth over its own wake, jarred the watercraft, sending spikes of pain through his head with every bounce. He could no longer deny the signs of a subdural hematoma. His headache was getting worse; a sure sign the hematoma was expanding. Any additional head trauma would most certainly be fatal.

He had blown his chance to escape, instead choosing to return in a futile attempt to save Charlie and subconsciously Jayco as well. Why? Maybe it had something to do with what was known as Stockholm syndrome.

CHAPTER TWENTY-NINE

December 28, 2007

7:00 a.m.

After a restless night, both men awoke almost simultaneously the next morning. The boat was adrift in a gentle current, banging occasionally against trees and sometimes snared by hanging vines.

The previous night Jayco had driven recklessly back and forth across the area where Charlie had fallen overboard. He searched the waterways even after darkness. His external demeanor could no longer mask his inner pain over the loss of his friends; first Tupac, and then Charlie.

The attempt to find Charlie after dark had not only been futile, but foolhardy. On one of the passes the motor's drive shaft extending below water level hit a cypress knee. The impact broke the shear pin, a device designed to prevent damage to the propeller. Without the pin in place, the propeller would not engage. They were stranded.

Rather than showing gratitude to Majorski for saving his life, Jayco became more belligerent, blaming Majorski for Charlie's death and virtually everything else. The situation was hopeless. Jayco would not accept the inevitable. Now there was nothing to do except sit and wait; but for what?

Majorski recognized Jayco was growing more unstable by the hour. He had to persuade the man to surrender. "It's time to give it up. Your deception didn't work. By now the police have figured out we are in the swamp. They can cover the entire area by helicopter and they have the boats and personnel to canvas all the waterways. At the very least they can wait you out and let you starve to death."

Jayco's scornful reply echoed across the vine-covered swamp. "They won't do that. They've got to worry about you."

Majorski snorted, his words reflecting his true belief. "I'm sure they assumed I didn't survive the first night. They just don't know what a nice guy you are—keeping me alive all this time."

"Shut the fuck up, Doc. I might get snake bit or something. I'll need you to fix me up."

"You really think I would? You've got no leverage anymore. I worried about the hostages, not about me. I even had some feelings for Charlie. But the two of us. We're both going to die in this damn swamp because you are so thick-headed."

Jayco grabbed the paddle, raising it ominously. "Don't try to fuck with my head. You're right about one thing. The cops most likely think you are dead. Maybe I should knock you in the head and dump your ass in the swamp. It would make the boat lighter and I can row myself out of here."

Majorski dug the needle in deeper. "You should have thought about those shear pins. The underwater cypress knees play hell with the propellers. All that extra gas doesn't help much when the blades are free-wheeling."

"I told you to shut up, you bastard." Jayco jumped up, moving toward Majorski with the paddle raised over his head.

Majorski flung himself from side to side. The sudden shift in weight to each side made the boat tilt only a few degrees, enough to make the boat unsteady.

Jayco stabbed at a tree with the paddle in an attempt to maintain his balance. The wooden oar missed and the momentum of his effort carried him out of the boat and into the black water. Fearing unseen creatures in the water, Jayco scrambled in vain to climb a nearby cypress tree. The slick surface made it impossible and in the attempt he lost the paddle, which drifted away.

Clinging to the tree, Jayco searched the water around him, certain a predator was on its way. One was. An alligator resting on one of the false islands of peat, slid into the water, its eyes just above the surface. It barely made a ripple in the water as it glided toward its victim.

Jayco did not see the alligator. He didn't need to. His imagination stirred him to action. Abandoning his efforts to climb the tree, he struck out for the boat, his adrenalin surge powering his arms and legs. He reached for the side of the boat, instantly jerking his hands back to avoid further pain from the blows rained down by Majorski.

"Let me in the boat. For God's sake, let me in." Jayco treaded water, his eyes searching the area around him. A few seconds later he saw the alligator approaching, the menacing eyes projecting just above the water. He reached up again, hooking his arm over the side and was rewarded with painful lashes from a doubled-up rope.

Majorski yelled at him with disdain. "If you plan to get in this boat, I suggest you do it from the stern so you don't capsize us. I don't care to join you for dinner with the alligator."

Jayco swam frantically to the stern, grabbing on at the motor housing, accepting the hand extended to him. He swung over the motor and collapsed in the bottom of the boat, sucking in great gulps of air.

Grabbing a blanket from the pile of supplies on the center seat, Majorski pitched it to the shivering man. "Wrap up and move to the bow. You won't be exposed to the wind as much."

"You ain't normal," Jayco screamed. "Ain't you afraid of dying?"

"I'm not anxious to leave this world, but no … I'm not afraid. I've been through hell on earth and nothing could hurt me worse. There was a time when I thought death would be a relief."

"Bullshit," murmured Jayco. He pulled the wet blanket over his head and curled up in the bow.

Majorski remained in the stern, leaning against the useless motor, watching the alligator circle the boat searching for his missed dinner.

CHAPTER THIRTY

8:00 a.m.

Watkins shuffled from the bedroom in the rear of the bus to the Communications area located in the center. He discovered Spalding sitting in front of a computer monitor, his face only inches away from the screen.

Watkins gave a cordial nod before continuing to the coffee maker. He was getting too old for manhunts. He needed eight hours of sleep every night and on a regular basis or his entire system got all screwed up. Especially his bowels; he couldn't recall the last time he took a crap. He poured a cup of the thick syrupy black liquid and sipped it, thankful it was at least hot, even if it tasted like it was brewed last week.

"Any news from the roadblocks?" he questioned Spalding.

Spalding screwed up his face in a snarl. "Not a damn thing. I've stared at this screen until I'm about to go blind. It's like those men vanished. Maybe Dubois has contacts with the alien world and they beamed them up."

Watkins chuckled, and then cut it off quickly. "I know I landed on Kimble hard when he was so pessimistic, but I really am worried about the doc. It would be easier for two men to evade capture if they weren't hauling a hostage with them. God help me. I can't believe I'm even thinking shit like that. Why can't we catch a break?"

"It'll come, partner. I'll sing your song. Got to be patient. Have you called Kathleen?"

"No. I hate to admit it but I'm afraid of her. If I get her on the phone she'll hammer me for being here. I will get pissed about her browbeating me, and then it will cost me big time to make up to her. Best if I just stay among the missing."

Spalding nodded that he understood. He fiddled with the adjustment knobs on the monitor, and sat back satisfied with the electronic picture. He spoke in an offhanded tone. "How come y'all never had kids?"

"Early in our marriage we were too caught up in our careers. Then we got selfish, enjoying the company of each other without the hassles of rearing children. Now it's a little late. Besides, things are bad enough; she worries about me all the time, without the possibility of becoming a single parent every time I go out. What about you?" Watkins asked. "Think you'll ever get married again?"

"What for? I've got you and Kathleen. If I'm not with one of you, I'm with the other."

"You want to explain a little further?"

"No, I'd better leave it alone. Don't want you thinking I'm hitting on your wife."

Watkins pulled up a chair near the console. "I don't have to worry about Kathleen running around with another cop. She still regrets marrying the one she's got, much less hunting another one."

"I don't think either of you have any worries. I've never seen two people so much in love after so many years of marriage. I'm a little jealous sometimes but I miss my Jenny too much to ever try to find a replacement. I'd always be comparing the new Mrs. to Jenny; wouldn't be fair."

"How long has it been since she died?"

"Twelve years."

"She was a real Georgia peach, no doubt about—"

"Base. Roadblock One."

"Base here. Go ahead, One."

"We got two guys fitting the physical descriptions of the suspects in a '03 Honda Accord. They are as high as a Georgia pine and refuse to open the trunk. Nothing inside the car to warrant a search for probable cause. Still looks suspicious. We need a warrant to breach the trunk."

"Go ahead, One. I'll make sure you are covered. I'll hang on here."

The minutes passed agonizingly slow for Spalding and Watkins who stared at each other, the same morbid thought in their minds. Finally Watkins broke the silence with a whispered prayer. "Please God, if Doctor Majorski is in the trunk, let him be alive."

Spalding lowered his head, his lips barely moving as he added, "Amen."

The radio barked again and Spalding snatched up the handset. "Base here."

"Base. Roadblock One. Nothing related to our search. Found a trunk full of marijuana. I called DEA and they are on the way. Sorry to disturb you. One is out."

Watkins sighed in relief. "I don't think I've ever been so grateful for a negative finding. The hair on the back of my neck stood up while we were waiting. I was so afraid they would find the doc's body."

"Come on, Grant. You've got to find the optimism again. You're making me depressed. Let's go over the map again and do a little brainstorming. Maybe we can come up with something else."

* * *

10:00 a.m.

"How did you get here, Jayco?"

Jayco shifted his position, a sullen look still on his face. "What the hell you mean? I came in the same damn boat you did."

"That's not what I'm asking and you know it. How did your life get so screwed up, you would get out of prison and immediately get involved in the same crap that will put you back in prison?"

"Don't preach to me, Doc. I wasn't born with a silver spoon in my mouth."

Majorski leaned forward, grabbed a flotation cushion and shoved it between his aching back and the motor. "Neither was I. My mother was a stay-at-home mom and my father worked two eight-hour shifts a day at a cotton mill. I started working at odd jobs when I was twelve and saved my money. My parents were insistent that I got an education."

"Well, ain't you special? My old lady worked as a secretary for a guy selling insurance. She was bonking him after hours, since she never got home until late at night. My old man spent most of his time on the sofa, at least when he wasn't at a bar or beating the hell out of me.

"I learned to use my fists at school—had to, or get my ass whipped every day. One day when I got home, my old man was plowed. He took a drunken swing at me; I ducked underneath and busted his nose with a left hook. He came at me with murder in his eyes. I tripped him and when he hit the floor, I smashed in the back of his head with a vase. I left home the same day. Been on my own ever since. I thought I'd killed the bastard. Year later, I found out I didn't finish the job."

The two men sat in silence for several minutes, and Majorski closed his eyes, emotionally and physically exhausted. Finally he said, "Being poor and having an asshole for a father is not an excuse for murdering people."

As soon as the words were out of his mouth, Majorski regretted his comment. He expected a backlash and the weak response surprised him.

"I didn't plan to kill that old man at the store. I just snapped when he shot Tupac. I thought he had killed my best friend."

A splash came from near the bow of the boat. Both men jerked toward the sound. The water was still. After a moment, when no additional sounds came from the area, Jayco turned back to face Majorski.

"Tupac is a better man than me. He saved my ass in Reidsville," he said. "I hadn't been there long—not enough time to get with a group. You need to be with a group to watch your back. The blacks decided they didn't like me; not from anything I had done, other than being white. Tupac stopped them from slicing me to pieces with their handmade shivs. Shocked me when he did it, me being a Georgia cracker, but he never hesitated. We been close like brothers ever since."

"How did the two of you manage to get out of prison at the same time?"

"We didn't. Tupac got out four months before I did. I was scared shitless every day after he left. His reputation carried a lot of weight. The blacks left me alone. I met up with Charlie right after my release and we looked up Tupac. I knew where he was 'cause he had a job roofing houses and was doing okay. He sent me spending money while I was still in prison. I wish now I hadn't found him. I talked him into helping me with the holdup. He didn't want to do it but I needed some seed money to get to Mexico.

"I didn't know anyone else to help me, and you know Charlie. I couldn't do it with just Charlie. He wasn't too bright. I had big plans and I was going to take Charlie with me. He needed someone to look after him. I hate myself right now. Tupac wouldn't be in the hospital and Charlie wouldn't be dead, if I hadn't dreamed up what I thought would be a perfect holdup."

"Shit happens," Majorski murmured.

"That's the God's truth, and it always happens to me."

The men fell silent again. Majorski thought of all the things he had learned since the episode started. In spite of the misery inflicted by Jayco, he felt compassion for him.

"You know, the men and women who serve on the jury are people just like us. They go through rough times. Members of their families get caught up in situations they didn't intend to happen. These days, people who make up the juries are liberal minded. Even with a public defender, I bet you won't be charged with more than manslaughter. Maybe sentenced to ten or fifteen years and out with a lot less if you show you've changed."

Jayco exploded with rage, his face red and spittle flying from his mouth. "Goddamn, Doc, you don't get it! You ain't listening. No way I go back. Too hard to survive in there. Piss off the wrong person—you dealing with ten crazy fuckers who want to stick a blade in you. Always have to watch your back, 'specially the first few weeks 'til you get made. I'm not going through it again. Either I get out of this swamp or I die here, and I take out anybody who tries to stop me."

Majorski slammed his hands on the seat in front of him, immediately regretting his action. The vibration from the blow sent waves of pain through his head. "Why? Why kill another person?"

"Shut up, Doc. Just shut the fuck up. No more talk. I'm tired of hearing it."

Majorski shook his head in disgust, threw up his hands and turned away from Jayco. He noticed the boat tilt and heard a swoosh of air. Then his world turned dark.

CHAPTER THIRTY-ONE

1:00 p.m.

Rodney Smith flipped his cellular phone closed. He punched his partner, who was dozing in a vinyl-covered chair near Tupac's bed.

Mark Daniels opened his eyes, grimacing as he stretched his arms over his head. "My back is killing me. How much longer we got to wait here?"

"I just got off the phone with Spalding. No luck with the roadblocks so far. The Georgia State Patrol is helping now. They have taken over the roadblocks and the units from the various counties are searching the streets in Folkston. Since no one has any idea what type vehicle the perps are driving it's hard to find them. The regional radio and television stations are broadcasting descriptions of the men."

Daniels got out of the chair and began pacing around the room, lifting his knees in an exaggerated gait—an attempt to ease the discomfort in his legs. He bumped the bed, momentarily causing Tupac to stir. "They must have sneaked past the roadblock in Folkston?"

"No way to know for certain, but based on the time factor, it would be unlikely. Spalding said they will continue the search and the roadblocks for a few more hours and if nothing happens, they'll pull out. They have an APB out for the north Florida area."

Smith heard a murmur from Tupac. He walked closer and saw the man's eyelids flutter. Smith placed his hand on Tupac's shoulder and gave a shake. "You say something?"

"Swamp."

Daniels joined Smith at the bedside. "Louder. Speak louder."

"Swamp. Jayco talked about the swamp."

"When?" Smith asked excitedly. "When did he talk about the swamp? Did he mention the swamp during the holdup at the convenience store?"

Tupac shook his head trying to clear the drug induced fog from his brain. "No. In prison. He talked about the swamp all the time. Said the Indians lived there a long time ago."

"Okefenokee?" Daniels asked.

"Sounds like it." Tupac's voice trailed off and he drifted off to sleep again.

Smith made eye contact with his partner and he hit the speed dial button on his cell phone. "I'm calling Spalding. Maybe the perps never intended to go south to Florida. There's several ways to get to the Okefenokee from Folkston."

1:15 p.m.

Spalding ran from the line of official cars parked adjacent to the southbound lanes of US Highway 1 back to the bus. When he jerked the side door open he caught Watkins, who was exiting. He attempted to speak, his heavy breathing making it difficult.

"Just ... heard ... from Smith at the hospital. The black perp is awake. He told Smith and Daniels about conversations in prison with Dubois. Said he talked about the Okefenokee all the time. Maybe he planned to go there all along. We've wasted nearly two days standing out here on this damn road."

"Fits with what I just learned," Watkins replied. "We got a call from Charlton County Sheriff's office. A boat was reported missing from Okefenokee Adventures, one of those outfits that rent boats and offer tours. A Jeep was in the parking lot and the tag number matches one reported stolen from Burnt Fort. Our boys are hiding in the swamp and we know where they went in."

"Okay. We're cooking now. Get a helicopter over that area. Have the pilot land in the parking lot of Okefenokee Adventures and pick up a park ranger. He can show the pilot the most likely escape routes through the swamp. Once we get a general idea of where they're headed, we'll get every boat available in the water."

Watkins rubbed his forehead, pinching the bridge of his nose, a mannerism which often occurred when he was about to relate bad news. "The call to the sheriff's office came from the son of the head ranger at the park. His father is missing. The son was out in the swamp all yesterday and most of the night looking for him. When he notified one of the other rangers, they promptly called the sheriff."

"Another victim on our conscience. Too sketchy to say for certain but I'll bet our 'boys' had something to do with his disappearance."

Watkins nodded his affirmation. "What about the Fargo side? We need additional rangers to start out from the Stephen Foster Park and patrol the waters where they intersect with the Suwannee River."

"Good idea. I'll leave it up to you to make the call. Kimble can call the people at Suwannee Canal and I'll get in touch with the helicopter unit. If lucky, we might get some fixed wing assets from the state."

Spalding reached for the phone but stopped short when he felt Watkins grab his arm. "What is it? Am I missing something, Grant?"

Watkins' voice squeaked when he tried to speak through his constricted throat. His emotions were running high. "No. You're right on track. I just wanted to apologize again for things I said earlier. I was wrong to doubt your sincerity in caring for the hostages. No matter how this turns out, you've done a superb job. If there's a battle with city hall, I'll stand behind you all the way."

Not willing to trust his voice, Spalding simply nodded and picked up the handset. He had always considered himself battle-tough, able to handle about any situation. This was different. Somewhere out there, possibly in the middle of an unforgiving swamp, a doctor who laid his life on the line for strangers was at the mercy of cold-blooded killers.

"The rules have changed, Grant. I don't care what it costs me personally; I will do everything I can to get the doc back alive."

CHAPTER THIRTY-TWO

3:00 p.m.

An OH-6 Cayuse helicopter, cruising like a dragonfly, skimmed the tops of the Spanish moss draped cypress trees. The forty-year-old chopper, a survivor of the war in Vietnam, still performed to perfection and was an excellent observation platform. The pilot, exceptionally skillful and confident in his ability, flew low to search the waterways for the suspects' hidden boat.

Ranger Al Carter wasn't as confident in the pilot's skill and prayed silently for survival. He knew the waterways like the back of his hand but this was only his second trip in a helicopter and the first at treetop level. If Stan wasn't missing and possibly in the hands of a maniac, he would be searching the swamps in a boat where he belonged. He promised himself this would be his last helicopter ride; if he made it back to the ranger station. He spoke nervously into the voice mike attached to his helmet. "Uh … we could see a larger area if we flew higher."

The pilot smiled, enjoying his position of command. "Won't do any good to fly higher. You can't see down through the trees to the waterways unless you are directly over them. Flying higher would create angles making it impossible to see under the canopies."

Carter gripped the edge of the seat when the pilot suddenly swerved the chopper around a lone tall pine tree, isolated among the shorter cypress. "It looks like you know what you're doing." Carter said.

The pilot replied while concentrating on the scene below them. "Had plenty of practice. I flew for DEA in Colombia for two years. It was even tougher there. The terrain was mountainous, not flat like here. Those Colombians down there were prone to shoot at snooping helicopters. Hell, they shot at everything, including weather balloons." He paused for a moment and then said, "You know these waterways better than I do. What's the chance of finding them by air and water?"

Carter tried to use the conversation to relax but found it

impossible. "To be honest, if they're well equipped and have the knowledge to live off the land, we may never find them. There are places down there where you can be ten feet from a boat and never see it. If the doctor and Stan are still alive, they've got to find a way to help us."

The helicopter dipped lower over the Chase Prairie where the water was clogged with floating green vegetation. Narrow water trails sliced through the endless floating mass. There weren't as many trees in the area but those present stood like sentinels, requiring the pilot to be constantly alert. He manipulated the cyclic and pulled back on the collective causing the large blades to bite into the air, lifting the metallic bird higher.

Carter, gradually acclimating to the flight, leaned out of the open-sided helicopter. The shoulder harness, though creating restriction, provided a sense of protection. He scanned the watery scene below him, testing the limits of his vision. From his lofty perch he soaked in the beauty of the swamp, noting the contrast between the floating vegetation in the prairies and the thick brush and cypress trees on the false islands of peat. The angle of the sun created rainbows of colors from the reflections.

The area was mainly populated with water fowl and occasionally he saw deer. Even with binoculars he was unable to find any alligators in the water or on the swamp banks. He regretted the absence of a camera. It would be great to share the scenery with his family when he told them of his wild adventure.

A dark shadow streaked across the placid water, mirroring perfectly the flight of the graceful egret gliding overhead. Carter's attention was diverted from the job at hand while he watched the bird ride the wind currents and then dip its wings to skim across the surface of the water. An object totally foreign to the area flashed across his field of vision.

"I see something," he yelled.

The pilot continued the climb, turning the nose of the chopper to return to their original flight path. "Where? What did you see?"

"Look at the northwest corner of the prairie. There's something orange caught in the middle of a patch of water lilies."

"I see it. Looks like a life vest."

The pilot flipped the switch on his radio to transmit. "Base, this is Dragonfly One. We've spotted something floating in the water at the northwest corner of Chase Prairie. No boat seen. Anyone close to this area?"

"Dragonfly One. This is Gator Three. We can see you. We're about a mile away. Continue to circle where you are and we'll be there shortly."

The uniformed officer at the control of Gator Three shoved over the handle on the Johnson outboard motor, swinging the boat in a one-hundred-eighty-degree turn. As soon as the boat was lined up in the center of the waterway he revved up the motor to its maximum of twenty-five horsepower. He throttled back when the radio barked.

"All boats, this is Base."

The five boats all answered Base in sequence.

"Everyone hold your position except Gator Three."

"Dragonfly One?"

"Dragon Fly One reporting to Base."

"Dragonfly One. When Gator Three reaches the target area, continue to circle in your present location until you hear otherwise from me."

"Dragonfly One copies. Out."

"Base. Out."

* * *

Spalding sipped from the hot coffee provided by the small café at Okefenokee Adventures. He looked over at Kimble, who sat in front of the computer bank, his head resting on the table. "Jesus, how long does it take to travel a mile on water? It's been twenty minutes. I can swim faster than that."

Kimble raised his head; his bloodshot eyes staring at Spalding. "Take it easy, Lieutenant. They have to maneuver carefully around those cypress knees or lose a motor. Should hear from—"

"Base. Gator Three."

"Base here. Go ahead, Gator Three."

"We found the body of a male Caucasian wearing a heavy camouflage jacket. Looks like blunt trauma to the head. Hasn't been in the water very long. The exposed flesh has been worked over by the critters in the water. Odd thing. Has a life vest tied around his leg? We'll bring the body back to Base for identification."

Spalding developed a sick feeling in his stomach. "Any form of ID on the body?"

"Base. Gator Three. Found nothing so far. The body and the clothing are waterlogged. It's hard to get into the pockets and maintain balance in the boat. Over."

"Okay, Gator Three. Make your way back to Base with the body. Base out."

"Gator Three—out."

Spalding stared at the handset wondering if Watkins in Gator One heard the communication. He placed the electronic device on the table and buried his face in his hands. If Watkins heard, then he would be feeling rotten as well. If he didn't hear, then no reason to tell him until there was a positive identification.

Spalding stood in front of the topographical map hung on a wall in the bus. He motioned for Bill Cafferty, a local "swamp guide" to join him. "Mr. Cafferty, I appreciate your willingness to help us."

"No problem. Glad to be of service."

"As you can see, I've marked the location on the map where the body was found." Spalding pointed to a red thumbtack on the map. "What we need to know is whether or not it was possible for the body to float to that area, or was it dumped there?"

Cafferty stroked his long white beard, carefully studying the map. "Can't tell you if the body was dumped there, but from what your people told me about the leader of the bunch, I think he would have weighted him down so he wouldn't be found so soon. What I can tell you is the current is not real swift in that location, but strong enough to move the body from anywhere northwest of Chase Prairie."

Spalding shifted his gaze to a spot higher on the map. "How far? I mean, how far could it have drifted in, say, the last twelve hours?"

Cafferty stepped closer to the map and pointed with his index finger along a line representing a waterway that branched off the Suwannee River. "Could have come from anywhere along this waterway flowing southeast. It would be unusual for it to drift very far without snagging on something, unless the current kept it in the middle of the channel. I'm not familiar with human bodies after death, but large animals, like deer, get bloated quickly and can drift unless they get hung up or worked on by the critters in the water."

Spalding shook Cafferty's hand. "Appreciate your help and if you don't mind, please hang around for a while. There's coffee, Cokes and sandwiches on the table by the door. Please help yourself."

Dealing with anxious family members of missing people was not Spalding's strong point. But often in the course of his job it was necessary. He motioned to the young man seated at the table to join him at the map.

"Hello Jeff. I'm Lieutenant Spalding. I'm sorry we haven't been able to locate your father but we're doing all we can. I need you to help me out. Are you willing to look at the map and point out exactly where you searched?"

"Yes, sir. I'll do anything I can."

Spalding gave Jeff a yellow marker. "Start from the marina and highlight the course you took in your search. Make sure you include any place where you deviated from the main channel."

Jeff was familiar with the map and promptly went to work. He used the marker to draw his course on the acetate overlying the map. His movements were precise and certain. His course was straight up the channel, no evidence of meandering or significant deviation. An occasional mark revealed places where he had traveled briefly into a small tributary.

"Understand I didn't travel fast and I was gone most of a day and night. I went all the way to Minnie's lake before I turned around. I didn't want to give up the search but I was afraid my mom would be frantic."

Spalding patted the young man on the shoulder. "You did a great job. You showed maturity way beyond your age. Don't give up hope. We have a lot of assets searching the swamp. Something should turn up soon."

He turned to the radio, picking up the handset. "This is Base to all boats except Gator Three. Move up the waterways in a northwest direction from your present position. Check out any tributary large enough to hide a boat. Respond."

The remaining four boats answered in sequence.

Spalding spoke again. "Dragonfly One. This is Base."

"Dragonfly One."

"I want you to fly northwest from your position to the Suwannee River, and then follow it southwest as far as Stephen Foster Park. If you don't see anyone on the river, return to the mouth of the waterway and work your way in grids back southeast to Chase Prairie. Do you copy?"

"Dragonfly One copies. Out."

* * *

5:00 p.m.

Base Command

"Lieutenant Spalding, you have a call." Kimble walked toward Spalding who was stretched out on the sofa.

"Not now, Sergeant. I'm whipped and I need about ten minutes of shut-eye. If it isn't a crisis then take a number."

Kimble remained standing beside the sofa with the phone in his outstretched hand. "No crisis, but the caller is Tracy Adams, the young lady who helped the doc in the store."

Spalding sat up quickly and took the phone from Kimble. "Lieutenant Spalding here. How may I help you?"

There was a brief pause before the soft voice spoke. "I know I shouldn't disturb you. I was wondering if you had any information about Doctor Majorski that you could share with me. I promise not to say anything to anyone. Oh ... I'm Tracy Adams. I was in the—"

"Miss Adams. I know who you are and I'm familiar with the role you played in helping the doc save the lives of all the hostages. I'm available anytime you want to call. I do have some information that has not been released to the press. We suspect the doctor has been taken into the Okefenokee Swamp. We are sure they had planned to hide out there until the heat was off, but we got a break and found out where they entered the swamp. We have search parties out as I speak. I will notify you if we get a confirmed location. I'm going to give the phone back to Sergeant Kimble and you can give him information on the best way to contact you. I might add you are a very brave lady."

Spalding didn't wait for a reply, just handed the phone to Kimble and settled back on the sofa. He was surprised at his ability to get through the conversation. His throat and chest felt like he was in a vise. He refused to believe the doc was dead until he saw his body with his own eyes.

CHAPTER THIRTY-THREE

5:00 p.m.

"Wake up." Jayco kicked Majorski's leg to emphasize his verbal command. "Help me spread the tarp."

Majorski struggled to open his eyes against a suppressive weight. His head felt as heavy as the rest of his body. He didn't remember falling asleep but for some reason the pounding in his brain was worse. As he attempted to pull himself upright, his left hand lost its purchase on the seat and he fell to the bottom of the boat. His left arm and leg moved sluggishly and it took several efforts before he was sitting erect.

"What's the rush? It's not raining." It took considerable effort to speak and his words seemed to hang on his lips.

"Ain't the rain I'm worried about. I hear a helicopter cutting circles in the sky and getting closer to us. The cops must have figured out where we are. We're sitting ducks without a working motor."

Using his right hand, Majorski untied his end of the netting and lowered it to the bottom of the boat. Hiding his worsening disability, he accepted the cord from Jayco and tied the loose end of the tarp to an overhanging limb. When finished he collapsed on the seat, leaning against the useless motor.

With anguish, he watched Jayco slam a clip into the AK-47 and jack the slide. At Jayco's feet was Charlie's weapon, also locked and loaded.

"I won't let you ambush the people who show up," Majorski said.

"Don't fuck with me, Doc. You start yelling and attracting attention and it will definitely get people killed, starting with you. Just stay quiet and maybe they won't see us. I figure a couple more days of searching and they will think we made it through the swamp to Fargo."

Majorski settled back against the motor. It was never his intention to attract the searchers to them. He didn't want to be responsible for anyone getting hurt, even Jayco; but if they did get close and Jayco made any effort to shoot them, somehow he would stop him. He looked around for any object he could use to incapacitate Jayco. There was a lightweight fire extinguisher, a tool box and the long metal rod lying in the bottom of the boat, partially covered by gear. He recalled Charlie saying he would use it to fend off gators.

Jayco lifted the tarp at the bow of the boat. He searched the channel and waters around them. His vision was limited by the advancing twilight. Darkness came quickly in the swamp; the sun seemingly submerging into the swamp. No matter how hard he concentrated, the quietness of the swamp revealed no untoward sounds. The helicopter was audible though not yet in sight. He lowered the tarp and relaxed against a stack of floatation cushions. "Play it cool, Doc. It might turn out to be a boring night."

* * *

6:00 p.m.

The parking lot at Okefenokee Adventures was cordoned off with orange cones, wooden barricades and bright yellow crime scene plastic tape. The efforts were in vain and did little to hinder the enterprising media and the curious. Cars, trucks, and media vans of every description lined the two-lane asphalt road from the entrance to Suwannee Canal Park to the log cabin facilities at Okefenokee Adventures. No empty space was spared. Vehicles jammed into every available spot from the grass lawns of the rangers' homes to handicap parking areas at the Park Information Center.

Located defiantly halfway under the yellow CSI tape used to mark the off-limits area was a fire-engine-red 450SL Mercedes Benz convertible. The owner, wearing a dark blue pants suit, white blouse and black pumps, stomped across the site marked with fluorescent crayon to indicate the helicopter landing pad.

Kathleen Quick paused outside the Crime Bus, took several deep breaths and knocked on the door in a manner that belied her emotional state.

The door opened and she was met by Trooper Ginn, who immediately stepped back, familiar with her notorious temper. With the absence of the cameraman, it was apparent her visit was not in an official capacity. Her calm voice shocked the young trooper. "May I speak to Lieutenant Watkins, please?"

Ginn recognized trouble in the making and promptly beckoned for their guest to enter. "He's not here at the moment. Uh … if you'll come in and have a seat, I'll notify Lieutenant Spalding you are here. Would you care for coffee or a Coke?"

The expression on her face was answer enough.

Spalding entered the monitor room drying his hands on a paper towel. He saw Kathleen seated by the door and acknowledged her presence with a nod of his head. "Kathleen, you know the media isn't allowed in the bus. You're pushing things a little."

"I'm not here as a representative of the media. I want to speak to Grant. He hasn't contacted me since the bus left the site of the attempted robbery. Usually when he doesn't call, it's because he's involved in something he doesn't want me to know about."

Spalding picked up a folding chair and moved it closer to Kathleen. He straddled the seat, placing his meaty forearms on the seat back. "He's not here at the moment."

Kathleen's green eyes flashed with anger, recognizing the stalling maneuver. "He's in the swamp, isn't he? You let him go into the swamp on a manhunt after a couple of psychopaths. He's not a kid anymore, Buddy."

Spalding bit his tongue, keeping his initial thoughts from escaping his lips. The wrong words could destroy a long-standing friendship and he was aware of the pain and anxiety Kathleen was experiencing. He felt it himself. "For Christ's sake, Kathleen. What did you expect me to do? I couldn't physically restrain him and that's what it would have required. He's doing his job. This is still a hostage situation and he's still the negotiator. He's not a novice. He knows what he's doing."

Silence filled the room, neither of them wanting to speak.

Kathleen broke first. Tears filled her eyes and spilled down across her high cheek bones. "I'm a tough bitch and you know it. But not when it comes to Grant. I know he's been in tough situations before but nothing like this. The man is not a good swimmer."

They stared at each other for several moments before both started laughing. Spalding stood, beckoned Kathleen to her feet and placed his arms around her.

"That's the dumbest thing I've ever heard you say. Let's hope his worst problem is treading water in the swamp."

CHAPTER THIRTY-FOUR

6:00 p.m.

The nurse in the Intensive Care Unit removed the blood pressure cuff from her patient's arm, rolled up the cuff and returned it to the wire basket mounted at the head of the bed. She entered the vital signs into her portable EMR attached to a cord around her neck before checking the intravenous drip setting on the IVAC pump. A pleasant smile was on her face at the wonder of electronic medical records. She was old enough to remember the days when she spent more time at the nurses' station recording information in the paper records than she did with the patient.

Satisfied with the vital signs and the IV rate, she smoothed the sheet covering Lucille Dixon and turned her attention to the young couple waiting anxiously in the doorway of the ICU cubicle. "You may come in now. She's heavily sedated so don't be alarmed if she doesn't respond to you."

Samantha and Jimmy entered the room, hand in hand. Samantha's lower lip trembled when she approached the bed. She clasped her hands together, tucking them under her chin and offered a quick, silent prayer. The numerous tubes leading in and out of her mother's body appeared surreal and the scene was more frightening than when her mother was lying on a makeshift surgical table in the convenience store. The past forty-eight hours seemed an eternity. The long wait in the family room during surgery had been torture. Jimmy's loyal presence had helped her endure it.

Lucille's eyelids fluttered when her daughter kissed her lips and whispered in her ear. The brief response meant the world to Samantha.

In a few minutes, Jimmy wrapped his long arms around Samantha and leaned forward, pressing his chest against her back. He hugged her tightly, and after a moment pulled her away from the bed. "We have to go. The nurse said we could stay only five minutes."

"Is time up already?" Samantha cried.

"We'll come back. We can visit for five minutes every hour and

I'll be here with you until she wakes up. And she will wake up, Samantha. She loves you too much to leave you. Remember, the doctor said she'll be okay with just one kidney. Now it's a matter of recovery from the loss of blood and the surgery."

Samantha looked into his brown eyes. "Promise me you'll stay with me."

He kissed her lightly on her forehead, her nose and her lips. "I'll be with you forever, if you want me."

"Forever," Samantha said.

Jimmy opened the door to the family waiting area and stood aside for Samantha to lead the way. He saw Samantha's face brighten with a big smile and followed her eyes to Tracy and Luke sitting in a chair in the corner of the room—an area they had virtually claimed as their own.

Samantha skipped across the room and scooped Luke out of Tracy's arms. "Hey little fellow, I've missed you."

Jimmy leaned over, placing his arms around Tracy. "Thank you for coming. Samantha really needed a diversion and Luke is the best one ever."

The two of them watched Samantha dance around the room with Luke in her arms. There were no other people present in the room so the joyful demonstration went on without disturbing anyone else.

Samantha held Luke to her chest and smothered the soft hair on his head with kisses. She finally relinquished the baby to Jimmy and sat beside Tracy. She gave a loving hug to Tracy, holding her tight as if to make up for the hard squeeze she couldn't give her mother.

"How's your mother?" Tracy asked.

Samantha dabbed at her eyes with the sleeve of her blouse. "She is still unconscious. The nurses reassured me that her condition is stable and her unresponsiveness is expected. I'd feel so much better if she would open her eyes and look at me. That's not too much to ask, is it?"

Tracy put her hand under Samantha's chin, lifting her head so their eyes met. "No, it's not too much to ask and I'm sure your mother will oblige. She's strong. Even though she's been through a terrible ordeal, she survived it because she has the spunk to fight through tough times. She'll get better. She has a lot of life yet to live. Hey! She doesn't even know she has a future son-in-law."

Samantha smiled. "I know she will like Jimmy. We're cut from the same cloth. It's amazing how fast we bonded. It's obvious the same happened with you and Doctor Majorski."

Tracy glanced at Jimmy, who was rocking Luke in his arms. Both looked contented. "Isn't it strange that from so much tragedy four lives have changed for the better?"

"Make it five at least. Jimmy received permission to talk to Tupac, the wounded black man. They talked for a long time. Jimmy swears the man has changed and plans to do something with his life after he gets out of prison."

Tracy remained silent for a moment. With a forced smile she spoke from her heart. "One of the lives we talk about is not yet safe. We are all alive because of him. I have prayed continuously for him since those men took him from the store. I know God answers prayers and I know He will take Doctor Majorski in His protective arms and keep him safe."

The two women embraced, sharing their love and their tears.

CHAPTER THIRTY-FIVE

6:00 p.m.

Watkins sat in the middle seat of the seventeen-foot fiberglass skiff designated as Gator One. His neck ached from the past three hours spent twisting his head from side to side searching the brush-covered inlets. Never in his wildest dreams would he have imagined the denseness of the cover in the swamp. Half-sunken logs became boats; tangled vines swaying in the gentle breeze resembled men scampering over the tops of lily pads and cypress stumps.

He looked away for a moment to allow his eyes to focus on something different. He noticed how Corporal Jeff Boykin, the young officer in the bow of the boat, kept both legs braced against the hull, freeing his arms to cradle the Heckler and Koch MP5 rifle. Watkins patted his shoulder holster to assure the presence of his own Glock nine-millimeter automatic. With the district park ranger, Hal Elberhart, armed with a Colt M-16 A2 rifle, they were prepared to defend themselves.

"Hal, how much time we got before things really get dark in here?"

"Maybe about forty minutes. A lot of folks have been fooled by sundown in the swamps. I've heard stories about people spending the night sitting upright in their kayaks because they wrongly estimated how much time they had to reach a shelter. Some passed up shelters to get in a few more miles before stopping. Then when the sun goes down, it's like turning off the light in a windowless room."

Watkins noticed the sun had started its night time dive into the swamp. A yellow-orange glow filtered through the tall cypress trees creating a surreal effect, thrusting everything into shadows. He was concerned over the late hour; not overly ecstatic about spending the night in the open boat. Returning to Base was not an option.

He looked away from the brush when he heard the *wop-wop* sound of the helicopter blades cutting through the moist air. Though he couldn't see the mechanical bird, the large beam from the searchlight mounted on the bottom of the aircraft was very evident, placing the chopper northwest of his present location. Since locating the floating body earlier in the day, Dragonfly One had come up empty.

Watkins removed the portable radio from the waterproof pouch of his heavy jacket. Each time he checked in with Base he said a little prayer, hoping to receive the good news that the body found was not the doc.

"Base. This is Gator One."

"Base here. Go ahead, Gator One."

"The ranger with me estimates less than forty minutes of twilight left. I suggest you notify all units to look for a location to tie up for the night. We can resume the search again at first light."

"Base copies. I'll notify the other units. Dragonfly One has already been instructed to return to Base." Then radio protocol was cast aside. "Grant—I know you want this information. The body has not been positively identified. The medical examiner is fairly certain it is neither the doc, nor the ranger."

A weak, almost forced voice replied. "Gator One copies. Out."

Watkins stored the radio in the zipper-locked pocket of his jacket. He shifted his weight, cautiously holding the side of the boat, and turned toward the ranger on the seat behind him. "Hal, you heard the message from Base. That means the doc is still out here somewhere. We better start eyeballing a safe place for us to spend the night."

The ranger slowed the boat and leaned forward stretching his back muscles. "The channel is too wide here. It narrows about a half-mile ahead. We've got to scout the location before it becomes dark. It's a total blackout when the sun sets."

Watkins felt around at his feet and located the two large battery-powered lanterns. They were brought along to serve as spotlights and would come in handy when they began their preparations for the long night ahead. For the first time in the long day he noticed hunger pangs and his dry mouth. So preoccupied with the search, he had blocked everything else out. Once they got tied up, he would break out the sandwiches and the large thermos of coffee.

A sudden movement in the bow of the boat caught his eye and he jerked his head up. Jeff was waving his arms to silently attract his attention. Watkins looked back at Hal, noticing he was already aware of the commotion and had killed the engine. The boat barely made headway since the current in their location was almost nonexistent.

Watkins moved to the bow and crouched behind the young

trooper, steadying his own position by grasping the side of the boat with both hands. "What is it, Jeff?"

Boykin had grown up in the rural areas of Brantley County where hunting for game was a means of putting meat on the table rather than sport. He had been born with hunter's eyes. He maintained visual contact of the suspicious area while he whispered to Watkins, "There's a large green glob ahead to our right. Definitely artificial. It doesn't blend with the vegetation around it; looks like a tarp. I think we've found them."

"Damn," murmured Watkins. "Why the hell couldn't we have found them an hour earlier? It's too late to call the other boats in. We either got to go in alone or sit here in complete silence all night."

"I don't know about you," Boykin said, "but I'm not crazy about approaching a boat containing an armed psychotic killer in the dark."

Ignoring Boykin's comment, Watkins retrieved his radio, now more aware of the near total silence since the engine was off. He cupped his hand over the radio transmitter. "Base. Gator One."

"Base here. Be advised Gator One, your transmission is weak."

"Base. Got you five by five. We've located the suspects. Conditions make it impossible to act. The ranger estimates only ten minutes of twilight left."

"Copy, Gator One. State position of suspects reference your location. Over."

"Base. Suspects' boat is backed into thick brush and covered with a tarp. We're tied up approximately thirty yards away. We were almost on them before we saw them. Good chance they heard us approach So far no activity on their part. If we remain in our location, it would be impossible for them to slip past us even in the dark. Over."

"Gator One. Sound travels a long way over water. Are you certain you haven't been detected by the suspects?"

"Base. No way to know for certain."

"Gator One. Are any of the other boats near your location? Over."

"Base. That's a negative. Recommend we wait until first light and get the other boats here before we attempt an approach."

"Base to Gator One. We concur with your plan. But thirty yards is too close. Get farther away before you tie down for the night. At first light, fire a flare to guide Dragonfly One to your location. A sniper will be on board."

"Gator One copies. Good news about the sniper. Negative on

moving tonight. It would be too noisy. If we haven't been detected, our chances are better to stay in our present location and remain silent."

The stress of the moment got to Spalding and proper radio protocol was ignored. "Listen to me, Watkins. Thirty yards is too damn close. You need to get farther away, even if you alert them to your presence when you move. If that maniac opens fire with the AK-47, you'll be sitting ducks."

Watkins turned toward the ranger, noting the negative shake of his head. He agreed. There was no way to move without cranking the motor. If they weren't heard coming in, then they weren't chancing it again.

"Watkins. Do you copy?"

Silence.

"Dammit, Gator One, answer back."

Watkins turned off the radio.

The three men waited in silence, straining to hear any noise that could give them a heads-up on what was in front of them. Maybe they were staking out nothing more than an abandoned tarp. Maybe—not probable.

Hal leaned forward, his voice a whisper. "Why the hell are you out here, Watkins? You're too old to be doing this crap."

Watkins twisted in his seat, his hand cupped over his mouth. "You sound like my wife. Always on my ass about doing things better left to younger men. At the moment I wish I was back at headquarters. But I can't stop thinking about the doc. He laid his life on the line for people he didn't know. Am I so much more important that I shouldn't do the same?"

CHAPTER THIRTY-SIX

7:10 p.m.

"What was that?" Jayco croaked, his voice cracking with nervousness.

Majorski lifted his head from the middle seat of the skiff. He was kneeling in the boat with his head resting on a flotation device to ease the constant pounding in his head. "Probably an alligator rubbing against a cypress tree," he answered. "I read somewhere about alligators marking their territory just like dogs, only they don't piss on the tree."

"Like hell. Not unless this damn alligator is made of fiberglass and speaks English. I know I heard voices and they ain't far away." Jayco picked up the rifle, using the barrel to push back a corner of the mosquito netting and the tarp. He narrowed his eyelids to small slits, staring into the near total darkness.

"Well, well, we have visitors. There they are," he whispered, "sitting still in their open boat like ducks on a pond. It's time to do a little hunting." He dropped to a prone position in the bow, maneuvering the tarp to obtain a better line of sight. He brought the rifle to his shoulder.

Without a thought of the consequences, Majorski launched himself the length of the boat, landing on top of Jayco, a millisecond after he fired. Majorski's momentum and the weight of the two men tilted the side of the skiff nearly into the water. Majorski frantically sought purchase on the side of the boat but the strength in his left hand was gone. He managed to grab the netting and the tarp with his right hand and it tore free from the overhanging branches.

He fell into the water beneath the dangling tarp. Surrounded by total blackness, he realized he was under the thick plastic material, trapped between it and the boat. He grabbed the top edge of the boat with his right hand, holding on while he used his weakened left arm and hand to free himself from the tarp. His thrashing created noise like large animals fighting in the marsh. He changed strategy and began working his way around to the stern.

He didn't make it.

Jayco recovered from Majorski's attack and threw back a corner of the overhanging tarp. He saw men in the other boat grasping overhanging branches, using them for leverage to pull their boat away from danger. They were silent. Jayco peered cautiously over the side of his boat searching for Majorski. He had heard the splash when the doc fell overboard. From the sounds in the water, the doc was trying to free himself from the entanglement with the cover. Jayco cackled maniacally under his breath, working his way toward the stern. Unable to see his foe, he followed the sounds.

When he saw a hand grab the rim of the boat, he raised the rifle and brought the butt down hard in the void just beyond the hand. The crunch of the rifle butt against bone brought an ugly grin to his face. He heard a brief groan, followed by silence. Jayco dropped to his knees and ran his hand along the edge. He felt nothing. He cackled again, enjoying the hunt.

Majorski was stunned, barely conscious. He realized he was beneath the boat. Instinctively he had held his breath, but now his lungs were about to explode. He reached upward, felt the flat bottom and worked his way to the outboard motor. He surfaced in the cutout between the motor and its mount. The motor was backed into heavy brush and provided concealment. His head throbbed with each heartbeat and when he placed his hand on his scalp, his fingers outlined an indentation in his skull. *Don't black out,* he admonished himself.

The intense pain in his head increased, followed by showers of sparkling colored lights dancing across his vision. Closing his eyes didn't help. The constant throbbing made it impossible to think. He struggled to clear his mind. Instead, the widely scattered lights narrowed to an ever-shrinking circle, which seemed to move farther away. He lost the grip on the cutout, slipping deeper into the water. His right arm, functioning independently of purposeful action, slapped in a hapless manner, desperately seeking purchase on the motor housing.

Jayco moved from the bow to the stern, shoving the tarp away from the skiff. He slid his hands along the sides. He sensed the doc was hanging on somewhere, but where? He needed to use his flashlight. No, that would make him a target. The suspense drove him deeper into insanity. He couldn't tolerate it any longer.

He stood upright in the boat, screaming at the top of his lungs. His voice echoed across the water. "Bastards. I've still got the doc. Turn on your lights. I want to see you throw your weapons overboard or I'll blow his head off."

There was no response.

"You think I won't do it. I got nothing to lose. Turn on your lights, crank up and start moving back up the channel."

Silence.

"Okay, I'm counting to three and if I don't see a light, I'm shooting the doc in the back of the head." He paused for a few seconds before he began counting. "One, two—"

A sphere of light, rivaling the brilliance of the sun, cast its illumination over Jayco and his boat. At the same time he heard an engine start, sputter a few times, and roar to life. The sudden action spooked him and he dropped to one knee. He swung the rifle up and centered it on the light. Something wasn't right. The sound of the motor was coming from a different direction than the light.

Everything behind and adjacent to the light was still hidden in darkness. His visual field was limited to the area between himself and the location of the light. "Fuck. They've got me spotlighted."

He opened fire on the light, shattering it, creating small missiles of Plexiglas and metal that sailed into the darkness. He swung the rifle in an arc spraying the entire area with projectiles until the rifle bolt locked open with a clang. He ejected the empty clip and searched around the seat for additional ammunition. He made a short, quick step to retrieve the bandolier of clips. He felt the boat rock and he steadied himself while he slammed another clip in place.

Using the barrel of the rifle, he ripped down more of the tarp. Crazed by his hatred of cops and the loss of his two friends, he began firing in a circle around the boat. As each of the clips emptied, he jerked it out, grabbed another from the bandolier and reloaded. His heart pounded against his sternum in sequence with the shell casings raining down on the floor of the boat.

The flash from tracer rounds created an eerie light and in his peripheral vision, Jayco saw movement. He stopped firing his weapon and swung the barrel toward the stern.

He realized his response was too late when a sharp pain pierced the center of his belly. Attempts to lift his rifle were futile; his arms suddenly so heavy he couldn't lift them. He dropped the weapon and with both hands grabbed the metal shaft protruding from his gut. It was covered with his warm, sticky blood.

He shrieked. "Doc?"

There was no response.

* * *

9:00 p.m.

The boat containing the men of Gator One drifted a few feet before jamming itself between two cypress trees. The motion jarred Hal Elberhart to consciousness although being awake did him little good. In the darkness he was unable to obtain his bearings, nor remember exactly where he was. Lying still, he fought against slipping back into the black void from which he had escaped.

The motion of the boat helped stimulate his memory and he spoke with a whisper. "Watkins, Boykin. You guys okay?"

There was no answer.

He needed his flashlight. He attempted to lift his right arm—it didn't respond. The effort shot searing pain through the shoulder into his neck. He had better success with his left arm, managing to pull himself to an upright position. His hand swept the seat beside him and then the bottom of the boat. At his feet he located one of the smaller flashlights. He grasped it firmly in his hand, and froze. The thought of turning it on terrified him.

He remembered the crazed man shooting out the large flashlight they had secured to a tree. That much of their plan had worked, they did distract him. The plan to ram him from his blind side had failed. The continuous hail of bullets chewed them up and they didn't fire a shot in return for fear of injuring the doc, if he was still onboard.

The silence and total darkness finally got to Elberhart and he turned on the flashlight. The scene in the boat illuminated by the light caused him to switch if off immediately. He had never seen so much blood in his life. He was covered in blood from his neck to mid-thigh. From the locations of his pain, he reasoned he was hit in the shoulder and right arm. He was breathing okay so his lungs weren't injured. He rubbed his head and face with his left hand and felt a thick mass of hair and blood and a sticky matter on the left side.

Mustering his courage, he switched the light on again, playing it over the middle and front of the boat. Watkins was crumpled on the floor behind the second seat. There was no sign of life. His jacket, head and face were covered with blood and a grayish-white matter.

Elberhart pulled himself forward and grabbed Watkins' arm. "Grant." There was no response. He shook harder. "Grant, wake up." This time he got a wheezing response.

"Hal, that you?"

"Yeah."

"I'm shot up bad, Hal. In the neck, chest, belly and I think most of my left arm is gone. My brain seems to be working okay. I'm lung shot. Hard to breathe. I'm getting weaker. Probably bleeding out."

"Can you see Boykin? The beam from this flashlight isn't very strong."

Watkins answered with a wet, wheezing cough. Finally he managed to speak. "He's gone, Hal. The first shot took off half his head. He never knew what hit him. He toppled sideways and his body kept going over the side."

"Can you reach the radio?"

"No need. It went early too. Saw parts fly all over the place."

Elberhart was silent. When he spoke his voice was choked with emotion. "I'm sorry, Grant. I'm really sorry. I can't help you. I have trouble moving myself."

"Don't worry about it. Out of our hands. Either we'll make it to dawn or we won't."

CHAPTER THIRTY-SEVEN

December 29, 2007

5:30 a.m.

Dawn in the swamp came in small increments, like a dark cloth dragged slowly from around a lamp shade. The initial light chased away the pitch-black darkness but did not offer enough illumination to provide definition.

Elberhart crawled forward in the boat, the pain in his shoulder almost unbearable. He pressed his fingers against the side of Watkins' neck; a pulse was present, weak and thready. "Grant. Are you still with me, Grant?"

Watkins stirred, wheezing his answer. "Not for much longer. If the helicopter doesn't get here soon, I won't make it."

"Don't give up. You hang on. You made it through the night; the rest will be a piece of cake. Dragonfly One should have left Base by now. It'll be overhead within a few minutes. Gator Two and Gator Three are probably on the way here as well."

Watkins grunted his response. "Can you see the boat that fired on us?"

"I can just make it out. The cover is shredded and pieces are scattered in the brush around the skiff. No activity in the boat. Impossible to see over the sides. The bastard may be lying there waiting for us to move closer so he can start shooting again."

"Why did he stop? Not likely he's out of ammo."

"Got me—maybe he figured he got us since we never returned his fire. I hate it about Boykin. My fault. Once we found the boat, I should've moved us further away."

"Knock it off, Hal. We didn't know he heard us. Sure didn't expect him to start shooting. The doc must be dead or he would have warned us."

Time passed with agonizing slowness for the two men as they awaited daylight and hopefully their comrades. The wait was made even worse by the presence of Boykin's body, which had surfaced adjacent to the boat. Brains and clotted blood covered the bow of the skiff.

Watkins hesitated for a moment, his voice catching in his throat. It took most of his remaining strength to speak. "Hal, don't ... don't let them take the bastard alive. Even if he surrenders, shoot him down like the mad dog he is."

The ranger didn't answer. Nothing he could say to Watkins would matter.

The moment was interrupted by the slapping sound of helicopter blades in the cool, moist air. Both men looked skyward as Dragonfly One zoomed over their location, followed by a US Army UH-1H Iroquois utility helicopter used for medical evacuation.

"He doesn't see us," Watkins said.

The noise from the helicopters lessened and was replaced by the roar of outboard motors as Gator Two and Gator Three sliced through the tea-brown water of the channel toward Gator One. Elberhart waved a white handkerchief with his uninjured arm while keeping a wary eye on the suspect's boat. He half-expected the cursed maniac to start blasting away at any second.

Gator Two and Gator Three saw his motions, reduced power and glided through the water.

Elberhart pointed in the direction of Jayco's boat. Since stealth was no longer needed or possible, he yelled at his colleagues. "Keep your distance. We've got one KIA and Watkins and I are both seriously injured."

Gator Two came closer, shouting to Elberhart. "We heard shots last night but couldn't tell from which direction they came. No way to help in the dark anyway. I'm going back to open water and fire a flare. We need Dragonfly One to recon the suspect's boat and let us know the situation."

Within minutes of the flare exploding directly above their position, Dragonfly One was on station. At first the chopper made wide circles, and then reduced the circumference with each pass until it hovered over the suspect's boat.

Watkins peered up at the helicopter and saw the sniper sighting through the scope of his H-and-K sniper rifle—no shots were fired.

Gator Two powered up and pulled alongside Elberhart and Watkins' boat. "Dragonfly One reports no movement in the suspect's boat. One person is down with a metal shaft protruding from his belly. The other person, ID unknown, is face down in the bottom of the boat. Lots of blood present. No movement discerned. Looks like no survivors."

Elberhart nodded his head in response. "Boykin's body is in the water on the other side of our boat; please make sure someone retrieves it before it sinks again."

The officer in Gator Two stared at the two remaining men in Gator One. "Damn, you guys look like you've been in a war." He grabbed the side of the ranger's boat, leaned over the side and ran his hand alongside Watkins neck.

"Base. Gator Two."

"Base copies. Go ahead, Gator Two."

"Did you copy report from Dragonfly One?"

"We copied five by five. Understand two bodies down in suspect's boat. No evidence of survivors."

"Gator Two. That is correct. Got one KIA and two critical WIA in Gator One. We need medevac overhead immediately with a basket."

"Base copies. Will relay. Out."

* * *

After conferring with the medic on the medevac bird, Spalding gently replaced the handset. Crestfallen he turned to face the exhausted woman sitting next to him. "I'm sorry, Kathleen. I didn't do my job very well. You heard the medic's report. It doesn't sound good."

Kathleen stared at Spalding, her usually beautiful green eyes swollen and red from crying most of the night. She had feared the worst since Spalding had been unable to get her husband on the radio all night. Her shoulders slumped and she answered with a whisper, without a trace of accusation. "You did what you could, Buddy. No one can stop Grant once he's made up his mind. I just hope he's using the same bulldog determination to stay alive."

CHAPTER THIRTY-EIGHT

December 31, 2007

11:50 p.m.

The bright light came at Majorski again, and like before, he couldn't react. His arms refused to respond to the commands from his brain. His legs felt heavy and useless. A voice came at him from somewhere distant. No, he decided, the voice wasn't talking to him, but about him.

"His pupils are equal now, and respond to light. I reviewed the most recent MRI of the brain. There's no evidence of new bleeding. His limbs respond to painful stimuli so there is no apparent paralysis "

Tracy covered her face with her hands, peeking out through her fingers at the heavily bandaged figure in the hospital bed. "Is there a possibility he will ever be normal?"

The doctor hesitated a moment, carefully considering his answer. "Head injury cases are similar in some respects and totally different in others. Time will tell if his brain will recover."

"Thank you, Doctor Miller. Is it all right if I stay with him a little longer?"

"Stay as long as you like, Miss Adams. Talk to him; let him know he's not alone. Patients have told us in similar cases they were able to hear us talking to them, long before we were aware of their consciousness. His EEG looks good so the brain is functioning well. It's just a matter of whether or not it can recover from the shock."

Majorski heard another voice, a soft one. *I know that voice. I know Tracy. What is she doing here? She shouldn't be in the swamp.* He struggled to open his eyes, to look at her, but his eyelids were too heavy. He wanted to talk to her. He fought hard before the dark veil fluttered down over him again.

CHAPTER THIRTY-NINE

October 28, 2008

1:00 p.m.

Helium filled balloons floated over every stationary object in the backyard of Tracy's apartment. A large plastic number one, almost three feet high, was nailed to a post driven into the ground in the middle of the yard.

Tracy pushed open the back screen door with her backside, both hands loaded with trays of uncooked hamburgers and hot dogs. She weaved her way through the guests, refusing the frequent offers of help. She placed the trays on the picnic table next to the brick outdoor grill.

Watkins gave a mock salute with a spatula. He scooped up cooked burgers and placed them on a platter held by a smiling Kathleen. He looked every bit the part of a backyard chef, complete with a Homer Simpson apron and a French chef's hat. His smile and buoyant manner revealed little of the near-death struggle he had endured nine months earlier; the empty left arm sleeve the only visible evidence. "Tracy, tell your lazy husband to give the birthday boy to someone else and get over here and help me."

Tracy laughed. She doubted Majorski would relinquish control of Luke to anyone. The two of them had been inseparable since Majorski had moved in with Tracy after he was released from the hospital. She drove him to therapy every day for three months before continuing his therapy at her apartment. When Majorski finally returned to work at the emergency room on a part-time basis, she did volunteer work at the hospital gift shop and took Luke with her.

After six months it was obvious Majorski was back to normal and she assumed a stay-at-home role. A month later, they were married.

A child's squeal cut through the adult chatter. Tracy turned in Luke's direction in time to see him bouncing in Majorski's arms. Following Luke's line of sight, she saw Samantha dashing across the yard toward him. Jimmy and Lucille followed in a more sedate manner with Jimmy supporting Lucille by the arm.

Tracy held her breath when Luke literally jumped into Samantha's arms. She was a frequent visitor and loved to babysit for Majorski and Tracy when they went out. Usually, it was a two-for-one deal since Jimmy came along as well.

After Luke was squared away with Samantha, Majorski used the opportunity to mingle with the others present. He sought out Buddy Spalding since it had been a couple of months since they last conversed. "*Captain* Spalding?"

"Doctor Majorski. It's good to see you again."

"It's good to see anybody. I can never thank you and the others enough for saving my life. Congratulations on your promotion."

Spalding shrugged. "Thank you, Doc. It was you who saved lives. Tupac Garcia and Lucille Dixon certainly owe their survival to your skills and tenacity. And from what Watkins told me, he and Hal would have died in the swamp if not for your action."

A line of crimson crept up from Majorski's collar to his face. "We do what we have to do."

The statement hung in the air, both men momentarily lost for words. Spalding understood that Majorski still struggled with being forced to kill Jayco, even though his action saved the lives of Watkins and Elberhart.

Majorski, anxious to change the subject, delved into another sensitive subject. "Any progress on locating the ranger's body?"

"Afraid not. Anchored down the way you described, it may never be found. Maybe someday a piece of clothing may surface and improve chances of discovery. There is good news. The coverage on CNN brought attention to the heroics of Jeff Rutledge. It made great story—a young boy searching the swamp for his father during a storm. Money poured in and a scholarship fund was started."

Majorski nodded solemnly. "I noticed he and his mother are here today. Seems like everybody involved in the tragedy showed up for this more joyous occasion."

"Speaking of which, I spoke to Dr. Elder a few minutes ago. It was nice of him to drive down here for the party."

Majorski chuckled. "It certainly was. No more small plane rides for him. He's sworn off."

"Anyway," Spalding continued, "he told me you have decided to complete your thoracic surgery residency."

"Uh … well, I didn't decide without a little help. There was some divine intervention and a good push from Tracy. In the end, the choice was mine. I think I can handle most anything now."

Majorski waved goodbye to the last of the guests as their cars disappeared down the street. He turned to Tracy, taking Luke from her arms. "This little fellow looks worn out; my turn to bathe him and bed him down."

Tracy smiled. It was a family joke. Every night was his turn if he wasn't on duty. She stopped at the mailbox and removed a plain white envelope. It was addressed to "Doctor Majorski." "Honey, this is for you. Give Luke to me and I'll start his bath water."

Majorski took the envelope, noting the return address. He opened it and removed a single sheet of notebook paper. His eyes became misty as he read. "Dear Dr. Majorski. I want to thank you again for saving my life. I'm working on my GED and I plan to start college courses next year. I won't be in prison forever and when I get out, I have a lot to repay to society. I got a letter from Jimmy and he told me about you and Tracy and Luke. I hope this letter gets there before Luke's birthday. I want him to know what a great man you are. I want to tell him something you taught me. We all got choices in life; it's what we do with them that's important. Tupac."

Majorski returned the letter to the envelope, folded it and slid it into the front pocket of his faded jeans. He smiled as he sauntered toward the apartment to join the two most important choices of his life.

ALSO FROM THOMASMAX PUBLISHING

Joshua Smith enjoys the world of hero worship as quarterback of a championship football team at a major university. He is intelligent enough to understand the hazards of the drug underworld, especially the street drug dealer. But he couldn't imagine the hell that ensued when he combined the two worlds. In danger of losing his professional and personal careers as well as his life and the love of the woman he cherished, he receives help from the most unlikely source leading to a discovery more painful than the other potential losses. Available through most bookstores and internet sellers for $11.95, and on Kindle or Nook for $4.99.

Look for John House's next novel, *Trail of Deceit,* in 2013!

www.ingramcontent.com/pod-product-compliance
Lightning Source LLC
Chambersburg PA
CBHW050730250626
47155CB00005B/1732

* 9 780985 925512 *